CHAOS KIN

A JORDAN ABBEY NOVEL

JORDAN ABBEY
BOOK 3

SHERYL R. HAYES

SHERYL R. HAYES

Chaos

A Jordan Abbey Novel

KIN

CONTENTS

1

___

The light of the waxing half-moon shone on the pack of young adult werewolves. The group was gathered in a loose circle, beneath the oak tree in the middle of the field, naked. This was the last thing Jordan expected when she was invited to a memorial for a fallen Pack member. And while she had been to a couple of funerals before, those had been for humans. This would be different.

She thought back to the text chat she had with Billy a few nights before. "You're only now having a funeral for Bryan?" Jordan texted in response. She swiped to her calendar app on her phone. "Six weeks after he died?"

She could see the shrug in Billy's typed reply. "It's not a funeral like you think of in human terms. That ceremony has already been performed by the entire pack. It's more like a memorial or a wake—a chance for us to honor his memory. This is supposed to be done by friends and can only happen on a waxing half-moon."

Jordan swallowed, remembering the last time she had seen Brian. "But I wasn't his friend."

"You knew him, and you helped return his remains to us, so

that's close enough." There was a pause as three dots appeared on his side of the messages, signaling he was typing more. "And Angela says you should be there."

Her eyebrow lifted. "And she thought I'd say yes if the request came from you instead of her."

The three dots stayed onscreen longer than was necessary to type the next five words. "So, will you be there?"

Jordan shook her head and sighed. At least he didn't try to deny it. She caught her lip between her teeth and then typed. "Yeah. I'm sure I can get the night off. Tell her I'll be there." Then she went to Montgomery to find out what she had just agreed to. At least he had warned her about the nudity.

Now, she stood in the loose circle with Tran, Maria, Billy, Ryan, and Angela. Without thinking, she reached for the missing weight of her Family necklace. She hadn't noticed how much the pendant that looked like a drop of blood dripping from a stylized fang had weighed until she removed it.

Angela spoke, breaking the silence. Her words carried the weight of a ritual. "We do this to honor our fallen."

Jordan blinked. She had thought that Ryan would be speaking, since he was Brian's twin brother. "No need to be so formal, Angela," Ryan interrupted. "My brother was a pain in the ass on good days."

There were soft chuckles from the entire circle. "True," Angela continued. "But he was one of us, and nobody deserves to die by a silver bullet."

Jordan closed her eyes, a memory flashing in her mind. She had been there when his pelt had been delivered to Elder Marcus, an attempt to start a war between werewolves and vampires. It had been timed, or had the misfortune, to arrive when Alpha Shane had been there to confront the leader of the Conclave of Rancho Robles about an assassination attempt against his daughter Angela. And it might have worked, if not for both sides realizing, almost too late, that a third party was playing them. "He wasn't the only ones lost," Jordan said. "Family members Emma and David were lost too."

The werewolves stirred uneasily. Even Billy took a step away from her. Angela fixed her with a glare. Ryan growled in an undertone to Angela's words. "Are you going to name the vampire that got staked too?"

Something about her gaze made Jordan want to sink into herself. While Angela may have helped her with the Animal Control incident, clearly, they were not friends. "His memory was already... honored." Or as much as the vampire community did for vampires with little power or status in the Conclave. She had a suspicion that the others were using Victor Claddan as an example of what not to do. "The others weren't." Montgomery and Thorn told her that outside of their Patrons, the death of Family wasn't acknowledged aside from a notation of change of staff or unless they were considered more than servants. And Marcus didn't seem the sentimental type.

She and Angela held each other's gaze for a moment before Angela nodded. "Very well. You've already said their names, therefore they're part of the ceremony."

Jordan dipped her head in acknowledgement. They were trying to get along, she reminded herself. She was a guest for this hunt. No reason to get her angry.

The submissive motion mollified Angela. She addressed the pack again. "From life comes death comes life in an unending cycle, mirroring blessed Luna's transformations. Honor Brian, Emma, and David's place in the circle." Jordan noticed the annoyance in Angela's pronunciation of Emma and David's names. "We dedicate this hunt to the memory of the fallen, and to affirm their and our place in the cycle of life. Who will join me in this hunt?"

She had the foresight for once to ask Montgomery to prepare her for what came next. While the impulse was to howl an affirmation, she had been firmly told that you never howled at the start of a hunt of any sort. "Why would you want to let your prey know you're coming?" he responded when she asked the reasoning.

Instead, the wolves of Black Oak shifted as one, Jordan following only a half second after. Angela also shifted and, without hesitation, bolted into the trees. The other werewolves followed with Jordan at the back of the pack.

She hadn't run with a pack before. Billy had invited her many times, but it always seemed to coincide with Conclave meetings she was expected to attend. And to be honest, she hadn't wanted to give Angela another chance to bully her. Other times when she had hunted, it had always been solo. But this was different. She heard the breath of her companions quicken, the thud of paws hitting the ground in rhythms, felt the brush of bodies as the pack wove around each other. There was a companionship, a joy to it that she had never experienced before. And for the first time, she understood a little of what it meant to be part of a pack.

But all that changed the moment they came across the odor of deer. All the werewolves locked on as one, Jordan included. It wasn't a large herd, about a half dozen members, if she was scenting them correctly. The wolves fanned out, moving into a loose arrowhead formation that put Jordan to the right and three strides behind Angela. She wasn't sure if that was deliberate or coincidence. Ryan flanked Angela on the other side, focused and alert.

On the trail ahead, the group of does and bucks nibbled at the sorrel growing at the base of the trees. They were smaller than the mule deer she was more familiar with, having black tails but the same gray coats. The pack moved silently as one, using the brush and trunks as cover. Jordan, eyes fixed on the deer, saw tails flicking up in alarm as they bolted. Angela glanced at Jordan, her lips curled in a silent snarl. She hadn't done anything to alert the herd, had she?

Deal with that later, she thought as the pack loped after the deer. She scanned the herd, trying to figure out which one would be the target. Angela yipped and dashed to the left, following a buck that had fallen behind the others. Target acquired, Jordan thought.

The arrow formation broke as Tran and Maria dashed forward, forming a rough U-shape with the deer between the arms. The buck broke left, trying to avoid the trap. Jordan and Angela both followed, Angela taking the left and Jordan the right. Angela snapped at the deer's shoulder. It jerked towards Jordan, who, not expecting that move, dodged away.

The buck cut in front of her in a wide arc. A chorus of yips and snarls filled the air. They had to be yelling instructions at her, but she couldn't understand them. Guessing at what they wanted, she bolted after the deer.

She cut across the inner arc, pounding as hard as she could to cut off the deer. Twisting to avoid a kick from razor-sharp hind hooves, she locked her teeth onto a foreleg. She heard a crunch and felt the snap between her jaws. The deer squeezed and tumbled. Jordan was pulled down with her. She leapt to her paws as the deer thrashed, immediately going for the throat to put the animal out of her misery.

The yelps became growls. Jordan froze as the buck continued to thrash. Every eye was locked on her, every lip peeled back into a snarl. Eyes wide, she crouched, tail tucking between her legs. Why were they turning on her? Even Billy looked angry. His eyes went from her to the deer as his growl deepened.

Then she understood what was going on. She had forgotten the primary rule about a ceremonial hunt. "The alpha is the one who will make the kill," Montgomery had told her.

"And if there is no alpha there?"

"The highest ranked wolf there. In this case, Angela."

She had messed up. Worse, she didn't know how she could apologize in a way that would be understood. All she could think of doing was how she had seen other dogs show submission. And she was sure as hell not going to show Angela her throat. Ears pinned, tail tucked between her legs, she backed away from the buck.

Angela darted forward and clamped her jaws around the deer's neck. A howl rose from all the werewolves' throats, including Jordan. Angela glared at her, snorted, and turned her attention to the buck, shifting to her werewolf form. The others milled around still as wolves while Jordan watched.

She debated melting back into the woods when Billy sidled up to her and growled something. Or she thought it was a growl. But there was a cadence to it that made her think of speech. She stared at him, hoping her ears tilted to the side and wide eyes portrayed her bewilderment as she shook her head. Billy cocked his head to one side, like that logo she had seen with a dog sitting next to an old-fashioned record player. His eyes widened. Between Jordan's blinks, he dashed over to Angela. Several growls were exchanged between the white and gray werewolves. Angela looked over at her, then back to Billy. She growled something else and walked to Jordan.

Jordan shifted up to a werewolf form. Angela looked her up and down. Jordan stiffened, fingers curling to better position her claws for defense. Angela glared into her eyes. And to Jordan's surprise, she shifted to human and put her fists on her hips. "You haven't understood a single thing we've said to you since we shifted, have you?"

Jordan nodded.

Angela rolled her eyes. "What the hell has that vampire been teaching you?" she muttered loud enough for the entire pack to hear. "Did he tell you who's supposed to make the kill tonight?" Another nod. "So, you know what you did wrong." She waited for Jordan to confirm her statement before continuing. "I won't hold it as an insult or take it as a challenge to my station this time, and I'll talk to Dad about getting you some language lessons."

Jordan's eyes widened, and her ears lifted. She nodded, her swishing tail hitting her flanks.

Angela's expression remained stern before turning to the other werewolves. "Ryan, the kill is yours to distribute as you see fit, in honor of your brother."

The way Ryan glared at Jordan, she thought he might be thinking about adding her to the kill. She tried to keep her expression non-threatening, or at least bland. She hadn't killed his brother, but they hadn't exactly gotten along either. He shifted to werewolf and hefted the black-tailed buck over his shoulder like a sack of potatoes. *Or a dead body*, Jordan thought. Angela dropped to all fours as a wolf and trotted off the way they came. Ryan, still as a werewolf, followed her. The other werewolves fell into line behind them, Jordan taking the last place. She wasn't part of the pack, but at least this time, she wasn't running away with her tail between her legs.

2

Jordan fought the urge to yawn as she stepped out of the bathroom of the Black Oak Pack's main house. Physical and emotional exhaustion blanketed her limbs, the left-overs of the hunt and the confrontation. At least it hadn't taken three attempts before she shifted back to human. Now that she was dressed, she felt better able to deal with what happened as she stepped into the main room.

Angela was the only one standing, staring into the fireplace. Jordan took a short, sharp breath, squared her shoulders, and stepped towards Angela."Look, before we start arguing, I know I screwed up and I'm sorry."

Then Angela did the last thing she expected. "It's okay," she said, still looking at the fire.

Jordan paused mid-stride, mouth hanging open. "I'm sorry? Did you just... apologize?"

Angela nodded. "We were yelling instructions at you the whole time and couldn't figure out why you were ignoring us. But now, it makes sense if you can't understand us."

Of course, they had a way to communicate when not in

human form. "How do you understand each other? I mean, it's a verbal language, right?"

"There's some body language involved, but we're not psychic if that's what you mean." Angela shrugged. "It's like growing up bilingual for me. I've always understood both languages whether I was a human or a wolf. Billy and Maria both had to learn it. They might be better able to answer your questions." She turned and looked at her. "Dad wants to talk to you in his office," she said. "I'll make sure you get your share of the hunt before you leave."

"I'm not sure I deserve any." Or more accurately, she wasn't sure Ryan thought she deserved any. "And I thought that was up to Ryan."

Another shrug. "I get a say in it. Go talk to Dad; it's best not to keep him waiting."

Like Marcus, Jordan thought. But she didn't have to pass down a long hallway filled with security countermeasures. Instead, she walked across the room to knock on a closed wooden door. The answer was similar. "Come on in, Jordan."

How did he know it was her? She opened the door and felt a breeze tickle the back of her neck. He had set up a fan so the scent of whoever was at the door was blown inside to the oak desk he sat behind. *Clever,* she thought but said, "You wanted to see me, Alpha Shane?"

If he was surprised by her respectful attitude, he said nothing. He stood and walked around the desk to lean against its front side. He gestured towards a set of brown upholstered chairs covered with a quilted blanket, giving it a relaxed, homey feel. "Have a seat, please, Jordan."

Jordan, for her part, sat and waited, wishing she had the chance to make a note of the books overfilling his shelves. Shane looked at her, his face neutral. She met his stare for a moment and then lowered her gaze as a sign of respect. But this was different than their usual stare down. There was something uncertain in his ice-blue eyes, something she hadn't seen before.

And if she had any doubts, they disappeared when he spoke, "There's something I would like to discuss with you."

Now, she knew something was wrong. Normally, he phrased things as orders, not requests, even though technically, she wasn't part of his pack. "What is this about, Alpha Shane?" Her eyes narrowed. "If you're going to reclaim Mount Ponderosa—"

"No," he interrupted. "I granted it to you, and you defended it fair and square from Angela. It's yours." Again, that uncertain look flittered over his face as he reached into the pocket of his jeans. "I need you to do me a favor."

Jordan arched an eyebrow. "A favor?" That was the last thing she expected. From what she had seen of Shane, alpha werewolves barked orders. Favor wasn't a word in their vocabulary.

He selected an envelope from the paperwork on his desk and held it out to her. "I need you to give this to your Patron."

She looked from his face to his hand and back to his face. "Why?" she asked. "Why can't you email him or call Montgomery yourself?"

There was a ghost of a mournful smile on his lips. "I can't be certain he wouldn't hang up on me. Or delete the email unread. There's a reason that every time I've reached out to him, it's been through his sire."

"Fair," Jordan said. Knowing Montgomery's feelings towards Shane, he had an email filter that routed anything from the werewolf straight to junk mail. "So, why me and not Elder Marcus?"

Shane paused for a moment, jaw working back and forth before he spoke. "He needs to be aware of this, and I don't trust that the Elder won't twist or withhold the information."

Jordan nodded and took the envelope. "I'll see that my Patron gets it, Alpha Shane."

"Thank you, Jordan Abbey." Even though his face and words were formal, there was a sparkle in the corner of his eyes. "I'm glad to see that you and Angela managed to not kill each other tonight."

Jordan shrugged as she tucked the envelope into her jacket. "It was a close thing, but we're learning to coexist," she said. "Is there anything else you need of me?"

"Just that you pass onto me Montgomery's response, if he doesn't wish to speak to me directly." He placed a hand on her shoulder. "May Luna's light shine upon you."

Jordan nodded. She then bowed her head. "And on you," she said, guessing at a response to what she assumed was a formal parting.

He made a little noise deep in his throat, something that sounded like a strangled snort. He lifted his hand, and she turned around and left.

Angela was still standing next to the fireplace, which was odd. Jordan was sure she'd be over by the door, listening to her and her father's conversation. "You okay?" Jordan asked.

She shrugged. "Butchering's taking a little longer than expected. I'll get you your share tomorrow."

She knew when the subject was being changed. "Um, yeah." It wasn't worth fighting over. She looked at the closed door, hearing the rustle of paper against her clothing. "I don't need it. Give it to Ryan for me. Say it's a small token of sympathy for what happened to his brother and an apology for the misunderstanding tonight." She slapped her hand to her forehead as a thought crossed her mind. "And please don't tell me that's the opening move of some sort of mating ritual."

Angela laughed, losing some of her tension. "No, it's not. But I'll let him know you're not interested too."

Jordan nodded, smiling also. "Let me know if you need anything else," she said and headed to the door. She was halfway to the gate in Montgomery's SUV before she let herself wonder what had Angela so upset and how it tied into the letter she was carrying for Montgomery.

3

The first rays of the rising sun chased her heels as Jordan stepped into the main lobby of the apartment building and made her way up to Apartment 310. Once she had slipped through the door, she glanced to make sure the light-proof curtains were sealed closed. She didn't want to accidentally cause any of the vampires burns, no matter how slight. It would take time in the sun for them to be severely hurt, but she didn't like it when someone shone light in her eyes, and she wasn't solar sensitive.

Of course, Montgomery was too smart for that. The pale, brown-haired man stood in the kitchenette, well back from where any rays of light would enter the apartment entrance, studying her with his warm, green eyes. "Good morning, Jordan. How did it go?"

"Hey, Montgomery. It went well... considering."

Montgomery's eyes narrowed, though she wasn't sure if he thought she'd done something, or something was done to her. "What happened?"

"In the heat of the moment, I forgot what you said about Angela being the one to make the kill." She shook her head. "I remembered at the last second, and we figured out that we literally have communication issues since I can't understand them when they're wolfish."

Montgomery had the good graces to wince. "I should have asked for help with that a while back. I can't speak werewolf any longer, but I can understand it." He shook his head. "Sorry, Jordan. That one is my fault."

Jordan looked at him for a second. "Angela's going to figure out language lessons or something to help me with it. And Alpha Shane wanted to talk to me after the hunt." She unzipped her jacket and grabbed the envelope before she peeled it off. She held it out to him. "He asked me to give you this."

He eyed the envelope as if she were offering him a venomous snake. Jordan couldn't blame him, given the nature of his relationship with Alpha Shane. She'd be reacting the same way if the letter had come to her from Rosanna, Montgomery's bloodsister. "He did say he didn't want this message to be distorted in any way." She hoped that he got her unspoken message about Elder Marcus. It was one thing for Alpha Shane to accuse him of manipulating the situation. If Jordan, who was already on his bad side, made that kind of statement, and it got back to him, she'd be in trouble. "And he wasn't sure you'd answer the phone if you saw his number."

Montgomery smiled, clearly amused at the werewolf's assessment. "He's not wrong." He took the envelope, handling it as if it were made of hot steel and extracted the letter. His smile faded as he read it. "Shit."

Jordan tensed. She could count on one hand the number of times she had heard Montgomery swear. "What's wrong?"

Instead of answering her, he read over the page a second time. "Go wake up Thorn," he said. "We all need to talk about this."

Jordan nodded. Normally, he phrased his orders in a politer way, making them sound like a voluntary favor instead of a direct order. Something had rattled him. Instead of questioning him,

Jordan turned away. It was only a few steps down the short hall to the bedroom they all shared. She poked her head inside, waiting for her eyes to adjust to the darkness.

The room was dark from both lamps being turned off and the blackout curtains covering the window. She could barely make out the lump lying diagonally across the bed, taking up the majority of the mattress. The only bit visible to her was the shock of blue hair, free from any stiffening product, flopping across a pillow. Jordan cleared her throat with a soft cough. When the figure didn't move, she spoke in a stage whisper, "Hey! Thorn."

The body twitched and scooted, taking up a position in the middle of the mattress. "Hey, Jo. You and Mac coming to bed?" It was more of a slurred mumble of "He O. You n Mac m-ing bed?"

"No. Why are you asleep already?" Thorn normally waited up for her to return when she was out this late. He and Montgomery hadn't had another fight while she was out?

"Long night at the shop. Wazzup?"

She jerked her head back towards the living room, knowing he could see better in the dark than she could. "Montgomery wants to talk to us about something."

"Gimmie a minute."

Jordan left him to stir. She walked back to the living room, where Montgomery still stared at the letter. His brow was furrowed in concentration, as if willing more information to appear. "Thorn will be out in a moment."

"Okay." His eyes never left the letter. "What's your game?" he muttered.

She opened her mouth to ask what was going on when Thorn's slightly groggy voice beat her to it. He padded up to stand beside her, wearing only a loose-fitting pair of jeans. "What's up, Mac?"

"Jordan brought home a letter from Alpha Shane," he said. He looked at her for confirmation. "He wasn't supposed to be at the memorial?"

Jordan shook her head. "Angela and I thought that he might have been checking up on if we were fighting, but his vibe wasn't quite right for that. He waited until we could be alone before he gave me that." She gestured to the letter.

Thorn's eyes brightened, as if he willed away the last of the sleepiness. "Mac?"

"Alpha Shane wants to talk with me," he said, as if trying to figure out a coded message. His eyes met Jordan's. "He's been told to expect a visit from an ambassador from the Green River Pack."

Jordan's brow wrinkled. "Why does that name sound familiar?"

"It should," Thorn said with an alien expression of solemnity. "Rhys was kicked out of that pack."

Jordan clenched. The werewolf who bit her against her will, the one who was convinced she was his mate without having ever exchanged words with her, the one she had killed to protect Montgomery. "Why are they coming now?"

"Probably they're looking for their wayward son," Montgomery said. "Bet there won't be peace when they're done."

Thorn grinned. "Didn't know you were a Kansas fan, Mac."

Confusion flittered over Montgomery's face. "What are you talking about?"

"Never mind." He looked over at Jordan. "You okay?"

She drew in a deep breath through her nose. "I will be. Give me a moment."

Thorn nodded. "What does the letter say?"

"First sentence tells me to read the rest of the letter instead of ripping it up," Montgomery said. "The rest is informing me that the Green River Pack will be sending an envoy and their Talespeaker to discuss what happened to Guinevere Lynden's brother."

Thorn raised an eyebrow. "She's not coming herself?"

"No. Apparently, she's Alpha now. I'm not familiar with Talespeaker Lucas. But we know the envoy. It's Enya Blevins."

Thorn's eyes widened. "You're kidding."

Jordan went back and forth between both men. "Who is she?"

"Someone from my past," Montgomery said.

"No," Jordan said into the following silence. "We're not doing this. You withheld the fact that you were a werewolf, and it came back to bite us."

"And you withheld the fact you were talking to your old teacher, and people got killed."

He was right. "All the more reason to get it out in the open now. Who is she?"

"She has a right to know, Montgomery," Thorn said. "You want her to hear it from Marcus? Rosanna? Or worse, Shane?"

"You're right." There was a note of defeat in his voice. "Sit down. This is going to be a long story."

They headed into the living room. Montgomery took his usual place on his recliner. Jordan and Thorn took positions on the couch. But this time, their usual positions were reversed, putting Jordan between him and Mac. "Okay, so who is Enya Blevins?"

"She's his ex-wife."

She looked at Thorn, her jaw dropped in shock. Her gaze snapped towards Montgomery as he sighed. "That's not accurate, Thorn, and you know that."

"Okay. Ex-fiancée."

"I'm not sure that's any better," Jordan said.

"It was a complicated situation," Montgomery said. "There's the human tradition of betrothing members of various kingdoms at an early age for political reasons. The same thing happens among Packs. The Alphas of Green River and Black Oak wanted an alliance. The easiest way was of blood. So, it was proposed"— he ignored Thorn's snort at the choice of words—"that I marry his younger daughter."

Jordan looked aghast. "You didn't have a say in it? That's awful!"

Montgomery put up his hand. "Like I said, it was a complicated situation. Mother had died when I was young, and I think he was worried about securing my future. I doubt that she would have stood for Dad doing it, especially since I was only two when he did it. As I grew older, he regretted his choice."

Jordan bit her lower lip. "Would he have let you out of it if you asked?"

Montgomery's eyes were hooded as he looked at the coffee table in front of him. "Maybe. I'm not sure. Anyway, before that was to happen, he had the idea about embedding me in Elder Marcus' court to learn more about their culture. And you know what happened."

She didn't, or at least she hadn't heard the full story from Montgomery's lips. She had pieced together enough from him and Thorn to learn that he had had fallen in love with Elder Marcus' blooddaughter Christine and forsook the Black Oak Pack. Alpha Shane had ascended to leadership at the same time as an assassination attempt on Montgomery and Christine. Montgomery had survived. Christine hadn't. And in his grief, he asked Elder Marcus to turn him. At some point, he had become involved with Thorn on and off, but she wasn't as clear on that part.

"Of course, when word got back to Green River, the engagement was immediately called off. It was more politically awkward than socially because Enya and I hadn't even met. In fact, we've never met."

"So, where does Rhys fit into this?"

"He is the brother of the current Alpha Guinevere Lynden," Montgomery said. "She has sent Enya Blevins and Lucas here to gather details about what happened to him. And most likely demand vengeance for his death, though I'm not sure if that would be from you or Alpha Shane."

"Why him?" Jordan snorted. "He didn't do a thing to help us when Rhys was killing in the city."

"That's part of why. They may attempt to overthrow Alpha

Shane since he bungled the situation so badly that it drew the attention of a hunter."

"Great. The other thing I was hoping they would forget I was involved with. Are they going to blame me for that too?"

"Hard to say," Montgomery said. "Probably depends on who feels like throwing whom under the bus."

"At least you're small enough, Jo, that if you curl up, the bus will run over you without touching you," Thorn said in a far-too-cheerful tone.

"So, what do we do about the letter?" Jordan asked.

"Did he ask you for a response?"

"Only if you didn't want to talk to him directly. He was more concerned that you got it." Jordan pulled her phone out of her pocket. "Should I give him a call and tell him you got the letter?"

Montgomery closed his eyes. "No. I'll give him a call."

Jordan blinked, not sure she had heard him correctly. Even Thorn looked surprised by his response. "You sure about that, Mac?"

He folded the letter and tapped it against his hand. "He went to the trouble to reach out to me. I should return the favor." He looked at the pair. "I'd prefer to do it in private."

Thorn nodded. He put an arm over Jordan's shoulders. "We'll head to bed. Join us when you're done."

Jordan let Thorn turn and guide her to the main bedroom. "I really should take a shower before I go to bed," she said.

"Wait until tonight," Thorn suggested. Once they were over the threshold, he closed the door. "It's going to be hard enough for him to talk to Alpha Shane. He doesn't need to be thinking we're trying to listen in."

She arched an eyebrow at him. "You're not going to?"

"Nope, and you shouldn't either." He looked at her, his expression one of rare seriousness. "I don't think I've ever seen Alpha Shane reach out to him directly. Or at least not through Marcus. For him to do this means something huge is going on, and he's worried. That means Montgomery, and by extension, us, should be too."

Jordan chewed on her lower lip. "So, I should get ready for trouble headed my way."

"No," Thorn said. "We need to get ready for the trouble that's already here."

4

———

The bedroom door shut, but Montgomery continued to stare at his cell phone. He should be making a different call first. The moment Montgomery had read the letter, he should have immediately informed his sire that a strange Pack was visiting, doing some threat assessments. Marcus would already be aware of it due to his extensive spy network, but it would prove his loyalty. Why he still had to prove his loyalty after twenty-odd years was something he didn't want to examine too closely.

But he needed more information first. There were details that Marcus would demand, and that meant that he needed to have a conversation with Alpha Shane. And he wanted to keep this one private. With one last glance down the hall to make sure that Thorn or Jordan had closed the door to the bedroom, he dialed his cell.

The phone rang once, twice. He was about to hang up when the third ring cut off mid-tone. Then a deep voice growled a response, "Took you long enough to call, Cooper."

He bit back a growl. There was no point confirming it was

him. Shane had to know who was calling. "You didn't have to give Jordan a note. You could have sent a text."

Alpha Shane paused and then rumbled in a softer tone, "I wasn't sure you'd respond."

So, Shane did have his cell number. Had asking Jordan for help been some sort of test? "Fair enough." Montgomery would have blocked the number out of sheer spite if he had tried to reach out. "So, do you know why they're sending the Alpha's 's sister and the Talespeaker?"

"Officially, they want to hear firsthand what happened to Rhys from the local Pack," Alpha Shane said. "Other than that, they see it as a way to poke at you for your part in it. I've heard about Talespeaker Lucas. He's a good man and is willing to listen and negotiate."

Negotiate what? Packs sending visitors was unusual. Normally, visiting members was in preparation for an inter-pack marriage, bringing in new blood. "And you're allowing this to happen?"

"I can't stop it even if I wanted to. They've asked politely and have followed all the old customs. If I said no, it would be an excuse for them to go after us. And by extension, Jordan and you."

Montgomery smirked. "I didn't know you still cared."

Shane's growl was broken off by a deep sigh. "I meant the Conclave. Although you specifically could still have a target on your back. And right now, I don't need to have both Elder Marcus and Alpha Lynden pissed at me."

Montgomery snorted. She was mad that he refused to marry his daughter to her son. "I'm glad someone learned from past mistakes."

"Don't be so bitter. That was your father's fault, not mine. He was the one who arranged the marriage you noped out of. And look how that turned out."

Was Shane actually daring to patronize him? Montgomery drew in a deep breath, shoulders squaring for confrontation, and then bit his lower lip to hold back his first reaction. There was no point in bringing up that old fight. In fact, that might be what Shane was trying to provoke him into. Keep him off balance and thinking through a haze of anger instead of with clear dispassion. Instead, he paced a circle around the coffee table to burn off his agitated energy. "I assume you want Jordan there."

"Of course," Alpha Shane said. There was a slight pause before Shane dropped the bomb. "And you as well."

Montgomery pulled up short, barking his shin against the coffee table. "I'm sorry, say that again?" He must have misinterpreted what Shane said. "You want me there as Jordan's Patron."

"No." He could picture his satisfied smirk even without being able to see Shane's expression. "All chaos wolves in the area are to attend. And that includes you."

Montgomery's jaw dropped. "Alex, you've got to be kidding," he sputtered, realizing belatedly he had used the Alpha's first name as if they were still friends.

And to his surprise, Shane sighed, as if he felt sorry for having to drag him into this. "Look, Montgomery, I know you don't want to be there in that capacity. But the wording of the request was specific. All chaos wolves, plural."

He couldn't be serious. "Yeah, and I'm a vampire, or have you forgotten that?"

"Trust me, I argued that exact point. You may be a vampire, but a lot of the packs also consider you a chaos wolf who abandoned his rightful position in the Black Oak Pack. And Envoy Blevins made it clear. If you don't come to us, she'll go to Elder Marcus to request a meeting. You won't be able to dodge her the whole time she's here." Shane paused, and to his surprise, his voice softened. "As awkward as it will be to face your ex-fiancée, I think Jordan is going to need your support on this."

He hit the mute button before he let out an annoyed huff. He didn't want Alpha Shane to realize how close to home he hit. And the most annoying thing? He was right in his assessment. Jordan would need his help navigating this situation. Montgomery unmuted himself. "Okay. You win. We'll both be there. When and where?"

"Tomorrow night at the main house. I'll leave it to you to determine how much you need to tell Elder Marcus. Oh, can you still understand werewolf?"

"Me, yes. I'd be more concerned about Jordan understanding."

"That's right. And be sure she's aware of the rules. Angela mentioned that she didn't seem to understand what she was telling her."

"When she was insulting her, you mean."

"Nah. Jordan would have understood that."

Montgomery chuckled, trying to stay quiet enough that Shane didn't hear him.

Shane continued, "I'll try to keep the conversation in English as much as possible. You need to make sure she's up on the rules so she doesn't accidentally make things worse."

"Hey, I went over everything with her before the hunt."

"Once, and you expected her to remember everything in the heat of the moment?"

Montgomery ground his teeth together, annoyed that Shane had a point. "I'll do better about going over etiquette in the future. Is there going to be a problem when she steps on your territory?"

"She made a pretty apology, so there should be no further problems, at least from Angela. So, I will see you and her tomorrow night." He heard the grin creep back into the Alpha Werewolf's voice. "And Montgomery, try not to antagonize Blevins too much."

He tapped the disconnect button before Alpha Shane could have the satisfaction of hanging up on him. He sighed and turned to the bedroom. At least Jordan and Thorn had the decency to close it and pretend they weren't listening in.

Or he was being too harsh. He opened the door in time to

hear Thorn say. "Oh, there was a message on the answering machine for you. Your mom called again."

"Jordan," Montgomery said. "You haven't called your mother yet?"

"I'll get around to it." There was a little too much lightness to her tone, which shifted to something weightier as she asked, "So, what did Alpha Shane have to say."

For a moment, he thought about accusing her of changing the subject. But Thorn shook his head, a bare movement back and forth. They'd return to the subject later on. "He wants me to show up with Jordan to greet the envoy officially."

"On Marcus' behalf?" Thorn asked. "Why'd the request go directly to you?"

"I'm not going in capacity as a vampire," Montgomery said. "I'm supposed to be there as a chaos wolf."

Both Jordan and Thorn rocked back. "But you're not a werewolf," Jordan said.

Montgomery waggled his hand. "There are arguments to be made that part of me still is." Mostly they were coming from his detractors, both werewolf and vampire, but that didn't make them invalid. "I've specifically been asked to be present."

"You think Shane is trying to pull something?" Thorn asked.

"No. I think this is coming from Blevins. Either way, Shane strongly suggests both of us are there. Otherwise, she may reach out to Marcus for a meeting."

Thorn scrunched his face as if he had bitten into a lemon. "We don't want that to happen."

"So, what do we do?" Jordan asked.

Montgomery shrugged. "We make an appearance at the Black Oak Pack. Hopefully, all the envoy wants is a look at the werewolf who killed her brother."

"Or the werewolf she was supposed to marry," Thorn said.

Montgomery rolled his eyes and shook his head. "She's never shown any interest in me before."

"You've stayed low profile among the Conclave, despite being the bloodchild of Elder Marcus," Thorn said. "Now, you've taken a famulus whose a werewolf. That makes you interesting."

Montgomery wondered why Jordan appeared to shiver at Thorn's words.

5

Montgomery stood outside the carved door, gathering himself to knock. It always felt like he was defacing the carving of the large bat soaring in a midnight sky over a distant wolf howling at the full moon. Right now, that was compounded by the desire to be curled up in bed with his lovers.

He had murmured to Jordan and Thorn as he slipped into bed that the call with Alpha Shane had gone well, and he would need to report it to Elder Marcus first thing in the evening. He wasn't surprised that Jordan had a text waiting on her phone when they woke, informing her to tell her Patron that he had an audience with the Elder of Rancho Robles. "How'd he find out?" he asked with a pointed look at Thorn.

The blue-haired vampire held up his hands as if warding off an expected blow. "I had nothing to do with this. I didn't tell him anything. Alpha Shane probably left him a message after talking to you."

Not that he'd ever find out. He took a deep breath, aware that he was putting off the inevitable. Montgomery raised his hand

and knocked. His fingers barely grazed the wood when he heard the baked command of his sire. "Enter."

Of course, he had been watching. Montgomery had spotted the hidden camera on his first visit so many years ago. Oddly enough, Marcus had never seemed to consider moving it.

He walked into the office that reminded him of something out of a science fiction control room crossed with a museum. A bank of monitors, some tuned to news channels, and others blank, lined one wall. Another had various art pieces that rotated in and out of display with every visit. This time, pride of place was taken by a rearing stallion carved in one piece, out of solid marble. A large, carved mahogany desk takes up the center of the room. Behind the desk sat a tall, bald man, light reflecting off his umber skin. Marcus, Elder of Rancho Robles, and his sire, watched him approach and gestured to a chair. "Have a seat, Montgomery. Alpha Shane contacted you?"

His sire wasn't one for small talk when he could avoid it. Montgomery nodded. "He reached out to me this morning through Jordan," he said. "He wanted to give me—us—a warning about the Green River Pack sending representatives."

"And he decided to send it to *you* instead of me," Marcus said.

He caught the warning note in his sire's voice. Marcus prided himself on knowing everything happening in his territory before it happened. The fact that he had been informed before his sire was an insult. And since Marcus couldn't strike out directly at Alpha Shane, he might redirect it to the closest target, currently sitting at the desk in front of him. "He was probably worried that Jordan would have been told something by the wolves she was running with. I was planning on telling you immediately on waking."

"And yet, I was the one who brought this up."

Montgomery held his hands to his sides in apology. "I didn't wish to disturb your sleep. I planned on informing you immediately upon sunset, but your staff had already reached out to my famulus."

Marcus stared at him, not blinking. Montgomery held his stare, remembering how he would have to hold the gaze of his father and other werewolves. After the space of three heartbeats, he lowered his eyes. Marcus' shoulders softened fractionally. "See to it next time that you contact me or my staff the minute you learn of news like this."

Montgomery kept his eyes appropriately downcast. "Yes, sir."

"This isn't to chastise you, Montgomery," Marcus continued. "There are mutterings about Jordan's loyalty to you, and by extension, your loyalty to the Conclave."

"I would have thought that Jordan's actions regarding the hunter would have quelled any doubt."

"She prevented Alpha Shane from being shot. Not me." Marcus leaned back in his chair. "That has just added to the rumors. They've been swirling around her since her induction into the Family."

Montgomery's hands were spread again, but this time in question. "And what am I supposed to do about the gossiping tongues of the Conclave?"

"A firmer hand on her leash would be a start." He leaned forward to meet Montgomery's eyes again. "She's far too independent, Montgomery. I know some of it is you wanting to cultivate the spirit of a wild wolf in her. But it would be much better for both of you if she remembers she wears a collar."

Montgomery held perfectly still to squash the urge to twitch. Had he heard about the incident with Animal Control? He had decided that Marcus didn't need to know. But if he knew that Montgomery was withholding something, they were both in trouble.

"That you can deal with in your own way," Marcus said. "For the moment, I'm more concerned about the Green River Pack. The emissary their Alpha is sending has a connection to you?"

"Yes," Montgomery said, relieved at the subject change even though the new one was just as fraught. "She was, in theory, to be my mate."

"And eventually, the Alpha alongside you?"

"Yes. We never actually met, and I'm sure if either of us had complained enough, another arrangement would have been made."

"I wouldn't be so sure of that. Your father was a shrewd negotiator. I wish he were here to negotiate with the Green River Pack rather than having to trust Alpha Shane."

Montgomery didn't bother to point out that if his father were here, none of this would be going on. His father would still be Alpha, or he would have stepped down at this point to allow Montgomery to take over, assuming he had the backing of other pack members. He wouldn't have been made a vampire since he wouldn't have been the only witness to Christine's death and deemed by Marcus too valuable to die. He couldn't say if Jordan would have been bitten because Rhys may still have made his way here, but she wouldn't have been his famulus. Instead, he stayed quiet as Marcus continued speaking, "What are the possible outcomes of this visit, Montgomery?"

"There are four I can think of off the top of my head." He ticked them off on his fingers. "A) there is a strengthened bond between Black Oak and Green River. B) Green River overthrows Black Oak, putting a potentially hostile pack in charge of their territory. C) Green River and Black Oak merge, also creating a potentially hostile pack. And D) inter-pack war with the Conclave taking side with the Black Oak Pack."

"How do you know that the Conclave would side with Black Oak?" Marcus asked in a mild tone.

Montgomery shrugged. "Devil you know versus the devil you don't. For all his bluster, Alpha Shane hasn't made a move against us. We can't say that Green River will want to keep the status quo Shane appears to value."

"That matches my assessment almost point for point," Marcus said. "What is your suggestion?"

"Right now, it doesn't appear that vampires will be directly involved," Montgomery said. "Alpha Shane has requested that Jordan and I be present when they formally welcome the emissary and the Talespeaker into Black Oak's territory."

Marcus arched his eyebrows. "I thought you said vampires weren't to be involved."

"We're not attending as Patron and famulus," Montgomery said. "We're attending as the local chaos wolves."

Marcus stared at him, his expression level. "Wolves. Plural."

"I'm not human. I never have been," Montgomery said. His hands fluttered as he explained further, "The argument that part of me is still a werewolf isn't only made by Conclave members who distrust me. In the eyes of many packs, I'm a chaos wolf now. The Green River'e emissary is asking to talk to all werewolves in the area, both pack and chaos. By that definition, I'm included."

"Convenient that, considering they've attempted to assassinate you in the past," Marcus said.

Montgomery shrugged his shoulders.

"When is the emissary expected to arrive?"

"Tomorrow morning, when she'll have a private discussion with Alpha Shane. Jordan and I will be joining the pack for the official greeting in the evening."

Marcus sat back, steepling his fingers. "You are to keep me updated of every statement that's made that has the potential to harm the Conclave. The emissary, Alpha Shane, your famulus, I don't care if that rude pup of his mutters something under her breath. I want to be made aware of it. Do you understand?"

"Perfectly, sir."

"Good. Now, I have another meeting. Please stop at Sarah's desk. She has something you need to address."

"Yes, sir." Recognizing he was being dismissed, he rose and gave a shallow bow. "I'll keep you informed."

"See that you do."

That was a definite dismissal. He didn't push it further and let himself out by the ornate door. Once the door shut behind him, he turned back to stare not at the flying Bat that took up most of the foreground, but at the Wolf howling at the full moon in the background. He shook his head as he walked up the hall to the main entrance. They were right. He was too focused on the werewolves.

A smile was plastered on his face when he stepped into the waiting area. "Sarah," he said. "Elder Marcus said that you had a message for me?"

The redheaded famulus looked up from the computer where she was typing. "Yes," she said. "I was asked to pass on a message from the Blood Bank. They're still wanting to know when you intend to replenish what you've withdrawn."

Montgomery made a face. That was still a sore point. Normally, Family would donate in cycles so no one vampire would be constantly taking advantage. It was a resource for emergencies and not to be meant as a regular food source. No vampire, even the Elder of the City, was exempt from this rule. "I suppose they haven't changed their stance about accepting Jordan's blood."

Sarah shook her head. "No werewolf. No animal. Human only."

It had been too much to hope for. He'd have to take on a human famulus. Jordan was enough to manage. Thorn was a handful. He didn't see how he could add another person in the mix. "I'll figure something out," he said. "How's your son?"

The change in topic worked. Sarah's eyes lit up. She grabbed one of several picture frames off the desk. "Max is growing like a weed!" She handed it to Montgomery. "He'll be talking in no time."

Montgomery politely studied the photograph of the cherub-cheeked baby. He had his mother's brown eyes and red hair, but the ears and nose must have belonged to his father. "He looks adorable," he said, handing over the frame. "You must be proud."

"I am." Sarah replaced the photo in the cluster of others. Her smile faded into a neutral line. "I missed all the mess when your famulus was introduced, but I've been hearing rumors."

Montgomery frowned. "What kind of rumors?"

"Your pet needs to be kept on a tighter leash. You need to be kept on one as well. You're only getting away with it because you're the child of the Elder." Sarah shook his head. "Be careful, Montgomery. You've always been kind to me. I would hate to see something happen to you."

Montgomery nodded. "Thank you for the warning. I'll take it under advisement."

Sarah nodded. She then turned back to her computer. "Do you need to schedule another appointment with your sire?"

Montgomery shook his head. "Not now. I'll call in if I need to."

"Then I wish you a pleasant evening, Mr. Cooper."

"And I you, Sarah," he said with equal formality.

Back straight, he left his sire's quarters and headed downstairs to his car. It wasn't until he was halfway home that the tension left his shoulders. All he could think was that Thorn would have a field day with this.

6

Jordan was used to the veiled hostility when she and Montgomery went to the Black Oak Pack's home territory. This time, it felt different because it wasn't directed at her. Or at least not all of it. She wasn't completely sure that Angela accepted her presence, although they seemed to have reached a state of neutrality. That didn't mean the other were-wolves felt the same way.

She pulled up to the gate with the stone wolves standing guard, driver window down, where Sentry Rodrigues waited for them. "Mr. Cooper, Chaos Wolf Abbey, please proceed to the main house. You are expected there."

Jordan nodded her thanks and rolled through the open gate. She glanced at the driver's window to make sure it was closed before speaking. "No warnings about behaving ourselves." She glanced at Montgomery out of the corner of her eye. "Are they being polite because they have guests?"

"Possibly. Looks like he'll be at the meeting too."

She glanced at the rearview mirror. The Sentry was following them up the winding road in a golf cart. "That can't be good."

"Nope."

Curving around the last bend in the road, they approached the large log building. Several cars were parked in front of it, in addition to a silver sedan she didn't recognize. The golf cart pulled to a stop beside them as they climbed out of Montgomery's SUV. Without a comment to her or Montgomery, Sentry Rodriguez hustled to the porch. Jordan shook her head. That was the kind of treatment she was used to receiving.

Montgomery came around to stand beside her. "Ready for this?"

"Nope, but I don't think I can stall until I am."

He looked at her, head tilted. "When do you think that will be?"

"Never."

A smile flittered over Montgomery's face. "Remember what I told you?"

Jordan nodded. "Yeah. Be polite and try not to piss anyone off."

Montgomery squeezed her shoulder. "Let's get this over with."

They walked up to the porch, where Sentry Rodriguez was waiting. He opened the front door and gestured them inside. "Welcome to the home of the Black Oak Pack."

Formal greeting for a formal meeting, Jordan thought as she stepped inside and walked down the hall. She and Montgomery followed the muffled sounds of people chatting to the main room. Jordan's eyes flicked around the room. The younger werewolves were present in one corner. Pamela stood in another corner. She met Jordan's gaze. She got the impression Pamela was trying to tell her something but couldn't say anything.

She watched as Angela drifted in their direction, trying not to look like she was heading deliberately towards them. Was this follow up for their near fight last night? Had she changed her mind and now wanted to punish Jordan for her missteps during the memorial hunt?

The blonde werewolf stopped in front of them, and to Jordan's surprise, dipped her head in respect. "Mister Cooper, Chaos Wolf Abbey, thank you for coming tonight."

Montgomery nodded. "Thank you, Ms. Shane. Where is your father?"

"He has been in a meeting with Envoy Blevins and Talespeaker Lucas since they arrived this morning." Jordan was certain that if Angela had been in her wolf form, her ears would have been tilted back in annoyance. "They should be joining us at any moment."

She was about to tell Montgomery that she was going to say hello to her friends when a hush fell over the room. The office door swung open, and Alpha Shane stepped out, followed by a woman and a man. The man, an inch taller than her, followed the woman a deferent three steps behind, much like Talespeaker Diana did Alpha Shane. The woman, however, stood evenly with him, something she hadn't even seen his daughter do. "Wolves of the Black Oak Pack, Chaos Wolf, and vampire of the Conclave of Rancho Robles, I present to you the Envoy Enya Blevins, sister of Alpha Guinevere Lynden, and Talespeaker Lucas of the Green River Pack in Auburn, Washington. They're guests in our territory and have all the rights of a member of the Black Oak Pack."

Half-listening to the rest of Alpha Shane's speech, she studied the pair. To her surprise, the Talespeaker was about her age, whip thin, and their eyes met for a moment. She had expected hostility. Instead, from his relaxed shoulders and neutral expression, the overwhelming sense she got from him was curiosity. She wasn't sure if it was directed to her, to Montgomery, or to both of them.

The hostility came from the envoy. Jordan didn't think she had ever seen light-brown eyes that managed to be so icy. She fought the urge to shiver as that gaze swept over her from head to toe and took in her measure. Enya's hard expression didn't shift a millimeter. She had the feeling she had just been found wanting. She wondered how Montgomery must feel, seeing the woman he was supposed to marry.

Her expression, as she took in Montgomery, was one of thinly veiled disgust. It could have been because he was a vampire, or he had chosen someone over her. *Most likely the vampire,* Jordan thought. She sneaked a glance up at Montgomery's face. His expression was neutral, one she had seen him wear when delivering news to Marcus he knew his sire wouldn't like.

At that point, Alpha Shane gestured them forward. She and Montgomery walked forward side by side. While as his famulus, she should have been at least two steps behind him. Here, he had told her that she should be his equal. She was a chaos wolf, which would be low enough in status to begin with. They had agreed that she needed every boost she could get. "Envoy, this is Chaos Wolf Jordan Abbey," Shane said. "And bloodson of the Elder of Rancho Robles, Montgomery Cooper. I believe you're familiar with both their reputations."

"Yes, I am." Her voice, a rich alto, didn't have the same coldness as her eyes. Arrogance, but not coldness. "So, we finally meet, Mr. Cooper."

"Yes," Montgomery said, offering his hand. He met her eyes without any hesitation. "I wish it were under different circumstances."

"Same." She didn't respond to his attempt at politeness, ignoring his outstretched hand. Instead, she turned her attention back to Jordan. "So, this is the chaos wolf who took down my brother." Again, Jordan felt herself being studied and found lacking. "This slip of a pup killed him? I expected someone more... imposing."

"I got lucky," Jordan said. And she had, as much as she hated to admit it. If Rhys hadn't made a mistake and left his throat wide open, things would have ended very differently.

"At least you admit that it was luck." She turned her attention back to Alpha Shane. "Is there anyone else you wish to introduce, or shall we get to the meat of why we're here?"

Alpha Shane didn't react to the rudeness, aside from a twitch of his eyebrow. "The letter of introduction Alpha Lynden sent indicated it had to do with your brother."

"Yes. When Rhys' body was returned to us, we were horrified to see that it had been desecrated. His fangs were missing." She glanced at Jordan. "I'm here to determine who performed this sacrilege, to retrieve them, and mete out justice for this indignity."

Montgomery took a sideways step closer to Jordan.

"I'm certain if that were done," Alpha Shane said, "it would have been done in ignorance. A trophy of a first kill, much as we keep antlers or horns of the first prey taken."

Erin's eyes narrowed. "Nonetheless, they were taken."

"Chaos Wolf Abbey, do you know anything about this?" Shane asked.

She quickly ran through her options. She could lie, say the hunter they had killed had taken them. Except that lie wouldn't hold up under the flimsiest of probing. She glanced at Montgomery, who gave her the barest of nods. Unvarnished truth then. "Yes," she said. "I did take his fangs."

She didn't expect Montgomery to speak up as well. Jordan had never heard anything as close to a werewolf's growl in his voice. "We were under the impression he was a chaos wolf of no importance."

Enya's gaze snapped to Alpha Shane. "And you allowed this?"

"I wasn't aware of it," he rumbled.

"Surely, you noticed the gaping holes in his gums where his fangs should be."

Talespeaker Diana stepped forward, hands raised to placate. "I was in charge of the body and didn't check it. I didn't think such a desecration would be performed. Jordan was still learning our ways and didn't know what she was doing." She shot a glare in Montgomery's direction. "Although someone should have explained the repercussions to her."

Montgomery stared back at her. "She was a chaos wolf

fighting another chaos wolf without any support from the Black Oak Pack. You made that clear to her many times."

Enya turned her attention to Alpha Shane. "And you tolerate this insolence?"

Shane took a half step forward, staring down at the Emissary. "First of all, she has passed every test I have thrown at her, even the ones I thought would be impossible for her to pass. She's surviving, if not thriving, among the vampires, which is more than some werewolves I can name. And third, what part about her being a 'chaos wolf' slipped your notice?"

Jordan blinked, surprised at Alpha Shane's praise, but not by the implied insult. But then, she had saved his life. That entitled her to a modicum of respect.

"So, you're siding with this arrogant lone pup instead of with an allied pack," Enya said. "You should have killed her the first time she mouthed off to you.

"No," Alpha Shane snapped. "I'm allying with someone who saved my life." His voice dropped to a rumble. "And no one dictates to me what I do within my pack's domain."

A growl rose from Enya's throat. Several of Black Oak tensed, crouching or shifting their weight so they could spring. Angela glared at the emissary, fury in her eyes. Out of the corner of her eye, she saw Montgomery shift his arm and felt a tug on the back of her shirt as he grabbed the loose fabric. She glanced at him. He shook his head no.

The male Talespeaker stepped forward, hands up as if keeping Enya and Shane apart by force of will. "There should be no talk of killings," he said in a calm voice. "Clearly, the chaos wolf didn't know what she was doing, and thus, she should be given the chance to make it right."

Both Alpha Shane and Envoy Blevins glared at each other. At the same time, as if coming to an unspoken agreement, they stepped backwards. The emissary's word had a hard edge. "How?"

"Recover the fangs, of course, and return them to their rightful pack."

Alpha Shane looked at Montgomery. "Can this be done?"

There was a hard edge to Montgomery's response. "Yes."

Jordan's eyes widened, but she knew better than to question him in front of the entire pack. Doing that was part of what led to this messy situation.

"You had better," Enya said. "Or else you and your little *pet* will pay the price."

Jordan's teeth ground against each other. She didn't realize she had moved around Montgomery and towards the envoy until his grip on her shirt stopped her.

Shane looked over his shoulder, fixed his eyes on her, and shook his head. Something about it didn't seem like an order, but a suggestion, even if she couldn't say exactly why. He turned back to Enya. "How much time does she have?"

"We return to Tacoma in a week," Enya said. "She has until then to make things right. The payment will either be the fangs or her blood."

Her shirt tugged as Montgomery's gripped tightened. But she hadn't moved. Maybe his grip wasn't to keep her in place.

7

Thorn knew there was a problem the moment two sets of feet stomped into the apartment. It was to be expected whenever the two of them had a meeting with the Black Oak Pack. So, he wasn't surprised when the door slam was followed by a furious outburst, "What the hell were you thinking?"

He lifted his head from where he had been lying on the couch, game controller still in his hand. He had expected to hear Montgomery addressing Jordan with those words, not the other way around. Both Montgomery and Jordan glared at each other, arms crossed over their chests in mirrored expressions.

"What happened?" he asked, expecting Montgomery to tell a story about how Jordan had pissed off Alpha Shane.

To his surprise, Jordan spoke, "You going to tell him that you've put us in the same position we were in six months ago, or am I?"

Montgomery rolled his eyes. "Jordan, it's not that bad—"

"Not that bad?" She threw up her hands. "What part of 'you'll pay the price' isn't that bad?"

"Whoa, whoa, whoa." Thorn sat up. "What do you mean 'same situation?' Who did you piss off now?"

Montgomery huffed. "Enya Blevins, of course."

Thorn scratched the back of his head as he digested that answer. "What about Alpha Shane?"

Jordan sat on the couch. Thorn noticed that she placed him squarely between her and Montgomery. "He seems to be on our side. Or he was more pissed at Blevins than at us."

"That's different," Thorn said. "Why?"

Montgomery flopped into the recliner. "Envoy Blevins has requested we hand over Rhys' fangs."

"The ones you gave to Rosanna as weregild." Now, the reason for Jordan's annoyance and Montgomery's irritation was clear. He asked the obvious question, despite the sinking feeling in his stomach. "Is that going to be possible?"

Montgomery nodded. "Yes."

At the same time, Jordan shook hers. "No."

Thorn merely raised his eyebrows.

"I didn't say it would be easy," Montgomery said. "But it can be done."

"I'm not so sure, Mac," Thorn said. "Even though she said she did publicly, she never really forgave you for what happened with her famulus."

"That was Rhys' fault. The only thing that Jordan had to do with it was that her famulus was carrying Jordan's dress, and they vaguely looked alike. It wasn't either of their faults that Rhys attacked her famulus, thinking it was Jordan."

Thorn gestured at him. "You know that. I know that." He pointed at Jordan. "She knows that. Now, try to convince Rosanna of that."

"Yeah." Jordan, arms still folded over her chest, stared at Montgomery. "Exactly how are you planning on doing that?"

"I'll have a calm, rational discussion with her and request them back."

Thorn snorted his opinion of that plan.

Montgomery ignored the sound. "If necessary, I will request Elder Marcus to step in."

"He didn't interfere when Rosanna made the request," Thorn pointed out. "What makes you think he will now?"

Jordan looked at him and arched an eyebrow.

"I'll be able to convince him if I can't persuade her," Montgomery reassured.

"We could have avoided this whole situation." Jordan crossed her arms and looked at Montgomery. "Why didn't you warn me about what Rosanna was asking? I had no clue that it could have serious repercussions with Rhys' family."

"That's not true," Montgomery said. "You saw how Shane reacted when we discovered the hunter had removed the dead werewolf's claws."

"That happened six months after I killed Rhys! You are not blaming me for not knowing better!"

The two glared at each other. Thorn was about to yell to catch their attention when Montgomery, to his surprise, deflated and sat back. "You're right, Jordan. I'm sorry. I should have handed the fangs over to Shane the moment I learned you took them," Montgomery admitted. "But I wouldn't humble myself to him. It's my fault you're in this situation, and I will get you out of it."

"You should have handed Jordan over too."

"Are we going to go over all my mistakes?" Montgomery snapped. At that point, his phone went off. "What now?" He jerked it out of his pocket and scanned the screen. "Great. Alpha Shane." He looked up at Thorn and Jordan. "A little privacy if you don't mind?"

Thorn rolled his eyes. "Come on, Jordan," he said, heading down the hall to the bedroom. "You can give me all the details, and we can figure out how to get you out of this mess."

With a sideways look at Montgomery, she followed Thorn to

the bedroom. She closed the door. "Okay. Tell me. How deep is the shit?"

Thorn shrugged. "Mac's the werewolf expert, not me. But if it were a similar situation with another Conclave, deep."

Jordan shook her head. "Then why did he let me do it?"

Thorn shook his head. "Like he said. He wasn't thinking of the consequences down the line. He was thinking about being forgiven by Rosanna and how it would tweak Shane's nose."

"While I get punched in the face." She dropped to sit on the edge of the bed.

Thorn flopped next to her and put an arm around her shoulders. "I know. And I'm going to do everything I can to help you."

Jordan curled one corner of her mouth as she studied him. "You make it sound like you have an insider who can help."

Thorn's grin was wide and toothy but without fangs. "Jordan, you have no idea." He rubbed her shoulder. "We're going to do our best to make sure you stay safe. We'll figure something out."

"We said that when Rhys bit me."

"Yeah and look how that turned out." Thorn smiled. "Or do you think it didn't turn out well?"

"Do you mean, do you think I'd be happier if I had broken my Family vows and joined the Black Oak Pack?" Jordan frowned for a moment, ordering her words. "I won't lie and say I haven't thought about it. I've wondered what it would be like to be part of a pack instead of being a vampire's servant. But given the situation, I think it would have been a worse choice. I'd be limited to staying on their hunting territory. Or be worried about someone taking a shot at me if I was in the city on my coffee run." She leaned against his side. "You know I can't live without my frou-frou coffee."

"True." He pressed a kiss to her forehead. "And I'm glad you don't have to." He followed her gaze to the closed door where they could just make out Montgomery talking. "Want to put our ears against it and see if we can hear what they're saying?"

For the first time that night, Jordan laughed. He grinned, wondering if she realized he was being completely serious. Then, nobody ever did. And that was how he would figure out how to get her out of this mess.

8

———————

Once the door to the bedroom shut, Montgomery tapped the answer button. He didn't bother with any niceties for the Alpha Werewolf. "What were you thinking? You were provoking Enya deliberately after you told me not to!"

"My pack, my land, my rules," Alpha Shane snorted. "Besides, she was going after Jordan. I thought you would protect your Famulus. If you wouldn't protect her, then I would."

"You know Jordan. Or did you forget the first time you met her?" This wasn't the first decision Jordan had made before she had all the facts. "Every other time I've stuck up for her, you've shot me down."

"That's because she was making stupid decisions that she needed to learn the consequences from. This one Blevins' using her to get at us."

Montgomery wondered idly when he and Alpha Shane became 'us' but didn't say anything about it.

Shane continued talking, "Anyway, how hard will it be to get the fangs back?"

Montgomery winced. He had hoped Shane wouldn't ask that. "Who said it would be hard?"

"You're answering the question with a question. You do that every time you want people to think you've got it under control, but you're winging it," Shane huffed. "I've been telling you for years that you need to work on your poker face."

Montgomery counted to ten and decided to tell the story instead of saying what Shane could do with his advice. "Rhys had killed the famulus of my bloodsister Rosanna, thinking she was Jordan. Therefore, Rosanna blamed Jordan, and by extension, me, for the loss of her favorite. She demanded his fangs as weregild in front of Marcus, and I told Thorn about it in front of Jordan without giving her the full context. When Jordan killed him, she took a moment to take the fangs, not knowing the consequences. I didn't know at the time because I was still out of it."

"And Jordan didn't know any better than to hand them over to keep the peace between the two of you."

He closed his eyes, steeling himself for Shane's response. "Actually, I did."

"What!"

He jerked the phone away before Shane's yell blew out his eardrums. He grimaced as he brought the phone back of his ear. "In my defense, we thought we were dealing with a stray chaos wolf, not the brother of an alpha, let alone Green River's alpha. And even if Rosanna knew, it wouldn't have made a difference to her."

"Like that should make a difference."

"You should have realized the fangs were missing when you made arrangements for the body to be returned."

That struck a nerve. Shane didn't attempt to hide the snarl in his voice. "We're not discussing my mistakes. This is about yours." He paused to take a growly breath. "Can you get them back?"

"Knowing Rosanna? What's plan B?"

Alpha Shane rumbled again. "Wonderful. So, did you tell her to do it? Or was she acting on her own?"

"She probably overheard me and Thorn discussing it and wanted to make things better. I hadn't told Jordan that taking trophies is frowned upon."

"And you thought you could get away with it since he wasn't one of us. What else haven't you told her?"

Montgomery wasn't sure whether he was included in that us or not. "I thought Diana was in charge of teaching her werewolf etiquette and protocol."

"She's teaching her history and stories," Shane said. "But Diana can't watch over her all the time. You're the one who has to guide her in these situations as they come up. Starting with how you'll get her out of this mess."

"I'm working on that," Montgomery reassured him. "Look, it won't be any worse than that time I had to get that elk antler back from Sablefur."

Shane barked a laugh. "Yeah, and I had to save your ass that time too."

9

————

Montgomery pulled into the entrance to The Row heading towards the hotel where his sire resided. He wasn't here to see Elder Marcus, but rather his bloodsister Rosanna Lombardi. And while protocol and etiquette had been followed, there was a minor breach. Jordan, as his famulus, should have been driving him. However, given Rosanna's feeling towards his famulus, he felt it was the smart move for Jordan not to be involved. While she made things easier getting things done during daylight hours, he liked the independence that came with driving himself around.

He pulled his SUV into his designated spot under the Hotel Cataluña in The Row, one of the few perks of being Elder Marcus' bloodchild that he actively used. Finding parking on The Row could be a nightmare with all the popular restaurants and bars open late into the night. Instead of heading into the hotel to see his sire, he joined the pedestrians migrating down the streets to the restaurants and movie theater. He paused to admire some of the faux European village, complete with arches and fountains and a small park dividing the two main streets. The fact he was stalling, and knew he was stalling, wasn't a good sign.

He had suggested they meet in neutral territory. Or at least something a little less territorial than Eleganza Discreta. His suggestion had been the coffee shop at the other end of the block or the restaurant in the Hotel Cataluña. Rosanna didn't even bother to consider it. If he wanted to see her, her responding text message read, he could come to her shop, without his famulus.

That should have told Montgomery everything he needed to know about how the meeting would go.

The second hint should have been the reception he was given when he entered the store. The towering display case of jewelry, the shelves filled with high-heeled shoes and tiny purses with large price tags were in the same locations as last time, even if their contents shifted with the seasons. Several plush red chairs for waiting companions formed a seating area near the dark wood doors of the changing rooms that could be accessed via a maze of racks of dresses. The redheaded woman rearranging the semiformal gown on the mannequin closest to the door greeted him as she would any potential customer. "Good afternoon, sir. How may I help you?"

"Yes," Montgomery said, returning her smile. "I have an appointment with Rosanna Lombardi."

She nodded. "Your name, please?"

"Montgomery Cooper."

The woman's smile turned from warm to frozen. As she recovered, she touched the pendant she was wearing, the finger resting on the ruby about to drop from the stylized fang on the black background as if for protection. "You're expected, of course, sir," she said. Now, her voice was filled with respect that bordered on fear. "This way, please, sir."

He was clearly expected, although he wasn't used to receiving this level of deference. Or at least not from his peers. He was the youngest of Marcus' bloodchildren and should be showing respect to Rosanna. But this woman was a famulus, and a recent one from how pale she had gone and the tremor in her hand. Was it because of who he was? Or what he was? He thought for a moment about reassuring her that she had nothing to fear from him, except he worried that him speaking might spook her more.

She led Montgomery through the curtain separating the public and private portion of the shop. Here the grandeur ended in a functional warehouse. He had been here often enough he could guide himself without any difficulty to the office, She opened the door. "Lady Lombardi will be with you shortly."

"Thank you." He looked around the cramped office. While Rosanna's desk was there, as well as the neat stack of invoices and orders to be processed, the chair that had been on the other side of the desk was gone. In its place was a three-legged wooden stool without any upholstery. "Okay," he said, perching on the seat, locking one leg to feel a sense of balance. Hoping this wasn't the third hint about how the meeting would go, Montgomery waited for Rosanna to make her appearance.

And waited.

And waited.

After forty-five minutes and shifting his weight between his legs twice in an attempt to relieve the pressure building at the base of his spine, Montgomery decided that he would give it another fifteen, then write a note, and leave. He paused when he heard the pok-pok-pok of stiletto heels coming closer. The woman with fiery red hair pulled into a painfully tight-looking bun swept into the room. "Sorry, Montgomery," Rosanna said, "but I had an irate customer who I needed to deal with."

He had been led through the main selling floor on his way to the office. There hadn't been any customers there, irate or other-wise. Either there was business she didn't want to him to know about, or she had been deliberately keeping him cooling his heels. He wasn't sure which, so confronting her wasn't a good idea. "I understand," Montgomery said with a forgiving smile.

Rosanna walked around the table and took a seat in her chair like a queen taking her throne. "So, tell me. Why have you come to see me?"

No further use of his name. No terms of endearment like she used to use. If she wouldn't indulge in small talk, then neither would he. "It has to do with the werewolf fangs, Rosanna. I need them back."

She blinked at him as if not believing the words he had just said. Rosanna shook her head. "No."

And he had the same tone and expression. "No?"

"No," she repeated. "They were the payment for the destruction of my famulus. I could have demanded the life of your pet werewolf in recompense. Instead, I asked for a minimal payment. And now, you ask that I return that pittance?"

Montgomery stiffened. "This is a matter of honor."

"Werewolf honor." She leaned forward into his face. "But let me take this opportunity to remind you. You are a vampire." Her eyes turned jet black as she spat her next words. "Act like one!"

He rocked back, startled more by the tone than the shift in appearance. "What?"

Rosanna blinked, eyes returning to ice blue. "Ever since you acquired your pet werewolf, you've been acting more like one of them."

"What the hell are you talking about?"

"How often are you in contact with the Pack? Without Marcus ordering you to talk to them?" She leaned forward again. "You've been protective of her. More so than any vampire should be after she's defied you on multiple occasions."

He leaned forward, matching her intensity. "What I do with my famulus is none of your business."

"As is what I choose to do with the weregild you provided to me."

Montgomery reeled back as if her words had been a physical slap. "You're unwilling to help me?"

"Yes. I'm not going to help you." The corners of her mouth

lifted in a bitter smile, but her teeth remained human. "Consider this the tough love Marcus should have shown you a long time ago."

"This isn't about me," Montgomery said. "This is about Jordan. She took the fangs, but she didn't know what custom she was violating at the time."

"Why am I not surprised?" Rosanna said. She leaned back, hands below the desk. "Ever since you came into possession of your little pet, she's caused nothing but trouble. Now, you're violating our traditions because another dog yapped at her, and she's run to you for protection." She shook her head in disgust or sympathy. Montgomery wasn't sure which. "Let her live out the consequences of her actions."

Montgomery rose, stiff from the ache in his lower back in addition to the need to be formal. "If that's your position, I will no longer waste your time."

"It is. And don't bother going to Elder Marcus. It would be a waste of your time," Rosanna said. "Oh, and I do have some news that you'll be interested in. You should be hearing from our sire in the next night or two."

He frowned. She was too gleeful about it if the gleam in her eye was any indication. "What?"

"Why, Nicolas Quinn is returning home. He's due in the next night or two." Her smile was precise, revealing her fangs. "Prepare to meet your older brother, Montgomery Cooper."

10

Thorn sat on the couch, in the quiet of Montgomery's apartment. On the coffee table in front of him was a spread of playing cards. Methodically, he laid down the cards in patterns of red to black in descending order. Solitaire allowed him to get his thoughts in order. And right now, he had a lot of thoughts to sort out.

The fangs, he thought as he placed a black three on a red four. *I should have seen it coming and stopped it.* The focus at the time had been on getting Montgomery somewhere inside before dawn, after rescuing him from the werewolf's lair. He hadn't noticed Jordan slip back inside. Or she had done it before the rescue party arrived. Either way, he had been there when Jordan learned of Rosanna's demands and knew the girl would want to help.

Unable to make any further moves, he flipped over a new card and paused. The queen of diamonds stared back at him with a benign gaze. The light caught the corner of the mouth, focusing on how the lips turned down. Squinted just right, they looked like vampire fangs. He had seen that look before. What *is your game, Rosanna? Is this really about your hurt pride? Or is it something more?* She wasn't without her ambition. While Montgomery had until recently seen her caring side, Thorn remembered more than one occasion when she had secured her position.

A key rattled in the lock. He put the card down as Montgomery stepped through the door. Montgomery's shoulders sagged, and he shuffled like a puppy who had been smacked with a rolled-up newspaper. His expression was pinched, the corners of his mouth curled down. His brow was furrowed as if in deep thought. Thorn sighed. Montgomery didn't have to say anything. "She said no," he said as he put down the card.

"She said no," Montgomery confirmed. He looked around. "Jordan here?"

Thorn shook his head. "Out grocery shopping. How bad is it?"

"Bad." Montgomery flopped down onto the couch next to Thorn. "Basically, she said that I got myself into this mess, so I should get myself out."

Thorn snorted. "Hate to say it, but she's not wrong." He held up his hands defensively at Montgomery's glare. "Doesn't mean I like it. I'm on your side, remember?"

"Doesn't feel like it." He leaned back, letting the couch support his neck as he looked at the ceiling. "Maybe I can ask Marcus to intervene."

"I thought he already said no."

Montgomery slitted open his eyes enough to glare at Thorn.

Thorn reached over with one hand to massage the closest shoulder. "He probably sees this as a test, a chance for you to prove how resourceful you are."

"I thought I had to do that when I was turned," Montgomery grumbled.

"You did, but Marcus likes it when there's drama between his kids. His way of making sure you're not getting fat and lazy." He nudged Montgomery's shoulder with his own.

Montgomery closed his eyes, thinking. "The pack won't be

happy about this. We have to figure out some way to shield Jordan."

"Any ideas?"

Montgomery shook his head. "Not a freakin' clue."

Thorn sighed and stared up at the ceiling. To be fair, he didn't have any ideas either. "You sure Black Oak won't protect her?"

Montgomery shook his head. "Same situation. Shane may not like it since it's a stain on his personal honor, but he has to look after the welfare of the Pack. A lone chaos wolf isn't worth the risk." He paused. "And we possibly have another situation."

Thorn rolled his eyes. "Because of course we do. So, out with it. How bad is it?"

"I wouldn't say bad," Montgomery hedged. "Except that Rosanna was too enthusiastic about sharing the information with me."

Thorn stiffened. "Oh, this can't be good."

Montgomery shrugged. "Nicholas Quinn is on his way to San Francisco."

Thorn swore under his breath. "You're kidding."

Montgomery shook his head. "That's all that Rosanna said."

"You ever met him?" Thorn made a face as Montgomery shook his head. "He's a piece of work. Stubborn, arrogant, sly, constantly plotting."

Montgomery shrugged. "Sounds like Marcus."

"Don't ever say that in your sire's hearing," Thorn snapped. "Marcus has the desire to protect all of us in his cold, unbeating heart, even if that means sacrificing individuals. Nicholas has no such emotion. He'll do what's best for himself and take what he wants, no matter who it belongs to."

"Great." Montgomery rested his head in his hands and then shook it. "First problem first. Protecting Jordan. What options do we have?"

Thorn blew out a breath and leaned back against the couch cushions. "Two options I see." He held up one finger. "Go to

Marcus and ask for protection for her. Basically, transfer her so she's his famulus and not yours." He added a second finger. "Get her out of here. See if we can make arrangements for another Pack to take her in for political favors."

Montgomery tilted his head. "A Pack and not a Conclave?"

Thorn looked at him with an even expression. "Do you really think another Conclave would accept her without huge political favors?"

"No. They wouldn't." Montgomery leaned back as well. He reached for Thorn's hand. Thorn interlaced his fingers and squeezed. Montgomery closed his eyes, body going limp. "I don't know what else to do."

"Don't know what to do about what?"

Thorn raised his head. Jordan was inside the threshold, putting her keys in the bowl. He hadn't heard the door unlocking. "You're way too sneaky."

Balancing a grocery bag against her chest, she kicked the door shut with her foot. "And you're avoiding the question." Jordan carried the bag to the kitchen. "She didn't give them back, did she?"

Montgomery's word was more a sigh. "Yeah."

Jordan's shoulders dropped. Turning away from them, she placed a packet of ground beef into the refrigerator. "So, what do we do now? Throw ourselves on the mercy of the Green River Pack?"

"What makes you think they have mercy?"

Jordan narrowed her eyes, jaw clenching and hand gripping a block of cheese. "I'm trying to figure out a solution here. Give me some guidance."

"There's not much I can give you." Montgomery slid over and patted the space between him and Thorn.

Jordan eyed him and then the spot on the couch. She sighed as she put the cheese into the refrigerator. She padded to the couch and sat between the two men, looking at neither of them. "That really doesn't reassure me."

"It's not meant to." Montgomery reached over to put an arm around her shoulders.

Her head snapped in Montgomery's direction, eyes narrowed. "Then you're doing a great job."

"Hey." Thorn tapped her shoulder lightly before reaching for one of her hands. "Enough snark from the both of you. You're not in this alone, Jordan. We're going to get you out of it."

She bit her lips, inhaling deeply before relaxing again. "Okay," she said. "How?"

"We literally get you out of here," Montgomery said.

Jordan looked from Montgomery to Thorn, lower lip caught between her teeth. "Don't tell me the two of you are staying behind to face the consequences."

Thorn shrugged. "It's going to be hard, but we'll have to find a Conclave that will accept you."

Jordan sighed, unable to come up with a good counter argument. "But where? Oregon?"

Montgomery shook his head once in a sharp motion. "Too close to Green River. You'd be within a couple of hours drive."

"Albuquerque?" Thorn suggested.

"I doubt that The White Ridge Pack will allow us to take up residence without Jordan joining and leaving me. Plus, Elder Hildalgo of the Albuquerque Conclave has no love for Elder Marcus."

Thorn pursed his lips. "We might be able to use that to our advantage."

"Yeah, if I betray Elder Marcus." Montgomery dropped his eyes. "The only way we'll be accepted by her is if I provide inside information on my sire."

Thorn put a hand on Montgomery's shoulder. "I know you've been taught since you were a child to put the good of the Pack before the good of the individual. Specifically, you. And you're treating the Conclave like the Pack. But there's no shame in choosing someone who actually cares about you. You've done it before."

Montgomery raised his head and nodded. "Okay. If things go south, get to the Hotel Cataluña. Marcus may not protect you long term, but he'll give you enough time to figure out your next move."

"Our next move," Jordan repeated firmly. "I'm not going anywhere without either of you."

Montgomery nodded, but the smile didn't quite reach his eyes. His hand reached down to join hers, holding Thorn's. "Of course, Jordan."

Thorn squeezed their joined hands but despite himself, his eyes fell on the Queen of Hearts and suppressed a shudder.

11

Jordan wasn't holding one leash but two. Rex was ahead of her by about a yard or two, leash pulled taut as he sniffed at this or that interesting spot on the ground. The giant black wolf heeled next to her with impeccable manners, lead hanging slack between her neck and Jordan's hand. Or as slack as it could be given that the wolf's shoulder was two inches above her head. Jordan glanced to the side and up, trying to make eye contact against her better judgement. "I'm surprised you're allowing yourself to be leashed."

She wasn't sure how a giant wolf managed to shrug while walking, but somehow, she did it. "It's your unconscious. Perhaps I'm trying to show that I'm not a threat."

Jordan shook her head. "I don't believe for one moment that I have control of the situation. Even if it is my dream."

"How do you know it's a dream?"

Jordan pursed her lips as she considered the question. "Well, first of all, the last thing I remember is falling asleep between Montgomery and Thorn. Second of all, if you're anything like me, there's no way you'd allow yourself to be collared if this were in the waking world."

Somehow, the Wolf managed a wry smile without baring her fangs in a threatening way. Maybe it had to do with the tail wagging at the same time. "I seem to recall a time in the recent past you did just that. It was pink and sparkly if I remember right."

Of course, the Wolf knew about that incident. Now, it was Jordan's turn to shrug. "At least this time, you're not chasing me through the woods like I'm some sort of prey to catch."

"Yes, we've done that several times, haven't we?" The ground shook from the rumbling chuckle. "We could have a change of scene if that would make you more comfortable."

Jordan shook her head. "This is fine. I know this route. We're going to the dog park. And I've always felt more comfortable in the city than the woods."

"Fair enough."

"And the third way I know this is a dream? I can understand what you're saying," Jordan continued.

The Wolf paused mid-stride, one forefoot in the air. "You don't understand the others when you're shifted?"

Jordan shook her head. "I've never been able to. Billy's confused because he picked it up fast where I'm lucky to distinguish a growl from a snarl."

The Wolf resumed walking. "Billy has also spent more time around other werewolves. Maybe you should do the same."

Jordan frowned. "That sounds like another argument to get me to spend more time with the Pack and abandon the vampires."

The Wolf chuckled again. "Maybe you should concentrate on what's being said."

"This won't be something out of an animated movie where I need to listen with my heart instead of my ears?"

The Wolf snorted. "I would just be glad if you listened, period."

Now, it was Jordan's turn to chuckle. She repeated the Wolf's words from earlier. "Fair enough."

They walked several blocks in companionable silence, Once they reached the dog park, Jordan let Rex in through the pair of safety gates. The Wolf stepped over the fence. Once they were inside, Jordan took off Rex's leash. As the dog romped away, Jordan reached for the collar on the Wolf's neck. She touched the latch, which was the size of a belt buckle that some bull riders won at rodeos. She paused.

The Wolf crouched lower. "Please."

It took a little angling and more straining than was comfortable for her to undo the buckle. After a few minutes of struggling, the collar slid off the Wolf's neck and landed with a dust-raising thud. Jordan backed off a few steps as the Wolf stretched, shook her head, and lifted a hind leg to scratch at her neck. "Good to have that off."

"I'll bet." Jordan waited until the Wolf placed that paw back on the ground before stepping closer. She noted that the bright gold eye never stopped focusing on her. "So," she said, trying to figure out the best way to ask what was on her mind. "Are you?"

The Wolf's lip curled in a teeth-baring smile. "Am I what?"

"The Wolf," she continued as the Wolf tilted her head at her. "Every time I've met you, it's been at a critical point in my recent life. First, when I had to learn how to shapeshift. Then, when the hunter tried to start a war between the pack and the Conclave. You're either my subconscious trying to tell me something I should have realized a long time ago, or you're a god who has decided to talk to me for some reason. So, which one are you?"

"Why can't I be both?"

Jordan shook her head. "My brain doesn't work that way. I may keep getting myself into these situations, but it's not because I have delusions of godhood."

The Wolf let out another one of those earthquake chuckles. "No, you don't. It would have made things so much easier if you did."

Jordan swallowed. "So, you're saying that you're..." Her voice faded out. She couldn't be.

The Wolf nudged her shoulder. "You once asked your friend Thorn if vampires believed the Bat still existed. So, why shouldn't I?"

"Then why are you talking to me and not Angela? Or Alpha Shane. Or even Montgomery." Her eyes widened. "Please don't tell me that I'm some sort of Chosen One meant to bring peace and unity to the vampires and werewolves."

"Gods, no!" It was disconcerting to see the canine face laugh like a human. It reminded her too much of a hyena's barking. "Trust me. You're not some predestined savior meant to unite the Children of the Wolf and Bat and redeem us in the eyes of Gaia, Luna, and Sol."

"Well, that's a relief." Despite her words, there was a tiny tinge of disappointment in her expression. Having a predestined purpose to live up to would give her some direction, or at least a reason for all this to be happening. She wouldn't feel like she was constantly flailing. Rhys' attack that got her into this situation, trying to figure out who was killing those around her in a way she would be blamed, even the incident with Animal Control—it would all be part of a predestined plan, ushering her towards a grand destiny for her to fulfill in a blaze of glory. Instead, she was lurching from one crisis to another without there being any meaning to it. "Then why are you here?"

The Wolf looked down at her. "It's been awhile since I've seen a werewolf that was willing to work with vampires to the point of almost abandoning their own kind." She tilted her head to one side. "That makes you interesting."

That makes you interesting. Where had she heard that phrase before? "Great." Jordan's brows knitted as she thought over her words. "You didn't speak with Montgomery? What he did fit your description as well."

The Wolf shook her head, hot breath gusting over Jordan's

skin. "I tried. He won't listen. He has closed himself off entirely to me."

"Then how are we talking? I thought you said I didn't listen either."

The earth beneath her shook at the Wolf's amused chuckle. "Something like that. I prefer to think that you're still willing to listen, despite what Alpha Shane believes. Otherwise, I wouldn't be able to speak to you like this."

"So, why are you here this time?" Jordan asked. "Normally, you've shown up during pivotal crisis moments in my life."

"This duel that you've found yourself in isn't a pivotal crisis?"

"Point." Jordan shook her head. "I don't know why I keep ending up in these situations."

"You do realize there's a common factor. Montgomery Cooper."

Jordan raised an eyebrow. The words slipped out of her mouth before she could stop them. "Same could be said about you."

The Wolf's head turned. She stared at Jordan with furrowed brows and bared teeth. Jordan was sure that she was about to be snapped up in that red maw like a hors d'oeuvres. Her dreams had ended like that before. The jaws parted, and Jordan tensed.

The Wolf barked a laugh.

Jordan's gut unclenched. She closed her eyes and slumped a little.

"You do have a mouth on you," the Wolf said. "You need to learn to rein it in. Or at least not to say the quiet part out loud."

Jordan dipped her head. "Yes, ma'am."

Now, the Wolf's eyebrows raised. "Ma'am? Are you actually showing me respect?"

Jordan shrugged. "It was bound to happen eventually."

The Wolf barked another laugh. "That right there is what makes you interesting. Not too many wolves would dare to sass me to my face, but then you don't consider me a god."

There was that phrase again. "No." Jordan picked her next words carefully. "Should I consider you a god?"

The wolf considered, her tail slowly wagging. "No. Don't. I like being questioned instead of being automatically deferred to. It's refreshing."

"Then how should I think about you?" Jordan asked.

Another thoughtful wag of her tail as the Wolf cocked her head at Jordan. "Think of me like your big sister."

Jordan smiled and shook her head. "But I'm an only child."

The Wolf shook her head, jaws opening to say something. An ear-splitting screech cut through the air. Jordan dropped to her knees, with her hands clamped over her ears. The Wolf leapt to her feet, scanning the sky, fur bristling. "How? How did he break in here?"

"He who?" Jordan looked up in the direction the wolf was staring.

The sky was filled with stars, brighter than should have been visible with the light pollution of the city. Instead, they were like diamonds spilled on black velvet, a backdrop for the full moon riding high in the sky. But there was a familiar shadow on the moon. An outline of spread webbed wings. And it grew larger, blotting out half of the lunar sphere, and then all of it. Stars blinked out as the shadow grew.

Not grew, Jordan realized. Approached. She backed up, tripping and falling on her butt as a large bat swooped towards her. "I needed to talk to her," the Wolf howled. "I've done nothing wrong!"

Jordan scuttled backwards on hands and feet, wondering what the hell the Wolf was talking about. Air gusted past her, blowing dirt into her eyes. The shadow blotted out the sky. Jordon screamed and shifted. She bit down on the cold bat claws closing on her with all her jaw strength.

Her eyes shot open, scream truncated into a gasp.

"Jordan!" It took a moment for her to process the whispered

hiss. She focused her eyes on Thorn. He lay on his side, facing her, worry reflecting in his eyes. "You okay?"

"Yeah." She took another deep breath as the last of the dream faded from her waking mind. "Yeah, I am. Just had a nightmare." She glanced back at Montgomery, who was asleep.

Thorn followed her gaze and shook her head. "He can sleep through an earthquake." His expression softened when he returned to her. "Go back to sleep, Jordan," he said. Gently, he ran his fingers down her cheek before kissing her forehead between her eyes. "You won't have any more dreams about the Wolf today."

She nodded and snuggled down into the welcoming mattress. Montgomery's arm was still wrapped around her waist, and she felt Thorn's hand rest lightly on her shoulder. She was drifting off to sleep when her eyes opened again, a thought buzzing through her head.

How had Thorn known she was dreaming about the Wolf?

12

"You ready for this?"

Jordan nodded. She and Montgomery had pulled over three blocks from the entrance to the Black Oak Pack's compound for one last quick discussion. "Got the Uber request programmed in to meet me here. If things go wrong, we run."

Montgomery shook his head, hand tightening on the steering wheel. "No, you run."

Jordan's expression tightened. "I'm not leaving you."

"Jordan, you have to run without me." Montgomery stared at her until she looked away. "I know you're afraid of what will happen to me. But they won't harm me. To do so is to risk open conflict with Elder Marcus."

Jordan bit back her response. Alpha Shane may have a vested interest in living in peace with the Elder of the Conclave of Rancho Robles. That didn't mean that these strangers who came from far away would have the same desires. Add to the fact things were personal between Montgomery and Enya, and the odds were that they wouldn't be thinking about insulting the vampires in the area.

She sighed and recited the plans they had come up with the night before. "If things go south, I run back to the Cataluña and wait for you or Thorn. If after twenty-four hours, neither of you show up, I ask Elder Marcus for help getting someplace safe. You and Thorn will join me once you're able to."

Montgomery smiled and nodded. She noticed a tear in the corner of his eye. "Hopefully, it won't come to that."

She didn't bother to say that he didn't sound like he believed it any more than she did.

Jordan closed her eyes but lifted her head as she and Montgomery drove up to the gate of the Black Oak Pack's home territory. As if by mutual consent, neither of them spoke as Sentry Rodrigues waved them through. There was no point hashing out their plans further. In the next ten minutes, they would know if she would have to run and hide with her tail between her legs.

The silence continued as they walked to the front door. Angela opened the door before she had a chance to knock on it, focusing on Jordan instead of Montgomery. The blonde blond werewolf arched her eyebrows in a question.

Jordan shook her head ever so slightly.

Angela's lips pressed together as she narrowed her eyes. Jordan could hear her thoughts. *Why am I not surprised?* Instead, she gestured them inside. "This way please."

The entire pack was gathered, clumping together in little knots around the room. Pamela met her eyes and then turned her attention back to her conversation with Tran. Alpha Shane, Envoy Blevins, and Talespeakers stood by the cold, dark fireplace. Angela took her place with the rest of the younger people in the room. The tension in the room ramped up as the four highest-ranking werewolves focused on her and Montgomery. Alpha Shane dipped his head in greeting. "Chaos Wolf Abbey, Mr. Cooper."

Enya was far less formal, not giving Montgomery and Jordan

a chance to greet them. She assessed Jordan, head lifted so she stared down her nose. "Were you able to retrieve the fangs?"

Jordan drew herself up to stand straight and as tall as she could. "No."

Everyone around her tensed, which she expected.

"This isn't her fault," Montgomery said. "She didn't know—"

"Silence, vampire!" Enya snapped. Her focus was on Jordan as she paced forward. "It's not completely your fault. I blame you as much as I blame him." She nodded towards Alpha Shane. "And him." Her gaze turned towards Montgomery.

Alpha Shane's shoulders hunched. He shifted his weight but said nothing.

She felt her ears flatten, an impressive trick as she was in her human form. Jordan opened her mouth, trying to force her words through her snarl. To her surprise, Billy, Juan, Tran, and Maria surrounded her and Montgomery with Angela taking the point in front of Jordan. Jordan couldn't see her expression, but the young woman stood stiffly, legs apart, and fists braced on her waist.

Confused, Jordan looked at Billy on her right, eyes wide. "What's going on?" she whispered as Montgomery put a hand on her shoulder.

"We're saving your skin," he said. "Now, shush."

Angela looked at Enya. "Jordan shouldn't be treated as a chaos wolf. She is—"

"Angela!" Alpha Shane barked, glaring at her.

His daughter didn't stop speaking. "—An alpha wolf in her own right."

Enya looked at Angela, to her, and back to Angela. She arched an eyebrow. "Territory?"

"Mount Ponderosa, which she defeated me to claim."

"Pack members."

"Depends on if you count him." Angela pointed at Montgomery. "I wouldn't since he's not informed her of her true status.

But there's also a Rottweiler who's a companion she spends time with on a daily basis."

"That's a dog."

"We allow wolves as members of our pack," Green River's Talespeaker said. "So, a dog would be allowed."

Angela lifted her chin higher, as if daring Enya to contradict her Talespeaker.

Enya narrowed her eyes, gaze shifting from Angela to Jordan. "If you are an , why are you going by Chaos Wolf?"

"My territory was only acquired recently," Jordan said. She felt Montgomery's hand grip her tighter. She wasn't sure if it was in warning or encouragement to follow Angela's lead. "Since Alpha Shane has the larger territory and Pack, it seemed wise to defer to his seniority rather than be perceived to challenge him."

There was a moment of silence while Enya absorbed her statement. Jordan was sure that the envoy was doing the same thing she was—searching for an out or a counter argument. "Very well," she said. "We settle this envoy versus alpha."

Every werewolf in the room tensed. Montgomery tightened his grip on her shoulder so much that she thought her clavicle might snap. Her voice was hard as she spoke a single word. "How?"

"A duel. I will accept her territory in lieu of my brother's fangs." Enya grinned. "Do you accept?"

Shane frowned and let out a low rumble.

Jordan turned her head towards Montgomery. "Let me guess. To the death?"

Jaw tense and eyes locked on Enya, Montgomery nodded.

Of course, there would be no small favors like it being to first blood. Jordan bit her tongue to stop her sigh. What was it with werewolves and vampires blaming her for breaking rules and customs she had no idea existed and then wanting to kill her for it? She didn't look at any of the other werewolves or Montgomery. Instead, she kept her gaze locked on Enya. "I accept."

The room erupted with growls and shouts. If her ears hadn't been metaphorically pinned before, they were now from the noise and the energy.

All of which seemed to fade when Alpha Shane stepped forward, making no effort to screen the growl from his voice. "This is unacceptable."

"You're saying she's not an alpha?" Enya raised an eyebrow. "Your daughter is lying to us?"

Shane's brow furrowed. His jaw thrust forward before he pulled back, clearly on the edge of shifting. "No."

"Has she been formally recognized?" Talespeaker Lucas asked.

"No," Shane and Montgomery said as one.

Jordan didn't like the gleam in Enya's eye nor her smile. Her bared teeth were human, and somehow more threatening than wolf fangs. "Well then, the first thing we should do is see if the Wolf recognizes her as one of her chosen alphas. Things may be resolved more quickly than we think."

She glanced at Montgomery. He shook his head in the smallest of movements and exerted a feather-light pressure on her shoulder. She recognized his signs for her to keep quiet.

Shane looked at her. "With your permission, we'll regroup at Mount Ponderosa for the ceremony. Not you, Montgomery," he added quickly. "This is for the Alphasalphas, Talespeakers, and high-ranking werewolves." He looked at Montgomery, jaw shifting back and forth.

"I'm her Patron," Montgomery said. His voice was calm, but Jordan worried that the bone under his hand would crack. "Where she goes, I go."

"This is only for werewolves to witness," Enya said.

Montgomery's chin raised a little. "My father intended for me to be alpha after him. While I never performed my ceremony, it was a known wish of his." He looked at Diana. "If I'm considered a chaos wolf despite being a vampire, I should still be considered a potential alpha as well."

Diana and Lucas exchanged a look. Jordan wondered if being telepathic was part of being a Talespeaker; they had an entire conversation by merely meeting each other's eyes. "He has a point," Lucas finally said.

"Very well," Enya growled. "Let us reconvene there."

Shane gestured towards the door. "I will see that you get to the location, Envoy Blevins, Talespeaker Lucas." He looked at Jordan and Montgomery. "We'll meet you there."

She felt pressure on her shoulder relax. Taking Montgomery's cue, she stepped to the door, head held high as she passed the group of werewolves. Out of the corner of her eye, she saw Shane shake his head as they passed.

Jordan waited until Montgomery closed the passenger seat door to speak. "What the hell just happened?"

Montgomery started the car. "You've just been promoted to alpha."

"That's what I was afraid of," Jordan said. "I didn't realize I qualified."

"I should have," Montgomery said. "It's my fault now that you have to perform the ritual."

"What kind of ritual?"

"A hunt," Montgomery said. "One performed by every alpha. In theory, you'll meet the Wolf, and she'll judge if you have the skills to be acknowledged as alpha."

"And if I fail?"

"In your situation, you go back to being a chaos wolf, and Envoy Blevins will demand your fangs as recompense for her brother's."

"I'd rather keep them where they are," Jordan said. "What do I need to hunt? Deer? Elk?"

"Anything you catch would be considered sufficient. Larger is usually considered better, but there are stories about alphas being crowned by the Wolf for catching a mouse. Remember, wolves are pack hunters, so being able to bring down something on your own is considered a great skill. And you have the advantage because you're used to hunting solo."

"Yay, being ostracized has a benefit for once." She shook her head. "So, why didn't you warn me about this?"

"I didn't even consider this a possibility," Montgomery said. "Angela is playing fast and loose with the definition of a pack. I mean, if you had a human lover who knew what you were, the argument could be made."

"I thought humans weren't supposed to know about werewolves," Jordan said.

"In theory, no, but for some practical reasons, there's no option. Shane prefers that the fewer outsiders who know, the better. Who told you that?"

"I got that impression from talking to some people."

"Who is dating... no, I don't need to know that. If that person wants to keep it a secret, don't say another word about it, Jordan."

"Didn't plan to," Jordan said. "It's not my story to tell. Now, exactly what have I gotten myself into?"

"This ceremony is supposed to be witnessed by werewolves only," Montgomery said. "And despite Alpha Shane arguing that I'm technically a chaos wolf, we all know I'm a vampire. Don't be surprised if they change their minds and say, 'No sense risking the wrath of the gods.'"

Jordan crossed her arms over her chest. "That sounds like an excuse."

"No use risking the wrath of Enya Blevins," Montgomery said. "I know you'll tell me everything I need to know to report to Marcus. We need to make sure this is done by tradition and is above board. I'll be waiting in the parking lot if we get separated."

Jordan nodded. "What if the ritual fails?"

"Then they won't consider you an alpha," Montgomery said. "It's not in Shane's interest to let Blevins hurt you. He'll make sure that you aren't harmed."

"In other words, evacuation plan two point oh if he goes down."

"Yeah."

"So, what exactly is supposed to happen?"

A small, bitter smile crossed his lips. "According to the legends, you're supposedly going to meet the Wolf."

13

———

They had been the first to leave the Black Oak Pack's territory for Mount Ponderosa. And yet she wasn't surprised that somehow she was the last to arrive. Alpha Shane was leaning against a sleek, black sedan, head tilting skyward as if communing with the moon and not looking at his daughter. Angela stood next to him, her arms crossed. The two Talespeakers were quietly discussing something, gesturing towards the woods. Envoy Blevins, standing next to a silver sedan, stared at her, following her every move with a predator's intent.

At least Montgomery was by her side. She needed a reassuring presence next to her as the Talespeakers lay out the rules. While he was allowed to witness the rite and had walked her through it, he wasn't allowed to participate. But that small comfort disappeared when they stepped out of the car, and Alpha Shane fixed his eyes on them. "Cooper. Over here. We need to have a talk."

Montgomery patted her shoulder. "Hang in there, Jordan," he said and then walked to where the werewolves had gathered.

At the same time, Angela drifted in her direction. "You ready for this, Jordan?"

"As I'll ever be." She hoped the way her hand twitched didn't give away her lie. Jordan tilted her head to one side, considering Angela. "Why are you here? Potential alpha hoping to steal my thunder?"

"That," Angela said. "And Dad said that I needed to see the mess I caused firsthand."

She rolled her eyes. That sounded like something Alpha Shane would say. "If he thinks this is your fault, he needs to have his head checked."

Angela jerked her head towards her. "What do you mean?"

"If it wasn't this," she gestured towards the forest, "it would be something else. I'm the excuse, not the target." Jordan shrugged and leaned against the car next to Angela. "That seems to be my life lately."

Angela nodded. "What do you think they're fighting about?"

Jordan looked over to where the other werewolves and the vampire stood. They were all talking but not loud enough to be heard. Their tight stabbing gestures punctuated their words. It was enough to tell from a distance that they were arguing about something, even if she couldn't hear what was being said. "What they always do. Me or Montgomery."

Angela snorted a laugh. "Yeah, I'd say the odds are fifty-fifty."

"Tell me something," Jordan said as she kept an eye on the arguing group. "Why are you doing this?"

"What do you mean?"

"You're helping me. As you pointed out, I'm an alpha, and you're going to be one. That makes us rivals."

Angela shrugged. "Maybe I'm trying to get you in debt to me. Is that going to be a problem?"

Jordan thought about it for a moment. "No, I don't think so. It's never gone easy between us. But I've made it clear that I don't want to be part of Black Oak, and I don't have any intentions of poaching any of your members. And while I appreciate you rescuing me from Animal Control, I would have preferred a less sparkly collar."

"The sparkly collar is kinda the whole point," Angela said. "Besides, we all go through that humiliation at one point or another." Her face scrunched as if she bit into something sour. "Dad says it helps keep us humble."

Jordan shook her head. "I wouldn't have minded if that lesson had been taught another way."

"Same."

At that point, Diana stepped away from the group. She gestured towards her. "Jordan, if you would join us please."

"Here we go." Jordan pushed off the car and walked towards the group. Whatever argument Shane, Enya, the Talespeakers, and Montgomery had just appeared to be settled. Both Shane and Enya looked unhappy, and she wasn't sure if it was a good thing or bad. Montgomery also looked unhappy, so that was definitely bad. Both Diana and Lucas had neutral expressions. "Has Montgomery informed you of what you need to do?"

Jordan nodded. "We discussed it on the ride over. I go into the woods and capture the first prey I can. Once I return with the sacrifice, you and Talespeaker Lucas will summon the Wolf. She may or may not appear, but She will make a sign that she approves of me as alpha or not."

Diana nodded. She and Lucas looked pleased at her response. Blevins did not. "You must complete this by moonset. If Luna is not visible in the sky, it doesn't count."

She glanced skyward. The waning moon dipped towards the western horizon, two hours from disappearing below it. But the trees were tall and would obscure the moon much sooner. "I'm protesting this again," Montgomery said. "She isn't being given the full night that most alphas have to perform this ritual."

Blevins smiled sweetly at him. "We don't recognize your words, either as a vampire or a chaos wolf."

Shane blocked Montgomery from stepping forward with a

hand to his chest. "It doesn't matter if she can't complete this tonight," he rumbled. "She has already met the requirements."

"Then she should have no problems," Blevins said with false sweetness. "The Wolf will bless her if she is the alpha your daughter claims her to be."

She saw Montgomery inhale, shoulders lifting, about to argue further. "Enough," Jordan barked, surprised at the command in her own voice. "We're wasting moonlight. Literally. Let's get this started if we're doing it."

Alpha Shane nodded and gestured towards the woods with one hand.

There had to be a way to quickly shift and drop her clothes. She had tried wearing them while shifting once, like the were-wolves did in movies. Jordan learned two things that day. Movie special effects lied, and denim was much harder to tear against the grain than she thought.

Stripping down in front of the group never seemed to get easier. She had no problems with Montgomery. She had a few times before with Angela, Diana, and Shane, but there was always a sense of judgement with them. She wasn't sure about Lucas given his open stance. But Enya, with her crossed arms and her cool stare, radiated waves of disapproval tinged with a desire to see her fail that washed over Jordan.

Like she would let that happen, Jordan growled to herself. Naked and trying to ignore all the eyes on her, she gritted her teeth and reached inward, focusing on her heartbeat.

For once, the shift seemed to come easily. Her skin prickled as fur sprouted across her arms and back. She inhaled, her body stretching as her legs leathered and her chest expanded. Her muzzle pushed out, and she snapped her jaws once to make sure her teeth were properly pointed. Maybe she was getting better at it. Or maybe she was just so pissed off at having to prove herself yet again that she was fueling her shift with her anger. Without another look at the group, she dropped to four legs and padded towards the wood line.

Once she was obscured by the trees, she closed her eyes and inhaled. Behind her, she could still smell werewolf and vampire musk. That would make hunting difficult, and she guessed that was part of the idea. If she could smell them, then any other animals would pick up the predator scent and flee. With a sigh, she shifted to full wolf and put her nose to the ground. There were enough human-made scents present that would scare off animals, other than ones habituated to scavenging the garbage left behind or were brave enough to beg a meal by sheer cuteness. None of those would be stupid enough to come near her.

Okay, then she would go to them. Jordan wove among the trees, working her way deeper and deeper into the trees. It was hard to spot the moon through the branches, but she kept an eye on it. The few glimpses she caught of it had it heading towards the western horizon faster than she liked.

She cast about, trying to find any scent. The ground was dry due to the drought, dirt and stale pollen ticking her nose until she snorted it clear. Jordan squinted, face wrinkling. She made noise that would alert any potential prey to her presence.

Which may not have been a bad thing. She heard a rustling in a bush to her right, then stopped. She stepped towards it, deliberately snapping a twig under her paw.

The rustling became scampering. A brown rabbit burst from the bush. It took off. Jordan leapt after it. The rabbit proved nimble, ducking and twisting every time Jordan came within a stride's distance.

Her one advantage was that she knew this land well. The disadvantage was that she knew the rabbit was heading for its warren. She scrambled after it. If the rabbit made it to the entrance before she did, there was no hope of catching it. And she didn't know if she'd have time to start over.

Something the size of a hawk swooped low, cutting off the rabbit's escape path. The rabbit pulled up and then bolted to her left. But hesitation was all Jordan needed. Haunches protesting, she pushed one last leap out of them. Her jaws encircled the rabbit's sides. Her jaws snapped shut. The rabbit squealed and then went limp.

Jordan dropped the rabbit and looked for the bird. Except she hadn't seen feathers on the wings, she had seen leathery skin. But bats weren't that big, at least not in North America. She studied the branches above her without seeing anything.

It didn't matter. She bent down to take the rabbit in her mouth. Her instincts said to crunch down and enjoy a well-earned meal. But aside from the killing bites, it had to be untouched. Or else this was pointless. It was a test of self-control, she realized. Proof that she could put her wants aside and provide for others. Ears high and tail up, she trotted a straighter path back the way she came, hoping that her drool soaking into the rabbit's fur wouldn't be held against her.

As she neared the clearing by the parking lot, she heard voices. She didn't need to make out the words to understand the angry tone. Her ears perked forward, hoping she wasn't coming back into a fight.

A hush fell over the gathered when Jordan stepped out of the trees. "See," Montgomery said with a smile. "I knew she'd do it."

"It's only a rabbit," Enya sniffed.

"And you know how hard it is to catch a rabbit solo," Montgomery countered.

"The Wolf will determine if it's a worthy sacrifice or not," Talespeaker Diana snapped. "It's not our place to say." She turned to Jordan and gestured towards a flat rock. "If you would place your sacrifice there, we can begin."

Feeling all eyes focused on her, Jordan walked to the stone slab that Diana indicated. She carefully lowered the rabbit onto the stone. Diana shifted to her wolf form and stood next to Jordan, shoulder to shoulder.

The elder gray wolf looked at her and wagged her tail once. Jordan had worried about this part the most. She didn't understand when werewolves spoke. How the hell would she understand what Diana said?

What Diana said. She thought back to what Diana and Montgomery said she needed to do. They hadn't said what form she needed to be in.

The Talespeakers howled to the moon. Jordan closed her eyes and listened. Diana had told her what the words would be, but it sounded like barks and growls. Mentally, she recited the words, trying to map them to the barks. "Great Wolf! Alpha Above All Alphas!" called Diana, "We call upon thee to witness the deeds of Jordan Abbey! She has claimed this land as hers, has fought to defend it from a rival, and chosen her companions to found a Pack." Diana and Lucas stepped back, leaving Jordan standing in front of the rabbit.

Jordan took a deep breath. Now, it was her turn. She heard a soft murmur as she shifted to human. Standing, she raised her arms to the sky. "I offer you this kill, Great Wolf, untouched by my appetite, in a humble request that you recognize me as alpha." Words said, she knelt and shifted. A pregnant hush fell over the clearing as they waited.

All six heads turned in the direction of a snapping branch. The outline of a giant wolf stepped into the glade, Montgomery and Shane's heads barely touched the ruff of fur on her chest. Her fur was midnight black, eyes the color of sunlight amber. All the werewolves knelt on one knee, heads bowed and exposing the back of their necks. Without thinking, Jordan took the same pose. The earth shook beneath her as the Wolf approached and bent down to sniff at the kill. A quick snap of her jaws, and the corpse disappeared.

Jordan sighed, some of the tension leaving her. At least the Wolf had accepted her sacrifice. Then her muscles locked up as she heard a familiar chuckle in her head. *It won't do for you not to understand what happens next.* Something warm and wet touched her forehead just above her eyes.

The Wolf studied the assembled gathering. When her gaze landed on Montgomery, she looked away, ears and tail drooping ever so slightly. Then the Wolf spoke, "Hail Alpha Shane, Talespeaker Diana, Envoy Blevins, Talespeaker Lucas. Why have you summoned me?"

Jordan's eyes widened. She understood what they were saying. But more importantly, the Wolf hadn't addressed her. Why give her this gift and not include her in the greeting? Had she made a critical mistake addressing her as a human? She heard the other werewolves rise to their feet. For some reason, it felt right for her to remain in a respectful kneel. Or maybe if she remained curled, head almost touching the ground, she wouldn't be noticed.

"We come to ask you who this wolf is," Alpha Shane said.

So much for not being noticed. The ground shook again. Two large forepaws stepped into her eye line. "Why do you ask, Alpha Shane? Your daughter has already spoken truly who she is." She felt a gust of warm air stir the fur on the nape of her neck. "This young one is Alpha Abbey, of the Mount Ponderosa Pack."

"No!"

Jordan lifted her head. The Wolf glared at Enya, one lip curled away from a fang. "Are you questioning my wisdom, Enya Blevins?"

For the first time, Jordan heard a deferential whine in Enya's voice. "No, ma'am. I mean no disrespect. It's just that it's not common for a chaos wolf to rise to alpha."

"But not unheard of." The Wolf turned her head to Jordan. She felt a wet tongue touch between her eyes. "Rise, Alpha Abbey, and join me in a howl."

Jordan slowly rose to her four feet as a wolf, then to her hind legs as a werewolf. The Wolf raised her nose to the sky and howled. Jordan tilted her head back and joined in. She was surprised when no other voices joined hers. When she lowered her head, the Wolf's form had disappeared, but her howl was fading in her ears. She stared at the others, wondering if that had really happened.

And from their stunned expressions, they were having the same thoughts she was. "I think," Montgomery said, words coming out in a stumble, "We have our answer."

Blevins spun on Montgomery, lips curling away from fangs, although her form was still human. "You are responsible for this!" she snarled. "I don't know how you pulled this off, but that can't have been the Wolf."

Shane arched an eyebrow. "Are you calling my Talespeaker a liar?"

Blevins looked at Alpha Shane and took a deep breath. Her voice was cooler, the words frosty. "I'm saying she may have been misguided."

"She spoke to us." Jordan had never heard the sheer level of awe in Montgomery's voice. If anything, she expected him to have been agnostic as far as the existence of the Wolf.

"Exactly," Blevins said. "She's never spoken to me before."

That snapped Montgomery out of his reverent state. "Perhaps you aren't as favored by her as you think you are."

"Enough, Montgomery," Shane growled. He looked at Enya. "You have your answer. She's an alpha. The challenge stands."

Enya's smile was something sweet and poisonous "Then there is no reason to protest. My Talespeaker will be in touch with yours to make the arrangements unless the... what was the name of her pack?"

"Mount Ponderosa," Jordan growled.

"Unless the Mount Ponderosa Pack has its own Talespeaker."

Diana clenched her jaw. "I will act as her Talespeaker until she can obtain one of her own." She looked at Jordan. "If you'll have me?"

"Of course," Jordan said.

"Very well. I will give you a week to prepare for the duel. My Talespeaker will reach out to you for the details of the location of the fight." Enya looked at Jordan and grinned. "I look forward to seeing if the rumors about you are true."

Jordan smiled and bowed her head in return, not rising to the bait.

"Unless we have anything more to discuss?" Alpha Shane barked. She knew when someone was hinting there wasn't anything more he wanted to discuss.

"No," Enya said. She looked down her nose at Jordan. "I've said all I have to say. Until the night of the duel." With that, she turned and swept back to her car, with Talespeaker Lucas following in her wake. The driver's door slammed shut after Enya climbed inside. The passenger side door closed with a quieter click.

Jordan exhaled a deep breath, shoulders slumping and knees unlocking as the rental pulled onto the road. Now that the immediate threat had gone, the reality of what had happened sank in.

She had met the Wolf. The Wolf existed. She hadn't been her subconscious trying to speak to her through dreams. She was real.

She glanced at Montgomery. Despite the snide remark to Enya, he appeared to be searching for words, glancing around as if figuring out what just happened. Their eyes met for a moment. He shook his head. Or it could have been a nervous twitch. Either way, she took it as a suggestion to stay quiet.

The reverence of the moment broke. Alpha Shane wheeled on Jordan. "Why did you say yes? What the hell were you thinking?"

"Did I have a choice?" Jordan snapped. "She would kill me either way. At least this way, I have a fighting chance."

"Emphasis on fighting," Montgomery said. She had expected worry in his voice but not anger. "Which you don't have a lot of experience with."

Alpha Shane coughed. "I'm not here for your couples counseling session," he said. He glared at his daughter. "This is your fault."

"Me?" Angela snorted. "All I did was point out the oblivious. It wasn't my fault they screwed everything up."

Shane's eyes narrowed as he stared down at his daughter. "You don't think I knew what she was? That I knew what happened the moment she defeated you? That I was trying to avoid this exact situation or worse? Do you think I'm that stupid, girl?"

Angela's eyes widened, but she said nothing.

"Smart choice," Shane growled. He looked back at Jordan. "You, I don't expect any smart choices from." He looked at Montgomery. "How's her fighting skills?"

Montgomery shrugged. "You saw her fight your daughter. She killed Rhys."

"She got lucky, in other words." Shane looked her up and down. Jordan stared back, chin lifted. "She's got attitude at least. I've got about one week to get you into fighting shape?"

Montgomery's eyebrows lifted. "You?"

Shane held his hands out to either side as if it were self-evident. "Who else?"

"Training Jordan is my responsibility," Montgomery snapped.

That got a bark of a laugh out of Shane. "You can show her how to fast shift? Quickest I've seen her do it is five minutes. Don't get me wrong. It's admirable that you got her as far as she's come on your own. But she needs lessons that you can't provide."

Montgomery's mouth pressed into a firm line. He crossed his arms over his chest as his shoulders dropped. He didn't say a word.

Alpha Shane turned to Jordan. "We're going to do all that we can to protect you. The problem is that our hands are tied. Normally, I'd suggest a champion to fight bet for you, but since this is between alphas, we can't do that. You have to fight for yourself.

"Wouldn't be the first time," Jordan muttered.

"You really need to learn to use your inside voice," Angela said.

Montgomery squeezed her shoulder, warning her to be silent. Under different circumstances, she would have. However, she spat out the words before she could stop herself. "I'm so sick and tired of the two of you insisting on riding to my rescue when it's convenient for you." She glared at Alpha Shane. "You weren't willing to help me when Rhys was around. And I don't want your help now."

Alpha Shane rolled a half step forward. "I owe you for saving my life."

"I know that," Jordan said. "And I will ask for you to return the favor when I feel it's necessary."

Shane snorted. "And who will get you ready for this fight?" He pointed at Montgomery. "Him?"

Jordan shook her head. She looked at Angela. "Would you be willing to teach me to fight?"

Angela curled the corner of her lip. "What's in it for me?"

Jordan grinned. "A chance to kick my ass on the regular for the next week."

Angela laughed. "Deal!"

Shane glared at Montgomery. "And you're going to allow this?"

There was a trace of a chuckle in Montgomery's voice. "You really think I can stop her?"

"You have a point." Alpha Shane rubbed his chin and looked at Angela. "You willing to do this?"

"You heard what she offered," Angela said. "Of course, I'm going to take her up on it. Be here tomorrow at sunset, Jordan."

Jordan nodded, wondering what else she had just gotten herself into.

14

───────

Jordan watched the Black Oak Pack pull out of the parking lot, leaving her and Montgomery alone. Her legs wobbled as a wave of exhaustion hit her as the last of her guard went down. She glanced to the east, assessing how much night they had before they had to get him safely home. "So," she said, not sure how to bring up what had just happened. "What was that we saw?"

"I... don't know." Montgomery stared straight ahead.

She didn't like that he was ducking the question. "Unless Alpha Shane somehow pulled a fast one, did we just meet a goddess?"

Montgomery shrugged. "Thorn's the religious one. Not me."

"Yeah, he and I have had discussions about the Bat, but we haven't."

"Haven't seen much of a reason to have that conversation before," he said.

"Are you okay, Montgomery?"

"I... I don't know." He shook his head. "I've been raised my whole life with stories about the Wolf. I never thought I'd actually see Her."

"You never dreamed about Her?"

Montgomery shook his head. "Not once."

"Did you not believe my dreams?"

"I figured it was your subconscious trying to tell you something."

"So did I," Jordan said. She looked up at the sky. "Life just got more complicated, didn't it?"

"More from you being an alpha than us having a religious crisis," he said.

Jordan shook her head. "I was trying not to think about that."

"We can hold that discussion until we get home. I'm sure Thorn will have a lot to say about it."

Jordan made a face. "What are you going to tell Elder Marcus?"

"I'll worry about that when I get home," Montgomery said. "You up to driving?"

"I think so."

"Good, cause I'm not sure I am." He looked her up and down. "Maybe you should shift back and get dressed."

She reached up, grabbing her muzzle and then her ears. "You're able to understand me?"

Montgomery nodded. "I never lost that ability, apparently. Can you shift down?"

She closed her eyes. It was easier to shift with only Montgomery watching. But then, he had seen her naked many times before. Once she felt the cool night breeze caress her skin, she opened her eyes. Montgomery stood in front of her, holding her clothing. "Thanks," she said.

"I should be thanking you," Montgomery said as she took piece by piece and put them on. "I never thought I'd get confirmation that the Wolf was real or not."

"You sure it wasn't Shane pulling a fast one?"

"Even if you're an alpha, you should be referring to him as one, for politeness sake," Montgomery said. His correction was half-hearted at best as he looked around the clearing. "But no. He may be many things, but a heretic isn't one of them. Besides, we'll search the area for projectors and speakers before we leave."

Jordan pulled her black tee over her head. "Trust but verify?"

For the first time that night, Montgomery managed to smile. "Something like that." He slapped her jeans against her chest. "I'll start looking."

Jordan scouted around the bushes, while Montgomery checked the shack inside and out. "Anything?" she called out to him as she trotted back to where the Wolf had stood.

Montgomery, on his knees checking under the building, shook his head. "Nothing."

She scanned for a string that could have held any sort of screen for a projector. "Same here," she said.

Montgomery's eye widened, wider than hers felt. "Unless we've been dosed with something, somehow, we saw the Wolf."

Jordan swallowed. "What do we do now?"

Montgomery looked around again. "We go home, and we discuss it there."

Jordan looked at him with an arched eyebrow. Montgomery shook his head again. Something had him worried, and she wasn't sure if it was because it looked like the gods were real, or he had just found proof they weren't. She held out her hand for the keys. Montgomery dropped them into her hand, and they walked back to his green SUV.

The drive back home was quiet, half due to Jordan's yawns and Montgomery's gestures to be quiet. They made it inside the building an hour before dawn. Jordan dropped her keys into the bowl and walked to each window, making sure the sun-proof shields were down and in place while Montgomery headed towards the bedroom. It didn't appear that Thorn had arrived yet. Once she was sure there wouldn't be any encroaching sunlight, she headed to the bedroom.

Montgomery was spread over his side of the bed, lying on his back, shirt off. Jordan kicked off her shoes and flopped onto her stomach. She inched up to lie next to him. "So, was the building bugged?"

"I didn't see microphones, but you can't be sure since so many different Family members had access to the building."

Jordan rested her head against Montgomery's chest. It still felt weird not to hear the steady beat of a human heart. Instead, she heard one beat every minute or so. Between the stress of the meeting and the hunt, all she wanted to do was snuggle in further and fall asleep. But she had questions to ask. "What makes you think this apartment isn't bugged?"

"I'm hoping it's not." Montgomery wrapped his arm around her shoulders. "We have to assume it isn't. Otherwise, we have no place we can talk in private."

"Is the cabin bugged?"

"I don't think so. But I saw some wires that I wasn't sure what they connected to."

Jordan sighed. "I'll talk to Alpha Shane. He might know someone who can look over the cabin."

She felt his lips brush across the crown of her head. "I'm proud of you, you know." He smiled when she twisted her head to look up at him. "You stood up to tonight's challenges with more grace and finesse than I would have. And you're clearly trying to make people who could easily be your enemies into your allies."

"It feels like I'm making more enemies doing that," Jordan grumbled.

"That sounds ominous," a third voice cut in.

Jordan lifted her head and looked at the door. "Hey, Thorn."

"Am I interrupting something?"

Montgomery waved a hand. "Come on and join us."

Thorn shucked his shirt and sat on the bed. He leaned over to untie his combat boots. "So, did everything go okay?"

"I'm alive and an alpha," Jordan answered.

Thorn blinked. "How?"

"A technicality," Montgomery said. "She has land to her name and Rex as a follower. But that's not the biggest news of the evening. We saw the Wolf," Montgomery added.

Thorn jerked back. "You saw the Wolf!"

Jordan nodded. "We both did."

Thorn shook his head. "You're going to need to explain that."

Jordan sighed and rolled onto her back, pillowing her head on Montgomery's arm. "I performed the ritual hunt and caught a rabbit. I brought it back. Talespeaker Diana and I called on the Wolf, and She appeared."

"Wow," Thorn said. He looked at Montgomery. "You saw her too?"

Montgomery nodded. "I can't say I honestly believed until that moment."

Thorn arched an eyebrow. "Despite being groomed to be an alpha yourself?"

Montgomery shrugged. Jordan's head raised and lowered, following the motion. "One of my many failings, besides becoming a vampire," he said. "The fact that I never claimed a vision of her was probably used as a sign that I was unfit to lead."

Thorn snorted and rolled his eyes. "Like She shows herself to every alpha."

"According to most of them, yes, she does," Montgomery countered.

"Does the Bat reveal himself to Elders?" Jordan asked.

Montgomery and Thorn both chuckled. "Oh, I'm sure they say that they have the Bat's blessing," Montgomery said. "But most don't want to acknowledge that they aren't the ultimate power."

"And the Bat hasn't kept his identity safe by revealing himself to every bloodsucker who claims to control a few blocks in the downtown area," Thorn said. "That would be a quick way for him to end up dead."

"But he's the Bat," Jordan said. "He's a god."

"Cursed god," Montgomery corrected.

"And immortality never equates to invulnerability, Jo." Now, it was Thorn's turn to shrug. "Don't think that an Elder wouldn't try to claim the Bat's power as their own, by enslavement, by captivity, or by attempting to drain him."

Jordan shivered. "That's a frightening thought." What she didn't say was what they were all thinking. Elder Marcus would definitely be on the list of those who would attempt it.

"Don't think there aren't those who wouldn't try to do the same to the Wolf if they had the chance," Thorn said. "Which explains why She's so cautious about who She reveals herself to."

"And why you have so many people like me who don't really believe until we're slapped in the face with her existence."

Thorn reached across Jordan to squeeze Montgomery's shoulder. "Don't beat yourself up, Mac. You're handling it a lot better than I've seen some handling learning that the Bat is real."

Montgomery squinted his eyes shut. "I hadn't carried the logic that far."

Jordan remained quiet. She thought of the giant bat from her dream. And the swooping figure that drove the rabbit into her jaws. Someone shook her shoulder. She twisted to look at Montgomery. "Huh?"

Thorn nudged her closest shoulder. "You looked like you checked out for a minute."

"Sorry. Lost in thought. Like what's the belief about when a werewolf dies?"

Montgomery exhaled. "There's a lot of variants, but most state that if the Wolf deems they have lived an honorable life, they'll run with her Pack."

"And if not?"

Montgomery shrugged. "Some say oblivion. We cease to exist. Our name is never spoken." He paused, brown knitting. "Others say we become the prey that the Wolf's Pack hunts."

"What about vampires?"

"Most, if they still have any religious beliefs, tend to hold to those." Thorn waggled his hand. "We're functionally immortal, which tends to make us more atheistic. But I've talked to a few who are concerned where they would end up if they did meet the wrong end of a stake."

"And what do you two believe?"

"The Bat's out there," Thorn said in a voice that would brook no arguments. "What happens after we die? I don't know."

She looked at Montgomery. "And you?"

"I don't know what to believe anymore."

"Did you not believe in the Wolf when you were mortal?"

Montgomery shook his head.

"If you can't deal with the thought of the Wolf, and by extension the Bat, being real, you can always tell yourself it was part of a group hallucination."

"That's not how group hallucinations work, Thorn," Montgomery pointed out.

"Then what did you think you saw?"

He sighed. "Because of the fact it didn't go her way, I'm sure Enya is saying it's some sort of trickery that Alpha Shane and I cooked up."

"That wasn't the question, Mac."

Montgomery's head fell back, eyes fixing on the ceiling. "I don't know. Even when I was a werewolf, I didn't have the greatest faith. None of the things I was told happened to future alphas happened to me. And then, when I lost Dad and Christine..." He turned his head away from Jordan and Thorn.

Jordan wrapped her hand around Montgomery's. His fingers curled around hers, and then Thorn's palm rested against the back of his hand. "You wondered if She was so concerned, why She didn't prevent it from happening."

He didn't look at them but nodded.

"I can't speak for the Wolf," Thorn said. "But I believe the Bat had as much of a vested interest in what happened." Thorn's hand squeezed hers, pressing it further against Montgomery's palm. "But I believe that as much as He wanted to intervene, he couldn't."

"Why?" Jordan asked as Montgomery refocused on them.

"The Bat has tried to interfere before," Thorn said. "Thought he knew best and tried to make things right, or at least what He thought was right. And every time, it made the situation worse. So, he stopped interfering." Thorn squeezed their joined hands again. " But I don't think He ever stopped caring. And I think the Wolf feels the same way."

"But you have no way of knowing for certain," Montgomery said.

"No," Thorn said. "But that's what having faith is about, isn't it?"

"You have," Thorn said. "Just not in the Wolf."

Montgomery raised his eyebrows in question.

"You had it in Jordan, that she'd be able to learn to shift."

"That's different," he mumbled.

Thorn arched an eyebrow. "Is it?"

Jordan looked at Montgomery. "Look, I'm in the same place as you. I wasn't raised with religion, so this is all new to me. I never expected to dream about a god, let alone meet her in real life."

"At least she acknowledged you."

"Is that what this is about?" Jordan asked. "I didn't ask for any of this. I don't want any of this. And you said you didn't even believe in Her."

"I know Jordan. I know. I just..."

"Look," Thorn said. "We've all had a shock. We won't figure it out tonight. Hell, we won't figure it out in a few lifetimes. Besides, it's almost dawn. How about we try to get some sleep?"

She felt Montgomery's chest arch, his mouth opening to protest. But instead, he deflated, seeing the wisdom of Thorn's words. "Okay," he agreed.

All three nestled down further under the comforter, Jordan's hand rested on Montgomery's shoulder, thumb lightly brushing back and forth. She felt Thorn press against her back, his arm shift against her side as his hand settled on Montgomery's hip.

As both men fell into the unnatural stillness that unconscious vampire shared, Jordan wondered, and not for the first time, if she should insist one of them take the center spot. Or that was what she chose to focus on. If she focused on the events of the evening, she couldn't get to sleep at all.

15

───────

Montgomery wasn't surprised when he, Jordan, and Thorn awoke to Jordan's phone beeping. On it was a text message summoning Montgomery to meet with Elder Marcus first thing this evening. Jordan's reaction had been a worried frown. Thorn threw up his hands and declared that he had nothing to do with it. And Montgomery believed him. While Thorn may have been acting as Marcus' spy in the past, and still was in some ways, he wasn't good enough to tell Marcus that things had gone south at the meeting before he was even aware.

After a quick drink and shower, he hurried to the Hotel Cataluña. It wouldn't do to keep Marcus waiting, especially with news that he knew wouldn't please him.

"...And she asked Angela Shane to help train her for the duel," Montgomery finished, bringing his sire up to date. Even with the warm leather and woods that made up most of the furniture of Elder Marcus' office, Montgomery had to fight the chill that crept up his spine whenever he sat in it. "She's meeting with Alpha Shane, Talespeaker Diana, and Ms. Shane about the details at this very moment."

Marcus sat behind his desk. He had remained perfectly still, while Montgomery recited the events of the prior evening and Jordan's interaction with the Black Oak Pack and the representatives of the Green River Pack. He leaned back in his seat, processing what Montgomery had said. "And the completion of this hunt and the sacrifice was successful?"

Montgomery nodded. "Yes." He wasn't sure how religious Marcus was—if he believed that the Bat and the Wolf were mere metaphors for the antipathy vampires and werewolves felt, or if he believed in them as living gods. He wasn't sure that he wanted to bring up to Marcus that there was something more powerful out there, and She had her eyes on Rancho Robles. "She performed it flawlessly. It's not so much that she can hunt. A big part of it proves her self-control. The rabbit she hunted only had marks necessary to kill it. If there had been any hint that she had begun to eat it, she would have failed."

"Would that she showed some self-control in other situations," Marcus mumbled. If he was doing what Montgomery suspected, he was running through every permutation of how the future could lead—if Jordan won, if she lost, and what that would mean for both Montgomery, the Conclave, and him. "I was under the impression that young Ms. Shane and your famulus did not get along."

Now, he had to tread carefully. Marcus hadn't been told about the incident with Animal Control, and he had no intention of ever letting him know. "The fight where Jordan defeated her seems to have relieved a lot of tension between the two. They seem to have settled their differences and understand where they stand with each other. They aren't best friends, but they are no longer actively antagonistic towards each other." Technically, what he said wasn't a lie, but it wasn't the full truth either.

"And this ritual that was performed?"

"Yes, sir."

"The one that convinced everyone Jordan is an alpha?"

"Yes, sir," he said. "Like I said, she performed it flawlessly. There was no reasonable argument that could be made against the outcome."

He knew that Marcus wanted the details of what happened. However, Marcus also knew there were certain things that Montgomery wouldn't tell him. Exactly how alphas were determined to be legitimate was one of the secrets that was still held closely. "Were you banned from observing because you're vampire?"

"It's a ceremony that only werewolves are permitted to be present for," Montgomery said, treading cautiously. He didn't know how his sire would react to him having seen the Wolf. The thought that the Wolf, and therefore the Bat, were real, could be seen as a threat to his power. "I made the argument that if they wanted me present as a chaos wolf to meet Envoy Blevins, then I had just as much right to be there."

Marcus gave no sign if he approved of that tactic or not. Or if he was angered that Montgomery wasn't giving him the details of what happened at the ceremony. But it was a relief that Marcus remained focused on Jordan's status. "So, Black Oak now considers her an alpha, or at least their Alpha does. Shane might be trying to manipulate her to his advantage, giving her a false sense of power."

Montgomery shook his head. "I don't think so, sir. That's not his style. Having acknowledged that she's an alpha makes her a peer with him. The pack will face dire consequences if they attempt to bully her as they have in the past. Or at least as long as she has Shane's support."

Marcus leaned back in his chair, considering Montgomery's statement. "Is Shane willing to back her?"

"He feels he owes her a debt of honor after the mess with the hunter earlier this year." No need to remind him that he, Thorn, and Jordan had saved his life as well. "I believe he was trying to position himself to aid her and challenge Blevins himself." He shook his head. "Unfortunately, with his daughter's maneuvering, it cut him off. Jordan's now considered an alpha in her own right as far as Green River is concerned, and that limits how he can aid her. Blevins and Jordan must resolve their conflict before any others can be considered."

Marcus nodded. "And what are her odds of her beating the envoy?"

"I don't know," Montgomery answered. "Jordan has killed a werewolf in the past. While Shane thinks she got lucky, I'm not so certain. Rhys may have not been fighting full-out since he wanted her as his mate. But I can't be certain."

Marcus arched an eyebrow in disbelief. "You were present for that fight."

"I was also half-starved from the lack of blood after Rhys beat me and jammed me into a footlocker. Everything until Jordan got me out of the cabin is a blur, and I'm not completely clear after that either."

Marcus leaned forward. "And what's your opinion. Is she legitimately an Alpha?"

The question had been asked in the mildest of curious tones. Montgomery knew better and chose his words carefully. He wasn't asking for Montgomery's opinion but for his assessment. "Yes, but it's a technicality. She has a pack in the loosest sense of the word. She has territory that's recognized by another pack. She completed the ritual hunt. Those three are the base requirements."

"But she is also your famulus. Won't that be a conflict of interest?"

He expected the next question to be who her pack members were. Was Marcus already assuming it was him? "That may be how some people consider it, yes," Montgomery confirmed, hating the catch in his voice. "Most of the werewolves are focused on the dog she walks on a regular basis as her packmate. But I have no reason to doubt her loyalty to me. In practicality, she isn't a threat to your domain or the Conclave."

"It's not her threat I'm concerned about." Marcus' expression hardened. "Her being an Alpha and a famulus might be the excuse a Pack needs to go on a crusade to wipe out our Conclave, either to free her from our tyrannical rule, or to destroy her as a traitor. Or worse, convince her to turn traitor. All she would need would be a decent following and she could destroy us all."

Montgomery rocked back in the seat, as if his sire's words were a blow. "Sir, do you really believe Jordan would do that?"

Marcus arched an eyebrow at him. "Do you believe you have that tight of a leash on her?"

"She trusts me," Montgomery said. "If I ask her to do something, she'll obey without question." The last part was a stretch, but she hadn't outright refused anything he'd asked of her so far.

"Oh yes, she's clearly obedient to you," Marcus said. "So obedient, she shifted within the city limits. Animal Control picked her up a few weeks ago, and the pups of the Black Oak Pack had to bail her out."

A trickle of ice ran down Montgomery's spine. He knew. Marcus knew. How long had he known? And who had told him?

Marcus continued talking as if he hadn't noticed his blood-child's sudden stillness. "Any other time, I would have ordered you to put her down for such blatant disregard of my orders. However, since she did help save my life in a public manner, I won't punish her this time. Nor will I publicly chastise you for having such lax discipline over her." His eyes narrowed. "I won't be as benevolent if she oversteps again. Have I made myself clear?"

Montgomery swallowed down his panic. "As crystal, sir."

Marcus' voice was softer than he expected. "I sincerely hope so." Then it hardened. "Get her on a short leash, Montgomery. And the sooner the better, for the both of you."

"And if I'm not able to?" he asked, dreading the answer he would get, but feeling compelled to ask it.

"Then I'll do it myself." He looked Montgomery in the eyes.

"And she won't be the only one I put a leash on." Marcus continued on as if he were now discussing the weather. "Now, onto other matters. Tomorrow night, you'll be introduced to your elder bloodbrother. Nicolas Quinn has returned to Rancho Robles and will be reintroduced to the Conclave. You and your famulus will be present for a private meeting before he's presented to the general assembly."

Montgomery nodded, trying to pull himself back into a semblance of control. "We'll be there, of course. And she'll be on her best behavior."

"As you should be," Marcus warned. "I know that you made a request to Rosanna, and she refused. Consider the matter closed. I do not want any visible friction between you and Rosanna. We are to present a united front."

"Yes, sir."

"I really wish you had shown some discretion, Montgomery, instead of irritating Rosanna with your request. While it would be a shame to lose your famulus, you must remember her job is to serve you. If her death is how that service is accomplished, then she will have performed her duties."

Montgomery's jaw clenched. He wasn't surprised that Marcus caught that small movement. "Do you have something to say?"

"I think she could serve a better purpose alive," Montgomery said. "If she pulls this off, she'll be considered an alpha, even if no werewolf joins her pack."

"There might be some who consider her your alpha, if you appear to be listening to your old instincts too much." Marcus' question was velvet soft and steel hard. "Do you consider her your alpha?"

Montgomery's chin jerked higher. "I'm her Patron, not a member of her Pack."

Marcus nodded, a faint smile on his lips. "Remember that always, Montgomery. And be ready to prove that if you must."

Montgomery didn't have to ask how he would have to prove it.

Jordan would be the one paying the price. There would be no way around it. And he would be the one exacting it.

He left Marcus' office without saying anything to Sarah this time. He held himself in a formal stiffness for anyone who was watching, and there were always people watching, until he reached his car. Once the door pulled shut, he allowed himself to sink into the seat, head leaning into the headrest. He blew out his breath. His first instinct was to go back to the apartment. Except he needed to talk to someone, and that someone couldn't be Jordan. Or not at least until he had a clearer grasp on what he and Marcus had just discussed. That left one option. Decision made, he started his car and pulled away from the Hotel Cataluña, escaping it for at least the rest of the night.

16

———

For once, when she showed up on the Black Oak Pack's home grounds, Jordan didn't feel like she was stepping into completely hostile territory. Or at least the ire normally directed at her was well hidden.

It started when she got out of her rideshare and walked up to the gate. Instead of having to hit the call box button and go through the ritual of asking for permission to enter, it rolled aside for her. Jordan arched an eyebrow but stepped through. If they wouldn't make her justify her visit, she wouldn't give them a reason to.

A dark-haired, dark-skinned male werewolf stepped out of the shack where the controls were housed. "Alpha Abbey," Sentry Rodriguez greeted her as he opened the gate.

"Sentry Rodriguez," she said, trying to hide her confusion. He called her Alpha and not Chaos Wolf?

Jordan resisted the urge to look around for someone else as he continued speaking, "Would you care for an escort up to the main house, or would you prefer a ride up there?"

She didn't want to make the long walk. Not having been ambushed the last time she took the long trail up to the main house, and Angela's ambush had left a definite impression, mostly on her backside. "A ride would be nice, Sentry Rodriguez."

"One moment, ma'am." The Sentry stepped back into the shack.

This time, Jordan did look around for her mother.

He stepped out again within fifteen seconds. "Someone will be down to transport you in a few minutes."

"Thank you, Sentry Rodriguez." If he could be formal, she would be in turn. She didn't think he was mocking her. He was being nothing but polite and respectful, but she couldn't be absolutely sure. Especially with the awkward silence and how he waited with her for whoever was coming.

After a minute, she heard a soft electric hum in the distance. It didn't have the weight behind it that Thorn's electric vehicle did. This was softer, less powerful, and somehow bumpily uneven. After another moment she saw why. Billy was driving a golf cart, one that reminded Jordan of the six seaters she had occasionally seen driven around Rancho Robles Community College by the maintenance people. Her mouth widened into a smile as she waved hello. "Hey, Billy."

Billy responded to her bright greeting with a seriousness she hadn't seen on him before. "Alpha Abbey.' He pulled the cart up within a yard of where she stood. "I'm here to escort you to the main house. If you would have a seat, please?"

She bit the inside of her lip but climbed into the front passenger seat. "Thank you," she said with equal gravity. She sat, hands folded and head lifted as if she were royalty riding in an open carriage before her subjects. Once she was settled, he U-turned and drove towards the main house.

And Jordan found herself in another awkward silence. Except Billy was her friend, and hell if she'd let that stand. Putting on her best royal voice, she asked, "May I inquire as to how you are doing, William?"

The cart jerked as Billy snort laughed. "Don't call me that, Alpha Abbey."

"And you don't call me that!"

"You don't want me to show you your due respect?"

Jordan rolled her eyes. "You saw me in that sparkly collar. I think we both know how much respect I'm due."

Billy laughed. "We've all worn that collar or something like it. Besides, Alpha Shane would have my hide if I were rude to a visiting dignitary."

"Dignitary? I'm not sure I like the sound of that. Reminds me too much of my great aunt. How about this? In public, be as formal as you want. But when it's just you and me, it's Jordan."

"Deal."

"So... can I ask about how things are going with your *friend*?"

The corners of his lips curled up, telling Jordan that he had caught the slight emphasis on the last word. "It's going well. I just wish..." He focused on the road in front of them, hands tensing on the steering wheel.

"I get it." It wasn't that Billy was dating another male, but that he was dating a human. One opinion that vampires and werewolves shared was that the mortal population, unless they could be absolutely trusted, couldn't know about the existence of paranormals. She had been trailed before when heading to the main house, and there was no reason to believe it wouldn't still be happening. "We should meet for coffee sometime. I'd like to get to know him when I'm not wearing a fur coat."

Billy straightened, shoulders dropping and fingers relaxing their grip. "Maybe next week, after this all gets settled?"

Now, it was Jordan's turn to tighten up and then force herself to relax. "Yeah," she said as they pulled up to the house. "Sounds like a plan."

Billy nodded as she slipped out of the cart. "Good luck," he said and pulled away.

She watched him head towards the garage. Jordan shook her

head. For the first time, she felt like an honored guest instead of a begrudgingly tolerated visitor. And a small voice in her skull couldn't help but wonder how long this would last.

The over-the-top politeness continued when Angela opened the door for her. "Alpha Abbey, we of the Black Oak Pack greet you and welcome you to our territory. May you have a full belly and sleep in a warm den."

This time, she didn't wince at the use of her new title. She'd never heard that greeting before but recognized a formal salutation when she heard one. Jordan did lift an eyebrow. "Are you going to greet me like that every time I come here?"

"Only when it annoys you," Angela said. "Or would you rather I say, 'Yo! Bitch! Come on in!'?"

Jordan shook her head as she crossed the threshold, grinning. "You have to admit. That fits our relationship better."

Angela actually smiled at that. "True." She gestured down the hall. "Dad and Talespeaker Diana are waiting."

"Thanks." She followed Angela to the main room, which seemed much larger than the night before. But that could have been when she was normally in it, it was filled with the entirety of the pack and any other guests who were there to discuss what she had done this time.

"Alpha Abbey." Shane and the Talespeaker rose from where they were sitting on the couch. "I trust you had a pleasant journey."

"Yes," Jordan said, drawing out the word. "Why is everyone treating me with respect suddenly? It's kinda freaking me out."

Shane chuckled. "Thanks to my daughter, you aren't seen as a chaos wolf causing trouble."

"Oh," Jordan said. "Let me guess. I'm now a leader of a rival pack causing trouble."

Shane actually chuckled while Diana shook her head. "Something like that," she said. She gestured to the smaller loveseat. "Take a seat, Jordan. We have a lot we need to go over."

Jordan perched on the edge of the loveseat, not fully comfortable with the situation. "So, you've made the arrangements for the fight?"

"How much has Montgomery told you about it?"

"Basically? Not much more than he said in front of you. Something about not wanting to give me bad information."

Shane shook his head. "Can't blame him. He's never had to fight in one of these, so he might be hazy on the details."

"Would the last one have been around when he was turned?" Angela asked.

Shane didn't say anything but nodded.

That was all the confirmation Jordan needed. The last challenge would have been when Shane challenged Alpha Cooper, Montgomery's father, for the leadership of the pack.

Diana shook her head. "Whose lesson is this supposed to be? Jordan or Angela's?" She fixed her bright eyes on Jordan's face. "Now, we've negotiated it the best we can for you. The fight will be at night so your Patron can attend. You'll be restricted to your bipedal form, so shapeshifting won't play a part. And there will be no silver. The fight is about proving that you're the superior werewolf, in theory."

"In theory," Jordan echoed.

"Yes, in theory," Shane said. "There's always an element of luck to these fights. Your battle with Rhys for example."

She was getting tired of everyone telling her it was stupid luck that she won that fight. But she didn't want to irritate Alpha Shane, since he hadn't been her ally until recently. Funny how saving his life had helped with that. "Was Montgomery wrong about it being to the death?"

"Technically, no," Diana said. "In the past, fights to the death weren't unheard of. These days, they are to first blood. That doesn't mean that first blood won't be a killing blow."

"Great," Jordan sighed. "I'm dealing with a traditionalist."

"Unfortunately, yes." Shane said. "Now, think about this,

Jordan. You've killed before. If you must, do you think you'll be able to do so again?" Shane shook his head when Jordan didn't immediately reply. "At least you're not overly cocky." He gave his daughter a sideways glance. "Even if you didn't know what you were getting yourself into."

"Telling me that I was an ignorant pup won't help me now," Jordan said. "So, tell me what I need to know. Like start with where this will happen."

"It will be in the meadow with the oak tree," Diana said, "under the light of Luna. Black Oak will be present, as well as any guests you wish to have present."

Jordan arched an eyebrow. "Vampire guests?"

Alpha Shane rolled his eyes as the Talespeaker answered, "Yes. And any humans who are aware if you want."

"No humans," Jordan said. "Montgomery for sure and probably Thorn. I won't know if Elder Marcus will want to attend until tomorrow."

"There will be an area cordoned off. The oak tree will make one corner. Alpha Shane, Talespeaker Lucas, and I will form the other corners. Your fight will be contained to that area. Step out of bounds, and it's an automatic forfeit. We'll call out any rule violations we see."

Jordan caught the inside of her lower lip between her teeth. "Do you think she'll cheat?"

Angela shook her head. "She won't think that she has to."

"Hey," Jordan snapped. "I've won fights. One of them was against you."

"And the other times I kicked your butt," Angela said. "You got lucky. You want to take a chance on getting lucky again?"

Jordan drew herself up, squaring her shoulders. And then, she deflated. "No. I don't."

Alpha Shane nodded in approval. "You're finally showing some wisdom." He looked at Angela. "Are you sure you can teach her in the allotted time?"

Angela looked Jordan up and down, considering her carefully. "I think it can be done. Maybe."

Jordan snorted. "Thanks for the vote of confidence." She turned her attention back to Shane and Diana. "What happens once I win?"

"If you win," Diana corrected, "she will acknowledge you as alpha."

Jordan frowned. "But that won't solve the problem about me taking her brother's fangs."

"No, but because you'll have proven yourself the stronger werewolf, she can yell all she wants. Nobody in your Pack will have to listen to her."

Pack, Jordan thought. *What Pack?* The only member would be a dog, and she wasn't even his owner. "What's to keep her sister Guinevere from coming down here and challenging me?"

"If Alpha Lynden were able to come down here, she wouldn't have sent an envoy. Her hold over the Green River Pack may not be as firm as she would have everyone believe."

"So, I'll still have to watch my back. Wonderful."

"Jordan, given the decisions you've made, you should constantly be watching your back," Alpha Shane said.

She sensed the waft of air against the nape of her neck. She whipped around, leg lashing out to hook behind Angela's knee and pull her down before she looked back at Alpha Shane. "What makes you think I don't?"

Alpha Shane chuckled. "Angela, I think you may be right about being able to train her."

17

______

Montgomery walked to the main entrance of The Wilted Rose, Thorn's tattoo shop. He pushed open the door and walked over to the display case where a young woman stood. "Welcome to The Wilted Rose," she said, pushing hair the color of a fire engine back from her eyes. Light glinted off a cobalt blue ring in one nostril. "Do you have an appointment?"

"No, actually, I'm not here for a tattoo," he said. "I was hoping I could talk to Thorn?"

"I'll see if he's free," she said. "Can I have your name please?"

"Tell him Montgomery wants to talk to him."

She nodded. "Give me a moment." She slipped through a curtain to one side of the counter, leaving him with the hum of tattoo guns and the stink of rubbing alcohol.

He bent over the counter, studying a sketch of a wolf's head poking through a circlet of ivy leaves. Although the wolf wasn't a solid black, it reminded him of Jordan for some reason. He wasn't surprised to see Thorn's initials on a lower corner of the page.

"Hey." He looked up to see the woman had returned from the back room. "The boss can see you now."

Montgomery nodded and followed the woman through the curtains. He walked past several alcoves, about half of them filled with clients and tattooists. None of which Thorn occupied. To his surprise, he was led to a back storage area instead of an office. "He's here, boss."

"Thanks, Charla," came Thorn's voice from the other side of the threshold.

He stepped through the door of a space that wasn't more than a glorified storage closet. Thorn had a tablet in hand. His eyes traveled between the stock of inks and equipment boxes and the tablet. "Close the door, Mac."

"Why are you back here?" Montgomery asked as he pulled the door shut, granting them privacy. "I thought you'd be up front, tatting."

Thorn winced. "First, the term is inking. Tatting is that thing where you make lace. Second, I can't tattoo if I don't have the supplies. And since I'm the boss, guess who is responsible?" He tapped something on the tablet. "So, how'd it go with Marcus?"

Montgomery shrugged. "The usual. 'She got herself into this mess. She can get herself out of it.' And I can expect to meet my elder bloodbrother tomorrow. Oh, there's one more thing." He paused for a moment, eyes on Thorn to gauge his reaction. "He knows about Jordan's incident with Animal Control."

Thorn put the tablet down on the shelf. He turned from the shelving to meet his eyes. "He what?"

Montgomery kept his voice even. They had already fought once about Thorn reporting to Marcus his and Jordan's doings. "Did you tell him?"

"Wait." He studied Montgomery before speaking. "You think I'm still spying for Marcus?"

Montgomery's voice was as flat as his expression. "That's not a yes or no, Kelly. Are you?"

"I swear to you, Montgomery, I told him nothing. If he found out, it wasn't from me."

Thorn never called him by his name unless it was serious. Even during their most intimate times, he was still Mac. The only time he used Montgomery was when he wanted to emphasize his point. "Any idea how he did?"

Thorn shook his head. "Most of it happened during the day. So, he either has a famulus in Animal Control..."

"Or a spy within Black Oak Pack," Montgomery finished.

"Would Alpha Shane have told him?"

"I'm not sure. It doesn't make me look good, which I'm sure he would jump at. But it could put his daughter in danger since she was involved."

"He still could have let something slip about the collar. Christine told me the story about what happened to you, so someone could have told Marcus. And if anyone mentioned that Jordan had a shiny collar, he could put two and two together."

"Or it could have been as simple as him spotting Jordan on their website and telling him. You saw that picture they took of her and Angela for their Reunited Pets section."

"Yeah, but you know how technically adept he is."

"One of his Family then."

"Still, that would mean he's keeping a close eye on you."

"I'm not surprised," Thorn drawled. "What about the Wolf being the one to declare she's a proper alpha? You tell him about that?"

He found it odd that Thorn used the word vision and not hallucination. "I left that part out. I just said that she could complete the ritual hunt, and that made it official. She's an alpha now."

Thorn blew out a breath. "Better hope he doesn't find out about what you left out."

"A visitation of the Wolf is considered sacred among werewolves and not to be talked about with outsiders." He stared at Thorn, hoping he wasn't making a huge mistake. "I'm trusting that you won't reveal this to anyone."

Thorn nodded. "Of course, Montgomery."

"Thank you, Kelly."

For once, Thorn didn't twitch when someone used his real name. "You know he's spying on you too."

Montgomery raised his hands, palms upwards as he shrugged. "Can you honestly say that he ever trusted me? He doesn't trust his own shadow. Why should I expect to be treated differently?"

Thorn shook his head. "You're not following, Mac. It's not that he doesn't trust you. It means he's actively spying on you and not with the obvious spies like me."

"Could that be part of why Nicholas is returning? A test of my loyalty?"

Thorn shrugged. "His brain is so twisty, I wouldn't be surprised if his ideas met themselves coming around a corner."

"What do you know about Nicholas?"

Thorn drew in a deep breath and tapped his fingers against the shelf. "He's a piece of work. Definitely wants to be the next Marcus. Only his relative inexperience has kept him from attempting a coup here."

"Is that why he left?"

"I never heard the exact why. The rumor mill said that he and Marcus had a huge blow up before he left."

"Any reason why?"

"You, actually," Thorn said. "This was when Marcus approached your father about bringing you into the Conclave as a bridge between our peoples."

"And look how that worked out." He leaned forward, resting his elbows on his knees and wiping one hand over his face.

"He won't be pleased to meet you," Thorn said. "Or Jordan, for that matter."

"How do you think I should handle him?"

"Wait and see how Marcus treats him. If he's being feted like the prodigal son—"

"The who?"

"It's a story in one of the human religions. It's about an estranged son returning to the family and his father pulling out all the stops to celebrate. His older son gets jealous and talked down to."

"Well, since I'm the younger one, that won't be happening."

"I'm serious, Mac. Don't make the mistake of taking this lightly. Nicholas is dangerous. Until you know how he stands with Marcus, stay polite but distant." Thorn paused. "He also has an eye for women. Specifically, dark-haired, dark-eyed women."

And that fit the description of someone he knew. "Like Jordan."

"Yeah, and rumor has it that being someone else's famulus doesn't act as a deterrent. That was the other rumor about why he left so quickly."

Montgomery leaned forward. "Whose did he mess with?"

"Some said Rosanna, some said Marcus. Some said both." Thorn looked him in the eye. "Just keep close tabs on Jordan."

"That'll be harder with what Blevins is trying to pull."

"And Angela," Thorn added, "You know that Marcus will call me in to report on you and Jordan."

"Yeah, I figured as much." Montgomery paused, looking Thorn up and down. "What will you tell him?"

"What I can without getting either of you into too much trouble."

Montgomery shook his head. "May be too late for that. He's already making comments about me needing to put Jordan on a tighter leash."

Thorn tapped a finger against his chin. "That might not be a bad idea."

"Come again?"

"Hope to later tonight," he said and ignored Montgomery's snort. "A public display of dominance might not be a bad thing.

Just a show, something we'd clear with Jordan ahead of time to prove you have a firm hand on her, and she's not running wild."

Montgomery inhaled through exposed teeth. "I'm not sure how well that will go over with her."

"It doesn't have to be for real," Thorn said. "Just something that will make Marcus and probably Rosanna happy. Prove that she doesn't have you completely hypnotized by her feminine werewolf charms."

"I dare you to say that to her," Montgomery said with a grin. "And that will go over so well with the Black Oak Pack."

Thorn frowned. "Actually, I hadn't thought about how Pamela would react to that."

Montgomery tilted his head, wondering why Thorn was talking about a mid-ranked pack member. "Why are you concerned about how Pamela would react? I'd be more worried about Alpha Shane finding out."

Thorn waved a hand, shooing his words away. "Slip of the tongue. She stopped by the tattoo shop earlier to see if I could identify someone's ink. You think Shane would react poorly?"

Thorn's answer was a little too smooth. But it was a reasonable explanation. "Yeah," he said, pulling his attention back to Thorn's question. "While he might not react as badly if it were any of his pack, he'll use the fact that we're picking on a werewolf to his advantage. Especially if he feels he owes her for publicly saving his life."

"Hadn't thought of that," Thorn admitted. "Maybe instead of a public censure, we ask if she can tone it down a little in public. Pretend that she's received a tongue lashing and acts appropriately meek."

Montgomery laughed. "This is Jordan we're talking about," he said. "Meek isn't one of the words I'd use to describe her."

"True," Thorn said. He shook his head. "It was a stupid idea."

"It's not that bad of an idea. We can talk to her when she gets home, assuming she's awake enough after whatever training regime Angela put her through."

Thorn shook his head. "Never thought I'd see them actually trying to help her."

"I'm sure part of it is that Angela gets to beat up on her in a sanctioned way. They may have come to some sort of peace, but I doubt they'll ever be best friends." Montgomery shook his head.

"Sort of like Alpha Shane and you?"

"We sparred, but we never beat each other up." A memory of an ache of Shane punching him squarely in the jaw said otherwise. But that was after Christine and his father had been killed. That didn't count.

"I'm talking about the two of you now. You don't pass up a chance to snipe at each other, but at least you're not as openly hostile as you were when Jordan first showed up." Thorn grinned. "If I didn't know any better, I'd say you might have a little crush on him."

Montgomery shrugged. "Maybe once but not for a long time. He's a political rival of Elder Marcus'. Nothing more."

Thorn nodded. "So political rival. How does this mess with Jordan fit into it?"

"We have to do what we can to keep him in power, as much as I don't like it," Montgomery said. "Aside with what happened with me and my father, things have been stable." He paused. "Have you found out anything about my father?"

Thorn shook his head. "Nothing concrete. Still waiting for some contacts to get back to me."

Montgomery shrugged. It was a vain hope he should have let go of a long time ago. "I'm not surprised the trail is cold."

"Doesn't mean it doesn't exist," Thorn said. "And it will just take time." Thorn put one hand on Montgomery's shoulder and squeezed. "And who has more time than a vampire?"

18

The burger joint they had agreed to meet at had changed some since the last time he had been here. Thorn looked around, taking note of the changes from the booth he had picked for privacy. While still serving hamburgers, hotdogs, chicken sandwiches, and french fries three times the size of what you could get at a fast-food restaurant, the decor had changed. The dining area had been gutted and redesigned. The plastic laminate tables with spindly wooden chairs had refitted with dark wood booths and tables with stools, replacing the laminates tables and chairs. The one screen for showing the most popular sporting event airing at the moment had replicated to six on two walls, each one tuned to a different event. But the biggest change was the full-service bar that dwarfed the register where food was ordered. Although the website still stated family friendly when he double-checked if they were open, the feel was more a pub crossed with a sports bar, emphasis on bar.

The waitress had left his drink and a basket of onion rings, the better to blend in, when the door opened. Thorn glanced away from the soccer game to note that Pamela entered. She looked around, searching for him and assessing the decor. He wondered if he had the same look of surprise at the changes. He lifted his hand and waved. Pamela nodded and then went to the register to place her order.

Then she was heading in his direction, her expression neutral. He watched as Pamela settled into the other side of him in the booth. He felt her surprise. "You're drinking a Tequila Sunrise?"

Thorn shrugged and slid the onion rings towards her. "I thought you would appreciate the irony." He snipped at the drink, knowing he wouldn't enjoy how his body would process it later. "Or are you shocked by me actually attempting it?"

Pamela shook her head. "Don't think that I'm going to finish that for you." She looked around the dining area. "It's a bit of an upgrade from the old place."

"They've stepped out of the eighties."

"Times change. We change." She gestured to the two of them. "Could you see us having this conversation five years ago? Ten? Twenty?"

A century? Thorn thought. *A millennia?*

From the distant look on her face, Thorn believed Pamela may have thought something along the same lines. At least she didn't say it aloud. No need to risk being overheard. "At least we're on a friendlier level now." The waitress arrived with her beer. Pamela took a sip. "So, what did you want to talk about?"

So much for the friendlier part. Thorn fixed his eyes on hers, trying to keep his voice quiet. "What the hell, Pamela? We agreed that we wouldn't interfere with her free choice."

Pamela shrugged. "I wasn't interfering. I needed to talk to her. Between Montgomery hovering and Angela training, I can't get anywhere near her alone."

"That's all you were doing?"

"On my honor. Besides, having her brought into the Black Oak Pack now would make things worse, especially since Angela has announced she's an alpha."

He hissed a breath out through clenched teeth. Now, for the real reason he asked to see her. "How legitimate is that, Pamela? Level with me."

Pamela waggled her hand back and forth. "Technically, it's true. If she defeats Jordan, she's got a toehold in the area and the right to attack Shane because she's no longer his guest."

"Wonderful," Thorn grumbled. He picked up his drink. "Let me guess, although everyone talks about the dog, they also consider Mac part of her Pack but won't say that part out loud."

"Pretty much. But there's someone you're forgetting." Pamela smirked and took a sip of her beer. "You."

Thorn's hand shook, sloshing some of the orange juice almost to the lip of the glass. "Me?"

Pamela shrugged, the smirk still on her lips. "You're sleeping with her. And even if you deny it, you're sleeping with someone who is considered part of her pack. Of course, the others will consider you part of her pack, even if you don't."

Thorn put down the glass. "You're loving this, aren't you? You get to acknowledge her for actually doing something that wasn't because a vampire pulled the strings for once? Oh, and that reminds me. What about that little gift you gave her?"

"Events are too critical for her to accidentally cause a larger incident because she mistook a curse for a growl. She can't continue if she literally cannot understand what's going on." She leaned forward, palms flat on the tabletop. "And if you're able to help her, I should be allowed to also. Or did you think I didn't notice you fluttering through the woods and helping cut off that rabbit?" She arched an eyebrow. "That's not helping me think you aren't part of her pack."

"Point, although I'm not saying I am." He took a drink to regain control. The orange juice burnt his throat, and he could already feel the first stirrings of nausea in his gut. "Speaking of packs, why didn't you stop her from agreeing to this insanity?"

"Couldn't. It was literally not my place to do so."

"And you're going to stand by idly while she gets herself killed?"

"You know I can't interfere any more than I already have. Not without giving away who I am. Same as you can't no matter how much you want to." She paused. "She actually means something to you."

Thorn looked away. His jaw tightened.

Pamela sighed. "You're not going to do to her what you did to my son?"

His head snapped back to face hers. "No! How dare—" He cut himself off and took a deep breath. "If she wants to be turned, that's Mac's responsibility. Not mine."

Pamela frowned. "If I didn't know you better, I'd say you were disappointed by that."

Thorn shook his head. "No, I learned my lesson a long time ago." He narrowed his eyes. "But this isn't about me. You're the one interfering with her dreams."

"It's the only time I can talk to her uninterrupted. Or it was until your little show. Anyway, she's only recently suspected who I am in her dreams but doesn't have a clue in the waking world."

"That's not the point. Showing up in her unconscious is interfering."

Pamela narrowed her eyes. His lips pulled a millimeter back from her teeth before they relaxed. "And you biting her wasn't?"

"That was an accident!" Thorn sputtered. "She offered while I was injured, and I didn't have the self-control to say no."

Her eyes didn't look away. "If you were that out of control, then she might have caught something. How much did she pick up from your memories?"

Thorn gestured, palm up without his arm leaving the table. "Not sure. She hasn't said anything to me about it. And I don't think she's talked to Montgomery, since he hasn't asked me anything."

Pamela snorted. "You should be more careful."

"Relax. If she did pick anything up, I'll convince her that she's mixing up one of the Talespeaker's stories while she was woozy from blood loss."

"You sure that will work? She's a lot smarter than you seem to be giving her credit for."

"If she's so smart, how did she end up in this situation?" Now, the acid he felt in his stomach wasn't only from the orange juice. "So, how do we get her out of it?"

"We can't." Pamela's teeth ground together. "The only way to end this is to forfeit. Jordan can't. Do you see Enya letting this go?"

"No." Thorn sounded as if he had been one defeated.

"Besides, it's not just her. There's the threat to Alpha Shane to consider. If Enya takes over the Black Oak Pack—"

"—The peace that's been built over the last generation goes up in flames," Thorn finished. "We're back to hunting each other in the streets."

"And those hunters will be laughing at us, waiting to sweep in and take us all out. Just like they tried earlier."

"Then we need to make sure she wins."

Pamela tapped her index finger against her lips. "The question is how. It has to be a fair fight. We've got no say in that."

Thorn bit the corner of his mouth. "You sure the Wolf can't show up and declare that she did no wrongdoing and awe everyone into accepting her innocence?"

Pamela shook her head. "Wish I could, but I reserve that trick for true emergencies."

Thorn leaned back against the faux leather of the booth. Now, it was his turn to smirk. "And that mess with the hunter wasn't an emergency?"

"As I recall, neither of us was aware of what was going on until it was too late."

"True." To hear Montgomery tell it, Shane and Marcus had been a sentence away from declaring war when Jordan had pointed out that the corpse's claws were missing. It had given them the heartbeats needed, even though some hearts didn't beat, to realize an outside party was playing them. "And that was Jordan's doing. Maybe we should give her a little more credit."

Pamela snorted and fished an onion ring out of the basket. "So, unless you've got something else to talk about...?" She chomped down on the onion ring.

"Actually, there's something I've been asked to look into," Thorn said. "Something you might be in a better position to find information on than I am."

Pamela's eyebrows rose as she swallowed. "You're asking me for a favor?"

Thorn's expression remained bland, although the corner of his eye twitched. "Yes."

She shook her head, a small smile curling her lips. "I know that has to be a blow to your pride. What do you want to know?"

"I can't get you to promise to do it before telling you?"

"Nope. Otherwise, how will I know what to ask for in return? Spill it."

Now was the time for a little delicate probing. "Were you part of the pack when Alpha Cooper was overthrown?"

She shook her head. "No. I joined the pack shortly after that happened. Wanted to see what was going on with Montgomery for myself."

Thorn tried not to exhale, but a whiff of air pushed through his nose harder than he wanted. Of course, it wouldn't be that easy. It never was. "I want to find out how Alpha Cooper died. Circumstances around his death and who was involved." He held up one finger. "Not the story that was told to us, but what actually happened."

"That... shouldn't be too hard to find out." She grabbed another onion ring. "Why aren't you asking the Conclave or Marcus directly?"

"Because I know what we've been told and who told us. I want to see how much it matches up to what you learn."

"In other words, you don't trust the Elder."

"Something like that," Thorn agreed. The acid was roiling in his stomach again. "Or I don't trust what was told to him."

"So, you won't tell me what you know?"

"Nope. Don't want to bias your investigation."

"Hey, I'm the trained detective, remember?"

Thorn smirked. "Don't worry. I'm not coming after your job. So, what do you want in return?"

"Favor to be named later," Pamela said.

"Can't pin you down any further?"

Pamela shook her head. "Not until I figure out how deep I have to dig, and how badly I have to piss off Alpha Shane."

"Deal." He knew he would regret that. He felt his stomach twist again as he looked down at the onion rings. "You want those to go?"

Pamela's smirk shifted to an amused grin. "You won't eat them." She stood and scooped up the basket of onion rings. "Give me a couple of weeks to find out things."

"Thanks." He watched as Pamela headed over to the side table where the condiments and to go boxes were. He stood, leaving the barely touched drinks on the table. He tried to tell himself that the unease in his stomach was due to having put something in it after decades of not drinking anything but blood. It wasn't due to worry about the situation Jordan had put herself into. But the main thing on his mind was whether he'd make it back to the apartment before he threw up.

19

———

"Ooof!"

Jordan slammed against the padded support beam so hard, she wasn't sure her spine wasn't permanently imprinted on the padding. Her stomach ached where Angela's kick had landed. At least the werewolf had flexed her paw so her claws hadn't sunk into her guts. Gasping for breath and ears flattened against her head, she pushed off the beam and charged for the white-furred werewolf, arms outspread to grab her shoulders. Finally, with a frustrated yell, she charged, intending to grab Angela by her shoulder and take her to the ground.

Angela, instead of backing away, stepped to one side. As Jordan sailed past, Angela cow-kicked, paw landing squarely at the base of Jordan's tail. Jordan yelped and stumbled, arms pinwheeling as she overbalanced. She crashed to the padded floor. Before she could roll over, a clawed hand gripped her scruff, jerking her head back. A set of claws curved around her neck, pressing against her windpipe. She froze, not even daring to breathe.

The claws then withdrew, and her scruff was let go. Jordan

took in a deep breath and rolled over. The claws that had almost sunk into her neck were now extended to her to help her up. "You're dead. Again." Angela's voice wasn't gloating or mocking. It was flat and a bit disappointed.

Jordan snorted and shifted to human. "At least you're keeping your end of the bargain. I'm sure that my ass has the bruises to prove it." She took the offered hand and levered herself to her feet.

"You're doing better," Angela continued. "You managed to land two blows before I knocked you over this time."

"Hooray," Jordan snorted. She took another deep breath and panted. Werewolves, like dogs, didn't sweat. But now that she had bare skin instead of fur, sweat seemed to be leaking out of every pore. "Can we take a break? I need a drink."

"You can't take a break in the middle of the fight.'

"Let's be honest," Jordan said. "The fight won't last the half hour we've been going at it.

Angela considered her words and then nodded. She grabbed a couple of terry robes from a nearby bench and handed Jordan one. "You're right. Let's get a drink."

The footsteps of both women turned from the squish of compressing padding to the slap of skin on tile as they reached the cooler. Angela tossed Jordan a bottle of water. Jordan snagged it out of midair. She didn't want to think that Angela was aiming at her nose, but the arc of the bottle had been a little suspicious. She didn't make any comment about that as she twisted off the top and took a long drink.

Angela looked her up and down. "Can I ask a question?" She had the grace to wait until Jordan. "Do your parents know about any of this?"

Jordan looked at her, squeezing and releasing the half-empty bottle in her hand. The vampires were paranoid about anyone outside of their mortal Family knowing about the existence of vampires. Was there something similar for werewolves? Billy had a boyfriend, but she assumed his reluctance to speak was due to potential disapproval from Alpha Shane. There had to be to avoid hunters or well-meaning people who wanted to destroy the monster and set their soul free. "No," she said, deciding that telling Angela couldn't cause any trouble. "My parents think I've dropped out of college and am living in sin."

Angela looked at her and then snorted. It took Jordan a moment to realize it wasn't a sound of disgust, but she tried to stifle a laugh. "Living in sin? Do people still use that phrase?"

"You'd be surprised," Jordan said. "Or at least my parents do. And they don't know there are two of them."

Angela's chest heaved as she suppressed another laugh. Then, her shoulders lifted and dropped in a sigh. "At least they love you enough to chastise you."

Jess blinked. That didn't make any sort of sense. She had seen him telling her off in front of her. "Your dad doesn't?"

Angela shook her head, looking at the far wall. "Not Dad."

"Oh." Now, Angela's willingness to stand up for her made sense. "You starting this whole mess isn't about me; it's about your mom."

Angela's jaws tightened. Her hand squeezed the plastic water bottle so hard, it creaked. Jordan wasn't sure if Angela would protest that Jordan's actions had led to the road they were on. But to her surprise, Angela said nothing. She nodded once.

"Divorced?"

"Never married."

"Oh." While there were some stigmas in the human world that were rapidly becoming antiquated, her parents aside, she had no idea if werewolf culture considered it the same. Mating for life was a myth, she learned, but that didn't mean they didn't have the same view of pups born out of wedlock? Matelock? She didn't have the right word. "Stupid question, but it's obvious she's not around here. Where is she?"

Angela shrugged. "Left about ten years ago and went up north where her family lived."

And didn't take me with her, Jordan finished mentally. "I'm sorry," she said. "But how does that connect to all this?"

Angela glared at her.

"Oh..." Up north, like Washington State. Where the Green River Pack was.

"She's not part of the alpha's family, but she's there. And she knows about this." She shook her head. "No emails, no phone calls, no letters. She didn't even tell the Talespeaker to say hello."

There was nothing to say, except for what she was thinking. "That sucks. What an asshole."

Angela lifted her head. "Did you just call my mother an asshole?"

Jordan shrugged. "Well, given what we are, calling her a bitch doesn't seem to be that much of an insult." She had just made a fatal mistake. From the dark expression on Angela's face, Jordan expected her to go for her throat. She tensed and braced herself, ready to get her ass kicked or worse. That would be the way she died—not at the teeth of a challenger from a rival pack, but from a supposed ally.

Angela broke out into a laugh. Jordan's mouth spread into a grin, then she laughed too. That set Angela off even more. For the next three minutes, they laughed nonstop, ending up sitting on the floor and leaning on each other. And when they stopped, one glance between them would start the giggles again.

After another three minutes, Angela elbowed Jordan hard in the ribs. "Stop it!! I can't stop laughing unless you do."

Jordan sucked in a sharp breath, laughter dying. She glared at the white wolf as she rubbed her ribs. "That wasn't fair, Angela!"

Angela, still grinning, shrugged as she stood. "You're an alpha now." She offered her a hand to help her to her feet. "Alphas protect their territory and have to be ready for an attack at any time."

Jordan eyed her, wondering if it was a trap. Once Angela rolled her eyes, Jordan decided to take the chance. "We both know that I had no idea what I was getting myself into."

Angela snorted. "Like I said I was trying to help. I didn't think she would go for the throat like that."

Jordan rubbed the nape of her neck. "So, what do you suggest?"

Angela's smile shifted from amused into positively predatory, all gleaming fangs. "Why, what I've been trying to teach you. To go for hers first."

Over the next hour, Angela showed Jordan how to go for the throat. She accomplished this by going for hers. While she hadn't done any major damage, she had come close more times than Jordan cared to admit.

At one point, she had thrown her arm in front of her neck a second before Angela's jaws clamped down. The white werewolf had bitten into her forearm, just below Jordan's elbow, so deep she felt fangs scrape against bone. Her scream had Alpha Shane and Talespeaker Diana running into the training room. "Back off! Both of you!" Alpha Shane barked.

And before she realized it, both she and Angela were six feet apart. Shane was yelling something unintelligible at his daughter, who was yelling back. She wondered if the urge to obey his command came from the force of his personality. Or an instinctive perk of him being an alpha? And no matter which ones it was, could he teach her?

Her legs buckled. Diana was by her side in a moment, guiding her to the ground. "Easy, Jordan. Let me look at that." Diana prodded the joint. She yelped and tried to pull away. Diana was using a light touch, but her fingers felt as hard as iron. The Talespeaker wrapped a hand around the wound, applying pressure. "Doesn't seem to be broken. Can you shift?"

Jordan scrunched her eyes shut. While she had mastered the ability to communicate while a wolf, she was afraid if she opened her mouth, all that would come out would be swear words. This felt worse than when Rhys had bitten her. Her lips peeled back from clenched fangs; ears flattened against her head. Part of what happened when she shifted was wounds healed faster. Healing faster didn't mean that the pain would be lessened any.

"Yes, it's going to hurt," the Talespeaker said, correctly guessing her thoughts. "But it'll be easier to deal with the bleeding if you're human."

Eyes still closed, she reached inside, past the pain, searching for that center of peace. It wasn't easy to find between the snarled, spat words of Angela and Shane's argument, the throbbing in her arm, and the copper smell of blood. She tucked her chin against her chest, flattening her ears and trying to block out all outside distractions. She felt her fur retract, her teeth dull, and the throbbing in her arm get worse, and then ease off.

Gasping, Jordan blinked her eyes open, meeting Talespeaker Diana's concerned look. She glanced at her left arm, which was perfectly human. So was her right, but it was awash with blood. "Hold still," Diana said. "Your body is still trying to heal. It will just take a few minutes."

Jordan nodded, still not trusting herself to say anything. Her arm was throbbing, but it wasn't the blinding white strobing it had been. She looked away, focusing on the two arguing werewolves.

Shane stared at his daughter. "Did you have to go that hard on her?"

"I wasn't trying to kill her," Angela protested. "Enya won't be smacking her on the nose with a rolled-up newspaper, Dad. Jordan needs to know what she's getting into. Coddling her won't do her any good."

"And you can't take her from zero to deadly in a few hours, Angela."

"Funny," she said. "That's what you asked that vampire to do when you first met her."

Shane growled at his daughter. "That was a different situation, and you know it." He looked over at Jordan. "You should stop for the evening. Go home and get some rest."

It was so tempting to do just that. Nurse her arm, get drunk to the point where she could no longer feel pain and hide under a pile of sheets and hope that when she woke up, somehow this had all gone away.

And of course, that was the one thing she couldn't do. "No," Jordan said as she pulled herself to her feet with Diana's aid. She felt a dew of sweat on her skin. Shock, or from the exertion of the fight. "She's right. This will be gentle compared to what Envoy Blevins does to me. So, I'll take a break for a half hour. But we've got to keep going."

Shane glared at her. For once, Jordan could meet his gaze. After ten seconds, Shane nodded. "If that is what you wish, Alpha Abbey."

And for the first time, the title didn't feel like a mockery.

20

———————

Thorn stepped out of the bathroom, wiping his mouth with a damp washcloth. There was a faint acidic taste in his mouth that he hadn't been able to get rid of no matter how many times he rinsed. At least the apartment was empty. Jordan was out meeting with Angela for her first set of fighting lessons. He wasn't sure where Montgomery was. Hopefully not getting into a fight with Alpha Shane, but he wouldn't put it past him.

And then he heard the noise he didn't want to hear. It was his phone beeping, indicating an incoming message from a specific number. He sighed and threw the damp cloth into the hamper. Thorn glanced at his phone's screen, but he could have recited the message without having to read it.

Marcus wants to see you ASAP!

With a heavy sigh, he picked up the phone and verified the message. His brows furrowed. He couldn't avoid checking in without causing more issues. At least he had made it home to purge himself of the alcohol. *Be there in fifteen, Sarah.*

He paused as he grabbed his keys. about to step out the door. When had he started thinking of this apartment as home?

Fifteen minutes later, he stepped through the door into Marcus' office. Or more accurately, the outer vestibule. For any unknowing mortal who somehow managed to get past the layers of security, they would be turned back here, escorted to the front lobby or one of the legitimate businesses on the lower levels. Or at least that was supposed to be the procedure in place. Thorn suspected anyone who made it to this point knew what they were getting into, and who they were going after.

He walked up to the desk and the young redheaded woman sitting there. "Hey, Sarah." Normally, he would half-sit, half-lean on the desk, flirting a little or asking what new milestone her baby had passed. But from the brusque summons in the text, those pleasantries could be seen as a disrespectful delay. "Is Marcus ready to see me?"

"Yes, Thorn. Thanks for coming so quickly."

He bit back his urge to joke about that double entendre, and instead, he stepped behind the desk and to the door. Sarah tapped in a code and opened the door. Nodding to Sarah, he stepped into the passage.

The door closed behind him with a louder, metallic thunk than its redwood appearance hinted at. Thorn walked down the hall at a measured pace to the other door with the frosted inset window. A bat soared in a sky graced with a full moon, while, in the distance, a wolf howled on the top of a hill. Thorn shook his head. He always thought the decoration was ostentatious, given that the only higher power Marcus appeared to believe in was himself. He wouldn't be surprised that the picture represented himself more than the Bat.

He stretched to calm himself. This wasn't the time to let a non-believer get under his skin. He knocked on the door the ceremonial three times and waited for Marcus' response.

"Enter."

Without any hesitation, Thorn stepped into Marcus' lair. Lair was the right word. Despite the monitors and the artwork and the plush furniture, there was a cave-like feel to the space. He walked to the desk where the Elder of Rancho Robles sat and bowed his respect. "Elder Marcus."

Marcus didn't waste any time with niceties. "Kelly," he said from his position behind his desk. Thorn suppressed a twitch at the use of his legal name. "It's good to see that you're back in Montgomery's good graces." He gestured for Thorn to take a seat at the other side of the desk. "Especially after the public display the two of you put on the last time you were seen together in the Conclave."

Thorn lowered his head, showing just enough deference as he took the indicated seat. "It was inevitable that he'd grow suspicious. "Probably a good thing that it did happen in public. If it happened behind closed doors, too many people would wonder if it was all an act."

Marcus arched one eyebrow, head tilting slightly. "And you believe they won't now?"

Thorn held his hands out to his sides. "They saw Jordan's reaction as well as Montgomery's. Neither of them is that good of an actor."

"True," Marcus conceded. He sat back in his chair. "Now, what can you tell me about this alpha wolf situation?"

"That caught us all off guard," Thorn admitted. "True, I'm not familiar with what constitutes an alpha wolf, but it's clear that Jordan was surprised, and Montgomery hadn't even considered it."

"I'm not concerned about Montgomery's reaction. I'm more concerned about Jordan's." Marcus steepled his fingers, then tapped them against his desk. "She's showing more of an independent streak than I prefer."

"She's young and still learning," Thorn said. "And she's learning." Not necessarily the lessons Marcus wanted her to.

"Is she learning fast enough?" Marcus asked as if reading his thoughts. "And the right lessons? There was the incident with Animal Control."

This would require some delicate handling. "Look at it this way," Thorn said. He hoped this would counter Marcus' argument before he made it. "She got herself into trouble, then got herself out of it without overtly drawing attention to what she was. It was another werewolf who recognized what she was." Not quite the truth, but close enough. "While she was disobedient, she didn't try to hide what she did from Montgomery or me and was contrite when confronted."

Marcus leaned forward. "I'm not sure that's a good thing."

"This wasn't a selfish act. This wasn't running at random through the streets as a werewolf. She did it to help a friend and was discreet about passing as a dog while searching for Rex. Mrs. Clarke loves that dog and was miserable without him," Thorn said. "She could have just cooled her heels until we realized something was wrong. Or had her friends contact us. But she knew she had to get out of her situation as quickly as possible and leveraged her allies so she could do so."

"And put herself into debt to Alpha Shane's daughter and is currently deepening that debt with every fighting lesson."

Thorn shrugged. "She'll have to learn to work with the werewolves, no matter how much we don't like it. I saw her and Angela together; they were at each other's throats in the middle of a grocery store parking lot. Then there was the conflict at the execution of the hunter. At least now they're polite in public to each other. It's a foundation to build on."

"Assuming Shane's pup lives long enough to become Alpha of Black Oak. I'm not convinced she's much smarter than Jordan is."

Thorn spread his hands. "Eventually, Alpha Shane will be no more. Wouldn't it be better to have someone who can speak with the new alpha on friendly terms? Someone who can convince her that going against the Conclave wouldn't be in her best interests while she solidifies her power? And then it would be more trouble than it's worth to upset the status quo?"

Marcus' eyes glazed over, and his body stilled. Thorn hoped that meant he was focusing on calculating the various paths of the future, determining the best ways he could manipulate the outcomes, and how Jordan would fit into that. "Perhaps." His gaze snapped back to Thorn. "I told Montgomery to punish the werewolf, and he's lucky that I'm not publicly censuring him. Same goes for you, Kelly. I'm disappointed that you didn't alert me to this situation."

"Most of it took place during the day when we were unable to do anything. By the time we knew what the problem was, she was walking through the front door," Thorn responded without raising his voice. "And since she is Montgomery's Famulus, it falls to him to report any misbehavior."

Marcus ached an eyebrow. "Since when have you cared about the rules, Kelly?"

Thorn met his icy stare with an even one of his own. "When telling you would have blown the trust I've been able to rebuild with Montgomery. I thought my orders were to get back into his good graces and do what it took to stay there." Now, it was his turn to arch an eyebrow. "Or did I misinterpret your instructions?"

Marcus' eyebrows drew into an even line. "It's not often that my own words are used against me, Kelly."

Thorn didn't blink, didn't allow himself to show any signs of weakness. "I repeat. If I had said something to you, Montgomery would never trust me again. As it is, he questioned if I had anything to do with you finding out. If he had an actual excuse, I would have been out on my ass before you could say 'leash laws.'"

Marcus stared at him for several more seconds, face unreadable. Then he dropped his gaze to the desk's surface. Thorn hoped his expression was a deferential neutral, but Marcus might even see that as a challenge. He didn't want to have to challenge

Marcus unless he absolutely had to. That time would come, but he wasn't prepared for it yet.

He looked up when Marcus spoke, "Having a set of eyes on Montgomery is important, but only if you report back to me." His gaze sharpened. "Do you understand, Kelly."

He nodded, the sparest up and down motion of his head. "Yes, sir," he said, swallowing his instinctive reaction.

"Now, tomorrow night, Nicholas will be reintroduced to the Conclave. Montgomery will meet him privately beforehand, while you'll be in the general assembly." He leaned forward. "You remember that Nicholas is not a fan of werewolves and was against Montgomery being sent to live among us. I do not want a fight to start between the two of them. The antipathy between Montgomery and Rosanna is bad enough."

"What about Sabrina?" Thorn said. Although not connected directly to her famulus' death, Jordan had been the last one to see him alive. She hadn't been vocal about blaming Jordan for losing David, the first known victim of the hunters. That didn't mean she didn't harbor those feelings.

"She'll be in the general meeting when I introduce Nicholas. As will you." Marcus leaned forward. "I know that Jordan is not popular among the Conclave. And her reputation is tarnishing Montgomery's. I need you to report to me any grumbling that you hear about them."

Thorn sat back. "For their punishment?"

"For further observation. And assessment if their complaints have any merit."

He nodded, knowing he had no choice but to agree.

"I want you to keep an eye on Montgomery's reactions. He has been accused of favoring his werewolf nature instead of acting in the interest of vampires. I want to know how much of that is bias given his origins, and how much of it is truth."

"And what's to keep you from coming to the conclusion that I'm not a biased source and protecting them?"

Marcus smiled. It was one of his rare smiles that he made more frightening by the fact his fangs were exposed. "You should make sure you are not."

Thorn hoped his shiver showed appropriate level of fear. "I will see to it, sir," he said.

Marcus studied Thorn for a second before nodding. "If you hear anything, report it to me immediately. No more delays under the pretense of keeping Montgomery's trust."

"Of course, sir," Thorn immediately replied. "Is there anything else you need to discuss?"

Marcus' lips pressed into a firm line. "Is there somewhere you need to be, Kelly?"

"Neither Montgomery nor Jordan know where I am at the moment," Thorn said. "If they make it home before I do, I may have some awkward questions to answer." Again, he noted with an internal wry grin, he referred to Montgomery's apartment as home.

If Marcus had caught his usage of the word, his expression didn't change. "Very well. I expect you to report in tomorrow night and every night thereafter."

Thorn bowed his head and rose from his seat. He was halfway to the door when Marcus spoke again, "And Kelly, do not disappoint me."

He paused mid-stride before he stepped out of the office. Let Marcus take his hesitation as a sign of fear. If he could see the compression of Thorn's lips, he would have been the one afraid.

21

——————

Jordan dragged herself down the hall, hoping she could make the last ten yards without falling on her face. Muscles she didn't realize she had ached. Ones that she knew she had threatened to peel off her skeleton and go on strike. And then, there was a thick blanket of exhaustion on her shoulders. She fumbled in her jacket pocket for her keys. It took her three tries to get them into the lock, and the door opened. She stumbled over the threshold and pushed the door closed behind her. Her keys missed the bowl and landed with a rattling thunk on the floor. She decided she'd pick them up later.

"What happened to you?"

Jordan winced at Montgomery's tone of concern and his light touch on her arm. She must have looked worse than she thought. "Angela kicked my ass, probably a little too enthusiastically since it's sanctioned."

Montgomery's hand shifted to her other arm, the one that didn't hurt as much and guided her to the kitchen table. "Thorn, go get some washcloths from the bathroom. And you, sit. How did you get home in this condition?"

Jordan sank down into the leather chair. "Billy drove me in your car. He called for a rideshare to get back home."

Montgomery frowned. "He knows where we live?"

"Didn't have much of a choice," Jordan said. "And he's trustworthy. Besides, I'm sure if Alpha Shane wanted to know where you live, he'd be able to figure it out."

"True." Montgomery stepped into the kitchenette and rummaged through the freezer on the bottom of the refrigerator. Thorn reappeared with two towels as Montgomery pulled a bag of peas out of the freezer.

Thorn's brow wrinkled as he handed over one of the cloths. "I thought those were for Jordan to eat."

"Yeah, but they make a great icepack." Montgomery wrapped the washcloth around the package. "Can you stretch out your arm, Jordan?"

Slowly, she unbent the arm. Montgomery laid the impromptu icepack on the swollen elbow. "Thorn, tuck the other cloth under her arm to cushion it."

Montgomery lifted her arm as Thorn moved it into position. Jordan hissed, face tensing and then relaxing as the pain flared and receded to a dull ache.

"You need protein and lots of it," Montgomery said. He went to the refrigerator and pulled out a jug of milk. Then he opened a cabinet and pulled out a container and a glass. "Thorn, can you see what steak houses or burger joints are still open?"

"None probably at this time of night. How about breakfast delivery?"

Montgomery poured the milk into the glass. "Anything high in protein would be good. Too bad nobody delivers an Irish breakfast." He added a scoop of the powder to the glass and stirred until the white milk turned into a tan color. He then placed it in front of Jordan. "Start with this. It will help your body recover."

Jordan looked at the glass and then at Montgomery. "You sure about that?" When Montgomery only looked at her in return, she grabbed the glass and took a cautious sip. Her nose wrinkled as her lips twisted. "Yuck! Why the hell did I chose the peanut butter flavor over chocolate?'

"I thought dogs liked peanut butter." Thorn held up his hands at the dirty looks Jordan and Montgomery shot in his direction. "Kidding, kidding. I'll go see who's still doing deliveries."

Jordan made a face and took another swallow as Thorn disappeared into the living room. She put down the glass. "I'm in trouble, Montgomery. If Angela can do this to me, what will Enya do?"

"Hey." Montgomery put his hand over hers. "We'll get through this, Jordan. You've survived one Blevins already. Facing a second one shouldn't be that tough."

Jordan smiled, equal parts exhaustion and hope. "If she's so easy to fight, you willing to do it for me."

"Not a chance," Montgomery said. "They won't let me step in for you."

Jordan sighed. "Had to ask." She took another drink.

Thorn stepped back into the kitchenette. "Fast food burgers, okay? It looks like there's two or three chains that might be open. Or we can set up an early order for breakfast delivery."

Jordan sighed, sinking further into the chair. "I'm so tired now, I'm not sure I could eat if you put a filet mignon in front of me."

"I know, Jordan," Montgomery said as he set a second glass in front of her. "One more. Then you can get some sleep."

She eyed the glass and then Montgomery. With a heavy sigh, she wrapped her hand around it and lifted it to her lips. She swallowed again. "Could you get me a straw at least?"

Thorn slipped over to the drawers and rummaged through them. "So, what's the plans for tomorrow?"

The sour expression on Jordan's face didn't change. "I have to be up early for a grocery run. Yours, Montgomery. Not mine." For a moment, the thought of how Thorn fed blinked across her mind, but it was gone before she could chase it down.

Montgomery nodded. "Then the pre-meeting for me and Jordan with Marcus and the other bloodchildren. After that, the meeting of the Conclave."

"Nothing with the Pack?" Thorn asked. He held up a paper-wrapped tube in triumph. "Aha!"

"If there is, Shane hasn't said anything to me," Montgomery said.

Jordan took the straw and unwrapped it as she spoke. "He and Angela looked disappointed when I said I couldn't practice in the evening," Jordan said, sticking the straw in the glass. She took another sip, this time her expression smoothing some. "Angela was about to argue with me before I brought up that it was a meeting with Elder Marcus. I think she would have still if her dad hadn't said it was more important, I put an appearance there than get my ass kicked more."

"So, the lessons didn't go well?" Montgomery asked as she sipped more.

She swallowed and shook her head. "I would have thought my arm would be proof of that."

"I was hoping Angela got in a lucky blow." Montgomery shook his head.

"More like the other way around," Jordan said. She slurped more up. The protein may have been helping because the arm did hurt less. Or it was the cooling numbness of the ice. Or it had to do with being away from the werewolves and where she felt comfortable.

She swallowed the last of the milk and protein mix and handed it back to Montgomery. "Do I need another?"

Montgomery shook his head. "You should probably get some sleep now."

"You heard the man." Thorn scooped her up and carried her to the bedroom. Montgomery followed, shutting off lights and making sure the light-proof curtains were drawn. Her duties, Jordan wanted to argue, but she was tired. Her arm wasn't hurting now, but a wave of exhaustion had broken over her head.

"You want to sleep on the outside tonight?"

"Yeah," Jordan said. "I need to get some stuff done tonight before the Conclave gathering."

"I really wish that Marcus wasn't insisting you be there," Montgomery said.

"Knowing him, he wants to see you squirm and test Nicholas' self-control at the same time," Thorn said. He lowered her to the edge of the mattress. "He has a type."

Jordan sighed. "And let me guess. I'm it."

"You're my famulus, Jordan," Montgomery said. He grabbed the oversized t-shirt that Jordan preferred to sleep in. "That should give you some protection."

"This is Marcus' eldest surviving bloodchild, and not just any member of the Conclave," Thorn said. "While the rules are supposed to be the same, he is your elder. Step cautiously."

Jordan winced as Montgomery helped her pull her shirt over her head. She needed to invest in some tops that unbuttoned down the front for the nights she was fighting. "Great. Someone else to look out for. You'd think I'd be used to it by now."

Montgomery chuckled as she wormed her way into the shirt, wincing as she bent her elbow. "I haven't yet," Montgomery said. Her head popped through the collar in time to see Thorn shoot a worried look at Montgomery. "I'll take the center. You sure you'll be up to running errands, Jordan, or do you want to sleep longer?"

"I'll decide when I wake up. The meeting with Marcus will be the first priority." She lay on her left side, staring over the edge of the mattress.

Montgomery spooned in behind her. "We didn't ask. Arm aside, how did the practice with Angela go?"

"Mostly, she beat me up, but it's not like it used to be. She wasn't picking on me."

Montgomery's hand worked on a tight knot of muscle at the base of her neck. "And?"

"And I'm starting to think they're right. I got lucky when I beat Rhys and Angela last time." Her chest deflated with that admission.

"Yes, that may have been true," Thorn said. He reached over Montgomery's body to rest his hand on her hip. "But I have faith that you can do this. You've been recognized as an alpha."

Jordan closed her eyes. "Alpha Shane actually addressed me as Alpha Abbey tonight," she murmured.

She heard the mattress creak as Thorn shifted his weight to look at her. "He did, did he?"

Montgomery's hand rubbing her back stilled. "The werewolves will honor that, but it might be best to keep it quiet among the Conclave."

"I don't plan on putting it on my business cards anytime soon." She sighed. "Can we keep it a secret from the Conclave? Elder Marcus knows and isn't happy about it. I can't see any of the others liking the idea."

"We have to play it that it's a technicality, because you fought Angela when she tried to claim Mount Ponderosa." Montgomery's hand moved to her shoulder and squeezed it lightly.

"You know, we might be able to convince Marcus it's a good thing," Thorn said. "At least Jordan, you're loyal to Montgomery. If you hadn't fought her and won, Angela would be the Alpha of Mount Ponderosa. And who knows what she would try."

"That... is something I hadn't considered," Montgomery said. "And it's a good point. With Jordan, there's stability, as long as others of the Conclave don't poke at her. With Angela, she could have led an assault against her father."

Jordan twisted around to look at the two vampires, although all she could see was Montgomery's chin. "Would she really do that?"

"It's a possibility," Thorn said. "Other than taking over the pack, I'm not sure what her motive would have been."

"I do," Jordan said. "She's got this need to impress her mother."

Montgomery looked surprise. "Her mother is alive?"

Jordan nodded. "She lives up in the Seattle area."

"Ohhhh." Both vampires nodded.

"She's not related to—"

"No. Or if she is, she's lying to me." Jordan shifted the subject. "Could she challenge me again in the future?"

"Only if the situation has changed," Montgomery said. "It's considered rude to repeatedly challenge someone you've already lost to."

"Change of circumstances," Jordan said. "Like?"

"Her taking a mate," Montgomery said. "Or her becoming the Alpha of Black Oak Pack,"

"So, I could be doing this again in another few years," Jordan said.

Montgomery didn't say anything, but kissed her forehead as Thorn made a sympathetic noise. "We can worry about that when she sends out wedding invitations," Montgomery said.

Jordan grunted. Her arm still throbbed, but while it maintained the beat, the intensity faded. "How long before my arm is healed?"

"Tomorrow, or the night of the fight at the latest," Montgomery said. "You can't use it to get out of it."

"Damn." She closed her eyes and although she wanted to open them, someone had smeared glue on the lashes. "I hoped I could," she mumbled. She felt Montgomery kiss her forehead again. Thorn murmured something, but she had drifted too far away to make out what he was saying.

22

Jordan pushed open the door to the coffee shop, anticipating the scents and tastes awaiting her. The dark, bitter aroma of freshly poured coffee drifted up her nose. She perked up as if she had already drunk a cup instead of just inhaling the scent wafting around the room. After double checking her phone to make sure her order was ready, she walked to the pick-up area and studied several labeled cups. At least this one had her last name correctly printed on her mocha latte. Correct cup secured, she claimed a table by the window and sat.

She sipped her drink and let out a pleased exhale. But as much as she wanted to sit and read a book until sunset, there was too much to be done tonight. She had already picked up the pork blood from the Asian market for Montgomery's meal. They really did need to figure out a way to get blood to replace what Montgomery had withdrawn from the Blood Bank. The vampires managing it had turned up their noses at the thought of werewolf blood being donated. There were only so many butchers and markets that Jordan could rotate her purchases among, and she didn't trust that internet orders wouldn't draw too much attention. He could drink her blood, but one famulus couldn't support a vampire. A combination of both would have to work if she could talk Montgomery into it.

Then there was the gathering of the Conclave and the private meet and greet before it this evening. This wouldn't be like the normal meetings. It wasn't every night that Elder Marcus' eldest bloodchild returned to his sire's domain. She knew she should be home napping. Or making sure the green dress she had worn when she had been presented to the Conclave was wrinkle free. She had argued for wearing a shirt, slacks, and blazer, and both would be free of dog hair, hers and Rex's. But Montgomery had insisted that she needed something more formal, and the fancier the better. And since she wasn't welcome in *Eleganza Discreta* and didn't have time to shop for anything else, the green dress would have to do.

Even with everything she needed to do, she also needed a few calm seconds to herself. She took another sip of the milky brew and closed her eyes.

"Hey! Jordan!" a cheery voice called.

Her eyes popped open. Jordan squinted at the woman approaching, frowning as she tried to place her. She looked vaguely familiar. Dark-brown skin, braids tight against her head. It took her a moment since she wasn't walking a white miniature poodle and holding a coffee cup. "Keisha, right? We met a few weeks ago at the dog park?" So much for time to herself.

Keisha nodded. "Good to see you again. Did you find Rex?"

Jordan smiled. "Yeah. Took a little while, but I did." She gestured to the empty chair across from her. "He was turned into Animal Control later that day. He's at home now, probably being spoiled rotten."

Keisha took a seat and put her cardboard cup on the table. "Great to hear. He is adorable, even if he isn't the sharpest crayon in the box." Her smile dimmed some. "What's with the bruise?"

"Bruise?"

Keisha pointed at a spot on her lower left arm. "Looks like you got hit with a softball."

She glanced down at the large purple tinged with green mark just below the bend of her elbow. She was surprised she hadn't noticed it in the shower. The pain was gone, and she hadn't paid close attention. "Oh, that." She tugged her sleeve down, but it didn't cover the purple and green blotch. She hadn't healed as fast as she thought she would from Angela's lessons. At least the bruise wasn't covering her whole forearm like it had been earlier. "I'm taking a self-defense class," she explained, tugging the sleeve down again. It was close enough to the truth. "My sparring partner was a little overenthusiastic, and I blocked the wrong way." Also, technically the truth.

"Huh." Keisha looked from the bruise to her eyes. "You'd think because you walk a Rottweiler that people wouldn't mess with you."

Jordan shrugged. She heard the note of skepticism in Keisha's voice. "You'd think. But Rex isn't mine, so he's not always with me."

"I get it." Keisha paused as Jordan took a sip of her coffee. "You need to talk about it?"

"No," Jordan said. "Yeah." She shook her head. "It's just... complicated."

Keisha grinned. "I like complicated."

"Okay." Jordan paused to get her story in order while leaving out the parts she couldn't talk about. "My mouth wrote a check that my body might not be able to cash."

"So, that's why the self-defense lessons?"

"Yeah." Jordan shook her head. "I was also given some bad advice that led to this mess. And I'm not sure I can get out of the situation without getting hurt."

Keisha gestured to her arm. "I'd say you already are. Boyfriend issues?"

Jordan shook her head.

"Girlfriend?"

"Nope. It's not a relationship problem," she said. "I got carried away talking with someone who's big into boxing, and I mouthed off and..." She shrugged.

"Can't talk your way out of it?"

"Not without causing a lot of other problems." Jordan shrugged again. "Thing is, I'm not so much the problem as the excuse." She frowned. "I might be able to get someone else to talk my way out of it."

Keisha held up her drink in salute. "Here's hoping so you don't end up with any more of those bruises.

Jordan lifted hers. "Agreed." Both women took a long drink.

"So, what are you doing out here?"

"Just did some grocery shopping and wanted coffee before I headed home." Without thinking, her foot nudged the half-open grocery bag.

Following the motion, Keisha glanced down and did a double take. "Is that... blood?"

Jordan glanced down at the bag by her feet. It had fallen open, revealing several sealed plastic bowls marked 'edible pork blood,' intended for Montgomery's next meals. She pulled it up so it covered the labels. "Pork blood for cooking," she confirmed. She thanked the powers that be that she had an excuse ready to go. "I've got an addiction to cooking shows. I wanted to try making some morcilla. It's a Spanish blood sausage."

Keisha studied her with a queasy frown. "I didn't take you for such an adventurous eater."

Jordan shrugged. "You only live once. And I figured if I didn't like it, I could always give it to Rex."

She shook her head, bemused. "I don't know if he'd enjoy that, or if I should report you for cruelty to animals."

Jordan laughed. "How's QT doing?"

"He's doing fine," Keisha said. "We should see about getting him and Rex together for a playdate. Rex is good with other dogs, right?"

"Yeah, he is," Jordan said without thinking. Rex was good with other dogs. The question was if QT would be good with her? Most dogs didn't react well to werewolves. Rex had taken some time before he was comfortable with her. And she wasn't sure that his chill attitude towards her would extend to other werewolves. "Maybe sometime next week?"

"Sounds great." Keisha pulled out her phone. "I'll text you?" Jordan rattled off her phone number. Keisha typed and a second later, Jordan's phone beeped. "I'll check my schedule and get back to you." She glanced at her watch. "Sorry, gotta run."

"Sounds good." Jordan kept her grin plastered on her face as Keisha got up and said goodbye. She sighed and looked up at the ceiling. *Why did I agree to that when I'm not sure I'll be able to?*

The sun was dipping to touch the horizon. Like Keisha, she needed to get moving. Grabbing her coffee and her bag, she headed out the door to the SUV. It was time to prepare for the night that was coming.

23

———

Jordan smoothed down the skirt as she followed Montgomery a respectful pace behind as a proper famulus should. "We're meeting a bloodchild of the Elder of the Conclave," Montgomery said. "We need to present our best appearance as a sign of respect."

"But that's the same dress I've worn twice, and Rosanna will be there." She didn't have to say that it was the reason Rhys had mistaken her famulus Bridgette for her and killed her in his disappointment. Which started this whole mess about the fangs.

"I know," Montgomery snapped.

Thorn put a hand on his shoulder. "We'll find you something new for the next time," he said. "But Mac's right. You need to be seen dressed in your best."

At that point, Jordan had sighed and held up her hands in surrender.

As they headed to the elevator where Richard waited, the elderly famulus held aside the rope blocking the private elevators, allowing them to pass. Once inside, Jordan swiped the security card and poked buttons 6 for Thorn and 7 for her and

Montgomery. After an all-too-brief ride, the doors slid open. "See you after the meeting." Thorn saluted them with a jaunty wave as he stepped out of the elevator car.

The doors slid closed. Jordan stepped closer to Montgomery, reaching for his hand. His fingers wrapped around hers. Neither said anything as they rode up to the next floor. As the seventh-floor indicator lit up, both let go and stepped apart. The doors slid open. Montgomery stepped out. Jordan waited for him to take three strides before she followed, as a proper famulus would.

They walked down the short hall to the entrance of the antechamber where the vampires gathered. Reginald stood by the door. How much he was there as announcer and how much as bouncer, she wasn't sure. He was older, unlike the three men she could smell secreted behind false doors on the room. Not that Reginald wasn't without his dangers as well, she could smell the gunpowder and the oil used on the gun. And she didn't doubt that he would be armed with silver bullets.

She wasn't sure if she should be worried or proud that she was considered that much of a threat.

Montgomery paused at the door. He nodded to Reginald and waited. Reginald turned to the room and announced, "Bloodchild Montgomery Cooper and famulus."

Montgomery stepped into the room, and Jordan followed. Elder Marcus stood at the far end, talking with Rosanna and a vampire she didn't recognize. The tall, blond man looked in their direction. She felt his gaze slide over her, dismiss her for the moment, and then focus on Montgomery. There was a predator's assessment of a fellow predator if she had ever seen one.

The stranger didn't speak. Elder Marcus smiled as they approached. Montgomery halted and bowed to his sire as she curtsied. "Elder Marcus."

"Montgomery Cooper, it's good of you to join us." Marcus' voice was warmer than she remembered him speaking before. And it made her think of the lure used to bait a fish, or worse—a leg trap. Marcus' hand swept towards the stranger. "Please allow me to introduce you to your elder bloodbrother, Nicholas Quinn."

Both vampires nodded formally to each other. "So, this is the infamous vampire who stole Christine's heart," Nicholas said.

"You're too kind," Montgomery responded. He stepped to one side and gestured to Jordan. "Allow me to present my famulus, Jordan Abbey."

Nicholas looked her up and down. "And this is the famulus that's also an Alpha Wolf," he said. She felt him assessing every part of her and fought off the urge to shiver. Being considered an object to be desired was an unfortunate part of being a woman. She could sense the hunger of another predator, except this one considered her prey, another morsel to be devoured and savored. And his words did nothing to assuage her feelings. "I must say, Montgomery, you do have fine taste in your famulus."

This time, when Montgomery put a hand on her shoulder, Jordan didn't have the urge to push it off. "I lucked into her," he said. "She has been nothing but loyal to me."

Even with her eyes cast down as a proper famulus should, she caught the lift of Marcus' eyebrow.

"Good to hear that you have her trained. I was under the impression that werewolves were hard to tame." He looked from Jordan to Montgomery. "I wonder if it's only certain werewolves."

The hand on her shoulder tensed, but Montgomery's voice remained neutral. "Think of it more as we give our trust to those who deserve it."

"So you say." Nicholas turned to the female vampire. "Rosanna, enchanting as usual."

To her surprise, Jordan heard warmth in Rosanna's voice. "Nicholas, you old flatterer."

He held his hands out to his sides. "Guilty as charged. But you're here alone? What happened to your famulus?"

Jordan fought to keep her expression still. Surely, he was

already aware of what happened since he had jokingly referenced her as an alpha werewolf.

"I recently lost Bridgette," Rosanna said with the barest of glances at Montgomery. "And her replacement isn't quite schooled enough to be out in public yet."

"My condolences for your loss," Nicholas said. "We should share a private meal and catch up. You can tell me the details then."

Rosanna's smile was as pleased as it was predatory. "Yes, we should."

Jordan didn't like the sound of that. But what caught her eye was a silver glint on her chest. Rosanna wasn't looking directly at her, but Jordan felt the weight of her gaze on her all the same, studying her for a reaction. What kept drawing Jordan's gaze was a silver necklace. The single chain looped around her neck to where the lower half split into two, each holding silver spacer beads that held four pointed ivory beads mounted in silver that looked like claws in place. Two larger ones hung on the upper chain, and two smaller lower ones pointed upward on the lower, giving the impression of a snarling mouth. Not beads, she realized, swallowing a wave of nausea. Fangs. Those were Rhys' fangs. And with that realization, any thoughts they might be able to retrieve the fangs and end the hostilities with the Green River Pack without violence died.

If Montgomery knew what he was looking at, and Jordan was damn well sure he did, he wasn't letting it show on his face. "Rosanna," he said in greeting. His voice was neutral, polite, and held a hint of caution.

Rosanna's voice had a frosty edge. "Montgomery." She looked Jordan up and down. She felt her taking in and cataloging what she was wearing. Of course, Rosanna would recognize the dress. She had provided it from her shop to begin with.

Marcus clapped his hands together and rubbed them. "Now

that we have the introductions out of the way, we'll continue the official introductions to the rest of the Conclave."

Which meant that she and Reginald would stay behind. Montgomery had prepped her ahead of time that she and Reginald wouldn't be on stage. It would be poor manners for two vampires to have their Family present while Marcus didn't. She took a step back as Montgomery lifted his hand and took his place after Rosanna. She glanced at them through her lashes, trying to look like a proper famulus. Nicholas gave her one more smirk of a glance as he followed Marcus to the door.

Once the door closed, only Reginald and Jordan remained in the room. She slowly relaxed, although the queasiness didn't leave her stomach. Her instincts were still screaming danger, although she could not put her finger on why exactly. Thorn's warning hadn't been thorough enough if this was how her instincts were reacting.

"You handled yourself well," Reginald said.

Jordan jumped. She had forgotten Reginald was there. She looked at him, about to ask what he meant when he continued. "But be cautious around him."

She didn't have to ask who *him* was. But could she trust Reginald, the highest ranking famulus of the Elder of Rancho Robles. Was he picking up on her nerves and had been ordered to play on those fears or confirming her instincts? She thought over her question carefully. If he were talking about something else, and she impugned Nicholas, Marcus wouldn't take it well. "Is there something specific I should be concerned about?"

"This information should really be coming from your Patron," Reginald said. "Just... be cautious."

"Okay. I'll talk to Montgomery." She noticed the light shake of Reginald's head. "Thorn?" she amended.

Reginald nodded.

Jordan bit back a sigh. Of course, Reginald couldn't come out and say it. He had sworn an oath to Marcus not to tell her. "I'll be careful, I promise."

Reginald nodded again, his face an impeccable servant's neutral expression. "We should join the other Family."

"Of course." And with that statement, she knew she wouldn't get anything further out of him. She followed him out to the room where other Family members waited for the meeting to be over.

24

There were times that Thorn thought a gathering of vampires shouldn't be referred to as a conclave, but rather a gossip. As far as he was concerned, they thrived as much on unsubstantiated rumors and speculations as they did blood.

He looked around the room at the gathered Conclave of Rancho Robles. Vampires milled here and there, talking in hushed tones and with subtle gestures of their hands, pointing to the subject of their discussion without being too obvious. There was an undertone of unease and worry. But they tended only to gather for negative news that had to be dispersed.

He caught motion coming in his direction. Sabrina, dressed in a business jacket and pencil skirt, worked her way towards him but wasn't so rude as to not stop and say hello to those she passed. But the fact that she would glance around, only stopping when their eyes met, told him that he was her ultimate target. The immaculate white clothing she had chosen to wear reminded him of hemlock blossoms—they were beautiful to look at but could be deadly to interact with. Better to meet her head on rather than letting her choose the high ground. "Sabrina," he said with a grin as she stepped into hearing range.

"Thorn." The dark-haired vampiress' smile was polite, but ice lurked in the upturned corners of her lips. "It's good to see that you and Montgomery have kissed and made up."

Thorn held his hands out to his sides, palms towards Sabrina. "A misunderstanding was bound to happen," he said. "But we worked it out. In a less public way than the blowup happened." He laughed.

"Yes, but there are still rumors," Sabrina said.

Here we go. This was what Sabrina wanted to talk about. He arched his eyebrow, playing dumb. "Rumors?"

"There are those who say the whole thing was an act between you and Montgomery. Of course, anyone who saw the two of you would know it was real."

Thorn laughed. "Tell my back that. I spent several days sleeping in the storage room at *The Wilted Rose*."

"So I heard." She paused, and Thorn fought to keep from tensing. "The rumor I don't give the most credence to has to do with the werewolf pup."

"Jordan? Montgomery's famulus." Clarification wasn't strictly necessary, but Thorn felt compelled to make it anyway. "What rumor would that be?"

"That Jordan is considered to be an alpha werewolf."

Thorn snorted, hoping that he was hiding his start. "Of what pack? An eighty-year-old woman's pet dog?"

Sabrina smiled, holding her hands to her sides much as he had earlier. "There are other potential members."

Thorn rolled his eyes. "If you're hinting at Montgomery, let me be the first to reassure you. He's loyal to Marcus first and considers her a famulus and nothing more." Okay, the nothing more part wasn't completely accurate, but sleeping with your famulus wasn't considered unusual.

"So he says," Sabrina said. "But we shall see. And for the

record, I hope the rumors are false. But you should be aware, Thorn, that he isn't the only one rumored to be so. There's another vampire he's close to who is also rumored to be a pack member."

Thorn's teeth clenched. "Care to name the person in that accusation a little more clearly, Sabrina?"

Sabrina's smile wouldn't melt a glacier. "Why, no, Thorn. If there's any traction to that rumor, I'm sure they'll resolve it one way or another." She nodded and floated onto her next victim.

Great. He wasn't surprised that the rumor about Jordan was already making the rounds. Nor was he surprised that there was speculation about Montgomery's status as a pack member. He hadn't considered that he would be seen as the same thing. Yes, Pamela had mentioned it, but she was attempting to get under his skin. He half-laughed at the idea, earning him side eyes from the vampires around him. Pamela had been right, and she'd never let him hear the end of it *If only they knew the irony of that.*

He debated walking up to someone else to ask what they knew about the situation with Jordan and Montgomery when the side door opened. One of Marcus' younger Family members, a blond woman with too-pale skin emphasized by her black dress, stepped on the dais. "Conclave of Rancho Robles," she announced. "I present to you Elder Marcus and his bloodchildren." Duty done, she didn't scuttle off stage before her Patron took it, but she did walk faster than was considered to be proper decorum.

Thorn kept his face neutral as Marcus stepped to the front and center of the dais, Nicholas, Rosanna, and Montgomery took positions behind and to the right, grouping themselves from eldest to youngest. Normally, the bloodchildren on the dais were named as they entered as well. That had to do with Marcus wanting to introduce his prodigal son. The vampire population, while it had remained stable, did have some new faces who would have no idea who Nicholas was.

Montgomery's expression was that of neutral support of his bloodfamily as he glanced over the crowd. Mentally, Thorn nodded. He was finally getting a better poker face. Or he was thinking that too soon. Montgomery's lips dipped into a frown when their eyes met, a micro-expression that you had to be watching for. Unfortunately, a lot of vampires would be watching for it.

Including Rosanna, or whatever spies she had placed in the audience. She hadn't seen Montgomery's shift, but she did have one of her own. At first, he thought the microscopic nod was meant for him. Except she wasn't looking at him but over his shoulder, in the direction Sabrina had headed. That explained some of Sabrina's interest. She had also lost a famulus in an event connected to Jordan. It would make sense that the two of them would ally.

And Nicholas made no attempt at hiding that he was scanning the room. If Thorn were in the same situation, he'd be doing the same thing. Determine who he didn't recognize, try to place names to familiar faces, and note who was no longer present to follow up on. Their eyes met for a fraction of a second, and he saw the slightest widening of his eyes. He had been noted and cataloged in Nicholas' mental index. He was curious where he was filed away—as ally or enemy?

There was no microphone to project Marcus' voice. There was no need for one. Everyone remained silent, giving the appearance of respectfully waiting on the Elder's words.

"Conclave of Rancho Robles," he began. "I wish to share my joy with you, for my prodigal son has returned home from St Louis." He held out one hand, and Nicholas stepped forward, joining Marcus by his side. "I present to you Nicholas Quinn, my eldest bloodchild."

"You are too kind, sire," Nicholas said. He was also projecting his voice but making it sound like he was only addressing

Marcus. "I thank you for allowing me to return to the safety I so foolishly fled from."

Thorn made a mental note of that. Who had Nicholas pissed off so badly that he needed to return to the perceived safety of Rancho Robles? And would that person feel the need to hunt Nicholas down? He made a mental note to reach out to any contacts he had in Missouri. Someone had to know what happened.

"The important thing is that you're back where you belong, under my protection," Marcus said. He then looked out over the group of gathered vampires. "I expect him to be treated as I would any of my other bloodchildren who are loyal to me."

And there it was, the reminder that Marcus' 'protection' could be withdrawn from any of them. He had thought that this was a reminder of who Nicholas was, and an introduction to those who hadn't met him. A new thought crossed Thorn's mind. What if this was a warning? More specifically, what if it was a warning to Montgomery? And was Montgomery picking up on it?

His attention snapped back to Marcus as the Elder addressed the room again. "Now, are there any questions?" For some reason, Marcus' gaze was on Thorn. No, it was on someone behind him. And he wasn't surprised to see Sabrina raise her hand. The vampires around her had backed away, leaving her in a defined circle.

Marcus acknowledged Sabrina's raised hand. "Yes, Sabrina, you have a question?"

"There are rumors that there are strange werewolves in the area," Sabrina said. While she stood there serene and poised, the vampires around her shifted away from her, as if the question would summon the bloodthirsty beasts.

Marcus didn't appear fazed by the question if the frown on his face was something to go by. "The Black Oak Pack has informed me of some visitors from the Seattle area."

"There are also rumors of a new alpha having established a pack near us."

"Let me reassure you that the visitors from Green River have done no such thing. If you're referring to Famulus Jordan Abbey, be at ease. She's only holding the title of alpha as a political faction. This envoy from the Green River Pack is playing a game with Alpha Shane. She is no alpha."

Murmurs spread through the group of assembled vampires. "So Famulus Abbey does not have a pack?" Sabrina asked.

Marcus looked to Montgomery to respond. He straightened up some but shifted his weight between his feet. "If you consider a dog that she walks regularly a pack, then yes, she does."

Laugher rippled through the gathering. How much of it was scornful and how much genuine, Thorn wasn't sure. But it diffused most of the tension. "As you can see, we aren't concerned about Famulus Abbey's new title. Let Alpha Shane deal with his visitor."

"But if Famulus Abbey aligns with this envoy?"

"Given that she killed the envoy's brother, that won't be happening," Montgomery stated.

"As I said earlier, politics don't concern us," Marcus said.

"But Famulus Abbey is just that, a famulus," Sabrina said. "She has a connection to us, therefore we're involved. And even if she weren't..." Her gaze shifted to Montgomery for a second before returning to Marcus. "There are others to be considered."

Thorn's focus was on Montgomery. *Don't fall into the trap.* Unfortunately, Montgomery took a step forward, only to be checked by a heavy hand landing on his shoulder. Smirking, Nicholas shook his head as Marcus spoke, "If you're questioning my bloodchild's loyalty, don't. Montgomery has been nothing but loyal to me."

Interesting, Thorn thought. He was certain that Nicholas would take a position against Montgomery, given his hostility against Montgomery being placed in the heart of vampire territory to begin with.

Sabrina's expression remained dark, but she dipped her head in submission. "If you say so, Elder." But Montgomery saw the fleeting glance to Rosanna before Sabrina submitted.

"I do," Marcus said. "Does anyone else have any questions?"

Silence echoed throughout the room.

"Very well. Then this gathering of the Conclave is over. Good hunting, everyone." With that, Marcus swung around and disappeared into the antechamber.

Montgomery sidestepped out from under Nicholas' hand. Nicholas, still wearing the same smirk, nodded to him and stepped forward to greet several vampires.

His fists were still clenched as Thorn stepped up to him. "Let's get out of here," he said. "I'm not sure if they're waiting to see if we break up again or kiss."

He felt several people watching them closely. "Probably both," Thorn said. Neither of them said the third option. They were waiting to see what the ex-werewolf would do. "You need to meet with anyone else?"

Montgomery shook his head. "I'm done here for the night."

Thorn nodded. "Then let's get out of here."

They stepped out of the meeting room into the hall, where the family members had lined up. Close enough to the door, Thorn noted, that they heard everything that happened inside. Jordan stood in the middle of the line, waiting properly for Montgomery to pass. She opened her mouth slightly and then shut it before taking her place three paces behind. She was learning to wait to ask questions until they couldn't be overheard, he thought with some pride.

25

Once the three of them were in the car, Montgomery turned to Jordan. "How much did you hear?"

"Most of it," Jordan said. "Mostly the question about Envoy Blevins and how I fit in." She shook her head. "I was hoping they wouldn't see me as a threat."

Thorn heard the weariness in Montgomery's voice, noticed how he looked down instead of at Jordan. "You always will be one, Jordan. If I'm seen as one, and I'm not even a werewolf anymore, there's no way you wouldn't be seen as one too."

"So, what do we do? Try to rehab my image somehow? Be even more deferential?"

"There's nothing we can do about that now," Thorn said. "You're an alpha now. And even if you could abdicate without causing a shitstorm, they'd still say it's an act, that you were planning something and using Mac as a sleeper agent."

Jordan bit the corner of her lower lip. "The Conclave or Rosanna?"

Thorn smiled. "Clever girl."

"Rosanna clearly has Marcus' ear," Montgomery grumbled.

"And probably Nicolas' too," Thorn said. "Trust me, he was

acting concerned about you causing a scene on stage, but that's all it was. An act."

"That reminds me." Jordan leaned towards Thorn. "Reginald warned me to be cautious around him but wouldn't say anything specific. He hinted that I should talk to you about it."

"Yeah," Thorn said. "I've already talked to Mac about this some. Being cautious is about all he can say. Nicholas left shortly before Mac came to live with us in that ill-fated exchange program."

"Who was supposed to go in my place?"

Thorn shrugged. "Not sure. Marcus never said. It could have been Nicholas, and that was the reason he left. That was the rumor at least."

"Still doesn't explain why I was warned against him."

"He has a type," Thorn said. "Female, young, brunette."

"But I'm a famulus," Jordan said. "He'd have to ask Montgomery before touching me." She turned to him. "And I know you wouldn't allow that."

"That's the other rumor about why he left. Or more accurately, Marcus asked him to leave. I'm afraid your status won't protect you. If anything, it might make you a bigger target."

"Okay," Jordan said. "So, I make sure I'm not alone with him if at all possible. Or is it not that simple?"

"In theory," Thorn said. "But think about how many times you've met with Rosanna alone. I wouldn't put it past him to arrange a situation where you would be alone with him."

"This is assuming he may try something," Montgomery pointed out. "Wouldn't Marcus have him on a tight leash?"

"I've seen it before where Marcus will pit one of his bloodchildren against another. He might sit on the sidelines to watch. His way of weeding out any weakness. Or weaklings."

"So, no protection there," Jordan said.

"Afraid not," Montgomery said. "But we won't solve that problem tonight."

26

Jordan approached the double gate to the dog park, scanning ahead for any dogs or other users. She made sure the gate behind her closed before she opened the other. "We're not having a repeat of what happened when that other person walked you."

Rex looked up at her and gave a soft whine.

"Don't give me that innocent look." Jordan bent down and unclipped the leash. "Go play, boy."

Rex glanced up at her, stump of a tail wagging. Jordan shook her head and produced the tug rope that was his favorite toy. "You want this? You want this, Rexie?" She flung it as far as she could. "Go get it!"

Rex tracked the motion of her arm. He was off and running towards the toy before she finished speaking. He scooped up the rope and trotted back to her, head held high.

"Hello, Jordan!" a familiar voice called.

Jordan turned and saw the Green River Pack's Talespeaker approaching. "Talespeaker Lucas," she said. She looked around for any other dogs using the park. She didn't see any, but that didn't cause the tension in her muscles to melt. While some of the local dogs accepted her presence with a show of growling, they might attack a strange werewolf. And that was a political mess she didn't want to be involved in. "What are you doing here?"

He gestured around to the fenced-in fields. "I thought I would see more of the territory that you and the Black Oak Pack call home."

"Right," she said, keeping an eye on the Rottweiler. She tried to show up when there were few dogs attending to minimize conflicts. Accepting her didn't mean that Rex wouldn't challenge Lucas.

"And I wanted to see your infamous pack," Lucas admitted. He was also watching the approaching dog. "Is this him?"

Jordan nodded. "Rex. Here," she called. Rex galumphed over but pulled up short, eyes fixed on Lucas. He growled, a sound Jordan hadn't heard since their first few meetings.

Or hadn't since she had finally asserted her dominance. Of course, he wouldn't show the same deference to a strange were-wolf. "Rex," she said in a soft, firm voice. "It's okay."

Rex kept his eyes locked on the Talespeaker, hackles raising. Jordan reached for his collar and tugged to get his attention. "It's okay. He's not going to hurt you," she said. Time to reassert her authority. "Sit, Rex."

Rex glanced at her, eyes locking. His hindquarters hit the ground with a thud. "Down." With a whine, he lowered his front. "All the way." Whining again as if wondering why she wasn't chasing away this threat in front of them, he lowered his chin onto his paws. Jordan smiled her approval. "Good boy."

Lucas looked at Jordan, then down at the dog. Rex was wagging his stump of a tail, eyes adoringly looking up at her. "You do seem to have him obeying your every whim."

Jordan reached down to dig her fingers into Rex's favorite spot behind his ear. "We have an understanding."

Lucas nodded, out of beat with the thumping of Rex's hind

leg. "I see. So, tell me," he continued. "What stories do you know of the Wolf?"

"Not many," Jordan said. "Talespeaker Diana usually tells me one that she feels is most appropriate to whatever situation I've found myself in the middle of."

Lucas chuckled. "That's one thing we all tend to do. So, what one has she told you about this situation?"

"Um, she hasn't this time." That was odd. They had been so focused on getting her ready for the fight that the Talespeaker hadn't pulled her aside to impart werewolf lore and wisdom.

"Huh. I figured she would have." Lucas looked at her out of the corner of his eye. "You willing to hear one now?"

Jordan shrugged, then tossed the tug. Rex looked at her, at Lucas, and then at her. When Jordan nodded, he ran for the toy. "Is that going to break some sort of taboo? Am I only supposed to listen to the Talespeaker of my pack?"

"You don't have a Talespeaker, unless your friend over there is a talking dog." He turned to face her, tilting his head. "You're not used to being treated as an alpha?"

Jordan shook her head. "I didn't even know I'd be considered an alpha until Angela pointed it out."

"What a way to learn. But despite young Ms. Shane's arguments, there are packs that wouldn't consider you a true alpha. Not until you had a werewolf swearing loyalty to you."

She sank further against the bench. "That won't be happening anytime soon, if ever."

"Never say never, Jordan." He clapped his hands together and rubbed them. "Now, do you want me to tell you the story?"

"Do we need to go to pack land or somewhere with less risk of being overheard?"

Lucas shook his head. "Nah, we can do it right here. You can keep playing fetch with Rex if you like," he said, nodding towards the dog trotting back proudly with the tug toy.

"Thanks. It's taken me two weeks to get the concept of

bringing the toy back to me in his head." As if to prove her point, Rex stopped in front of her but didn't put down the toy. "Rex, drop it."

Rex wagged the stump of his tail, teeth clamped firmly around the toy.

Jordan sighed. "Rex, I can't throw it if you don't let go of it."

As if he understood what she was saying, Rex dropped the toy. "Good boy," Jordan said, remembering to hit the clicker in her pocket. She picked up the tug and stood. Rex crouched, butt in the air, and his whole rear wagging in eagerness. Once she was sure his eyes were fixed on her, she tossed it a good distance out. "Fetch, Rex."

"You do have a bond with him. That's highly unusual."

"So I've been told." She sat again. "So, do I need to sit at your feet?"

Lucas raised his eyebrows. "She has you do that? How old school." As Jordan suppressed a snorted laugh, he continued, "Nah. No need to have you get down so I can dispense wisdom from on high. Besides, the bench is a lot more comfortable. As long as you don't snore in the middle of my tale, it's fine with me."

"According to Talespeaker Diana, I tend to ask annoying questions then."

"You can ask me whatever questions you want, but just hold them until the end."

"I do have a question though, and it's not about the stories."

Lucas nodded. "Go on."

"I've been having weird dreams about a large black werewolf, even before I encountered the Wolf at the ceremony. My latest one involved being snatched from her by a huge bat."

He chuckled. "It's not uncommon for Talespeakers and alphas to dream of meeting with the Wolf. It's a sign that Angela is right, and you are an alpha, or an alpha-to-be. But it's rarer to dream of the Bat also. You've managed to pique both their interests. But beware. Their interest can be both a blessing and a curse."

"Of course." Jordan sighed and let her head fall back on the edge of the bench. "Story of my life since I've been bitten," she mumbled.

"So, tell me of these dreams. Have you spoken to them?

"Only the Wolf, and mostly to tell me what I'm doing wrong. I was too busy screaming when the Bat picked me up in his claws." Jordan shrugged. "I thought it was my subconscious trying to tell me something about my werewolf self versus my friendships with vampires."

"It could be your subconscious," Lucas allowed. "But I think my interpretation is the correct one. You're touched by both the goddess of werewolves and god of vampires."

"I didn't believe they were real, until the other night," Jordan said.

"All of us feel like that in some way or another," Lucas said. "Before I met the Wolf, I thought they were some fancy metaphor for an excuse of why vampires and werewolves hate each other."

"That's what I thought too, except now, I'm not so sure." Jordan's eyes widened. "Wait. You've met her before the other night?"

"Not exactly. I didn't dream of her like you did." The Talespeaker leaned back against the bench as Rex trotted back. "I was trying to figure out my place in the pack. I knew I wasn't meant to be an alpha, but I felt a calling in my spirit. So, I meditated under a full moon, and She appeared to me."

"Wow." She felt a wet nose nudge her hand. Rex sat politely in front of her, tug in his mouth. Jordan grabbed the end that had been slobbered on not as much. "Drop it." Much to her surprise, the dog let go immediately. She scratched Rex behind the ears. "Good boy." She lobbed the tug again. Before she could tell him to fetch, he scampered after the tug. "So," she said, returning to the earlier conversation. "The Wolf told you that you were destined to be a Talespeaker?"

"More like she confirmed a trail my paws were already treading. I had an interest in going deeper into our culture. If you were meant to be a Talespeaker instead of an alpha, you'd already know it."

"I'm not even sure I believe that I'm an alpha," Jordan said. "Everyone else seems to believe it."

Lucas studied her as if she just spoke a foreign language he only half-understood. "Even with the Wolf's blessing?"

Jordan shook her head. "I thought She was a voice of my subconscious trying to get me to accept my situation. I'm still coming to terms with the fact that She's real."

Lucas frowned, then nodded. "That would be a shock if you haven't grown up with the myths and legends," he said. "Which reminds me. Do you know how the werewolf tradition of dueling came about?" He sighed when Jordan shook her head.

"No. One time, I asked Talespeaker Diana if there was a book I could read, and she looked at me like I had grown a second head."

"They're only supposed to be passed down orally." He grinned. "So, let me continue the tradition of telling you the story that could have helped avoid the situation after you put your foot smack in the middle of it."

"Guilty." Jordan chuckled. "She didn't react well to me saying that if they're supposed to be preventative tales, it would help if I knew about them beforehand."

"You were supposed to learn all this as a pup. And I'm sure they expect Vampire Cooper to tell you. Not sure why, since it's not his place, even if he had been a Talespeaker."

"Probably my fault, since I chose him to train me instead of joining the Black Oak Pack back... god, it's just under a year ago."

"Well, let me fill in this gap in your education. You see, the Children of the Wolf grew more numerous, gathering in groups and forming in the first Packs. Now, despite everyone being connected to the Wolf, be it child, grandchild, great-grandchild, and so on through blood or bite, squabbles arose. But unlike family, these tended to be deadly. Packs fought over territory, over game, over mates. Packs would wipe out rival Packs in bloody battles.

And the Wolf watched it all, sorrowing at the loss of so many of her children. As she watched the battles progress, she noticed more often than not, the Alphas of the Packs survived, most often by not taking place in the fighting. And sorrow turned to anger. She decreed that if Packs were unable to come to a peaceful agreement, they would be allowed to battle. However, the battle should be between the challenging Alphas, with the Packs to accept the outcome of the fight. Suddenly, the number of fights between Packs were greatly reduced. While fights to the death were still allowed, they became fewer and fewer. Unfortunately for you, they still are allowed." Lucas tilted his head. "Any questions?"

"That's the whole tale?" Jordan shook her head. "Sorry, I was expecting something more..." She paused, searching for a phrase that wouldn't insult Talespeaker Diana, and decided to just say it, "...Long winded."

"And old timey?" Lucas laughed. "Like I said. She's old school."

"Shouldn't you be with her arguing over the details?"

Lucas shrugged. "We've got that all settled. There's not that much to do until the night of the fight."

Jordan pursed her lips. "So, why are you here? It has to be for more than just to tell me one of the tales of the Wolf."

"I wanted to see if there was another way, if I could talk you into not fighting."

Jordan looked at him, her eyes wide. "I'm not the one who started this fight." She held up a hand. "I know I started it with the fangs. But I didn't say that the only way to settle this was by ceding my territory."

"Why are you keeping it?" Lucas asked. "You're the only werewolf using it. I can't see him," he nodded towards Rex, "running with you under a full moon. Never mind the vampire, even if he is technically a chaos wolf."

Jordan's eyes narrowed. "If he were a werewolf, would you be advising me like this?"

"No," Lucas said. "If he were a werewolf, you wouldn't be in this situation." He leaned closer to her. "You could cast yourself at her feet, give her your territory. She would let you live, given what we've learned about how you've been taught our ways."

That sounded similar to an offer Rosanna had once made her. She didn't like it then either. "And I'd have nowhere to go." Shane might keep her safe, at least for a while. He owed her that much after she saved his life from the hunters. But Marcus would see it as a betrayal of her oath of Family and could potentially use it as reason to wipe out the Pack. Or he might not have to.

"Tell me something," Jordan said. "If she takes Mount Ponderosa, would she attempt to claim Black Oak as well?"

He looked at her, holding her gaze. But his stare didn't have the same power behind it that Alpha Shane's had. His eyes shifted away to focus on the bench between them. "Yes."

"Thought so." She looked out to the field where Rex was romping around. As if he felt her eyes on him, he galumphed back to her, tug toy in his mouth. "I appreciate your offer," Jordan said. "But I've made my choice."

"I was afraid of that." Lucas stood and bowed his head. "I take my leave of you, Alpha Abbey. And should the worst happen, I'll howl the death song at your funeral."

She tried to hide the shiver running through her spine at his words. Then she felt the warmth of a large Rottweiler pressing against her legs. At least one canine had her back. "May that be a long time coming, Talespeaker Lucas."

27

———

After returning Rex to Mrs. Clarke, Jordan returned to the apartment long enough to scribble a note about where she was going. She left it pinned on the refrigerator, again with a small smile. She still found it highly amusing that they used a food storage system as their central communication point like any other family. Her phone beeped that her rideshare was five minutes away. Still smiling, she grabbed her purse and her keys and went down to meet it.

The gray electric sedan pulled up just as she opened the door to the outside. She double-checked the license plate and the driver before slipping into the backseat. "Hi."

"Hi," the driver said. "Just to confirm your destination. Peaceful Oaks Cemetery,"

Jordan nodded as she buckled her seatbelt. "Yes."

The driver tapped a few spots on the comically oversized screen. He then hit the green start button. The engine purred to life with a whisper whine. It was quiet compared to Thorn's hybrid. "Going to see a loved one?" he asked.

The question caught her off guard. "Yeah," she said after a moment. "Something like that."

The rest of the ride was quiet. The driver pulled up to the main gate. Jordan thanked him and slipped out of the car. Tapping at her phone to increase his tip, she walked into Peaceful Oaks Cemetery.

The sun was setting as Jordan walked up the paved path to the back area. The last time she had visited Peaceful Oaks Cemetery, she had been in a half-panic, trying to locate Montgomery, following his scent in darkness. This time, as she walked along the lit path, she was a lot calmer, at least for the moment.

No, that wasn't true. She was a lot better at stuffing down her panic in front of others.

It took about ten minutes for her to reach her destination. Not that she could have gotten lost. The weeping angel crouched on top of the grave was the most notable monument in this corner of the cemetery. It rose above flat markers and upright gravestones, a silent, mourning sentinel.

When she was last here, the darkness had obscured the writing on the plaque. Jordan bent down, squinting to read it in the last of the dying light. "Christine Brooks. Beloved daughter, devoted spouse, and dearest friend." The name that connected to daughter was obvious. Marcus, of course, would want top billing. But she wondered about who was the spouse and who was the friend? Montgomery? Thorn? Rosanna? Somebody she hadn't even heard of? Those questions tumbled through her mind as Jordan sat on the bench opposite the memorial. "Who were you?" she whispered softly.

Although the light faded, nobody came to shoo her out of the cemetery. It was quiet, though surrounded by the memories of those who died. If there were ghosts, they seemed at peace.

She heard footsteps approach. The tread was light but familiar as it crunched up the gravel path. Her discreet sniffing, even in her human form, of the breeze confirmed what her ears told her. Even if she hadn't scented him, his voice would have confirmed who it was. "What are you doing here?"

She turned to Montgomery. "I wanted to see it," Jordan said, gesturing towards the angel. "I mean, I saw it that night when I was tracking Rhys, but I didn't get a good look at it."

"Okay." Montgomery sat on the bench next to her. They both sat there silently for several seconds. "What are you thinking, Jordan?"

"I was wondering if my death would make such a mark. If I'd be remembered like this." Jordan waved at the statue again. "It's flashy and probably draws more attention than it should, but yet, here it is."

Montgomery sighed. "The cenotaph was Marcus' idea. She didn't want anything this flashy. A simple marker in a mausoleum, for example. Or her name engraved on a memorial wall. But Marcus wanted to make a point with her death and my transformation." He slipped an arm around her. "But that's not what you're really thinking."

Jordan nodded. "I know I've faced death before, but this threat feels more real for some reason."

"You've got some experience under your belt now. You have a better idea of what you're facing. And although she's teaching you all the tricks you need to know, losing regularly to Angela can't be helping."

"Yeah." Jordan bit her lower lip. "Is Thorn coming?"

"No, he said Marcus wanted to talk with him. Probably off giving his misdirection, er I mean report. Something wrong between you and him?"

"Not exactly." She took a deep breath, diving in. "I've been thinking about what you've told me about vampires, about what I've seen from you. And something feels... Off with him."

"Off with him," Montgomery repeated. "How?"

Jordan stared at the statue. "It sounds stupid. But when Thorn bit me, I got this vision of a bat. And the other night, I was having one of those dreams about the Wolf. But this time, the Bat was involved too." She turned to look at him. "When I woke up, he was watching me. And he knew I was having a dream about the Wolf before I said anything."

"That's odd timing," Montgomery said. "But you do tend to wake up with a certain look when you have one of those dreams. And as for the visions, he's an older vampire, although he doesn't like to advertise that fact. I've heard rumors about some older vampires having mental abilities. Like that time his mind whammied the guard and got us into Shane and Elder Marcus' meeting about the hunters."

"I hadn't even thought about that one." She had noticed it, but in the whirlwind of the attack and tracking the hunter who tried to assassinate the two leaders of the Rancho Robles factions, then dealing with the fallout from that, it had slipped from her mind. Montgomery accepted it, although he hadn't hinted that vampires had those kind of powers. "So, what does it mean?"

Montgomery sank against her. "I'm not completely sure," he admitted with a shake of his head. "He's older than he wants us to think he is. And by us, I mean the Conclave, not just you and me."

"So, can we trust him?"

Montgomery thought for a moment before answering. "I trust him. He wouldn't have admitted that he's spying for Elder Marcus if he didn't care for us." He paused. "Speaking of which, Elder Marcus knows about the incident with Animal Control."

Jordan stiffened. She had been caught. She closed her eyes, took a deep breath, and opened them. "Do you think Thorn told him?"

Montgomery shook his head. "No. Marcus has a spy in Animal Control. Or someone pointed out the picture of the black wolfdog on the reunited part of the website and connected it with the only known werewolf in the area who has black fur."

Jordan made a face like she bit into a lemon. "I couldn't stop them from taking that picture. And Angela was too keen on getting a picture she could embarrass me with in the future." Damn that pink sparkly collar.

"I know. And I don't blame you for that part. I wish you had figured out how to find Rex without shapeshifting." Montgomery paused. "He's worried that you're going to realize that you really are an alpha and cause trouble."

Jordan snorted. "Like I haven't before?"

Montgomery froze, then shook When she arched an eyebrow, his laughter bubbled out. Then she giggled, which set him off further.

It took them three minutes to get back under control. The giggles would fade, then one of them would snort and start another cycle. The cycles faded into a companionable silence before as they both studied the sculpture.

Jordan was the one to break it. "So, now that he knows, am I going to be punished?"

"He's leaving it to me to see you're put on a short leash." Montgomery rested a hand on top of hers. "Hopefully, I can keep it metaphorical instead of literal."

"I hope so." She rubbed her throat. "That collar was embarrassing enough."

"I know you want to treat it as a joke, Jordan. I do too." He sighed. "But you have to step lightly. If you give him any excuse, any hint of stepping out of line, he'll come down on you hard. I've seen him do it before."

"Even though I saved his life?"

"Especially because you saved his life, Jordan." Montgomery twisted to look at her. "You exposed a weakness. That hunter Elias Campbell should have never been able to live for so long in Rancho Robles without being found out. Now, he has to prove he isn't weak. And allowing a famulus to openly break his rules, even if she did save his life, will be seen as another weakness."

"So, how are you going to punish me?" Jordan asked.

"I haven't figured that out yet." Montgomery shrugged. "Got any ideas?"

"I'm assuming a rolled-up newspaper is out of the question."

"Yeah, it is."

Their gaze shifted again to the statue. "Tell me about her," she said softly.

Montgomery didn't answer right away. She was about to tell him not to if it was too painful. Then, he spoke, "I don't know what Dad was thinking when he sent me to stay with Elder Marcus. I know he thought it would bring peace between our peoples, and I would somehow be responsible for it. And to this day, I don't know why Marcus said yes. Maybe he found it amusing and thought I'd be an exotic pet. Or he thought he could use me as leverage against the Black Oak Pack, either with Dad or maybe once I took over." Montgomery shrugged. "But he couldn't be bothered with me on a daily basis, so he handed over that duty to Christine."

Jordan smiled. "And the two of you hit it off?"

"Yeah. I met Thorn at the same time, but things didn't start between us until much later." Montgomery leaned back some, looking at the sky. Jordan did too. The first stars were peeking out. "She was the first woman I met who wasn't interested in me because of who I was. Or more accurately, who I would be."

"I thought you were in an arranged betrothal," Jordan said.

"Oh, I was. It didn't mean that werewolves from other packs weren't throwing their daughters at me. And if one of those daughters ended up pregnant, well, the arranged betrothal is over and done with."

Jordan chewed the inside of her cheek. "But she didn't care about you being the future alpha?"

Montgomery shook his head. "No. She wanted to know all about my life in the pack. And I know what you're thinking. It may have started as her extracting secrets for Marcus. I wouldn't be surprised if Marcus hadn't ordered her to do just that. But it didn't stay that way for long. I taught her things about the pack, and she taught me about the Conclave."

"And you fell in love."

"Yeah." Now, Montgomery was studying the statue. "I called off the betrothal and took the oath of Family, pledging my love and loyalty to her. Dad was furious, of course, and cast me from the Pack. At that time, I didn't care. Marcus probably was also, but he always had a hard time denying her anything. And things went like that for a few months, until that night."

Jordan leaned against him, offering reassurance. "If you want to leave it there, that's fine. Thorn's told me some of what happened." Pamela too, but she didn't think that Montgomery would be too interested in the werewolf perspective.

"No, I'm talking about it for once. I should get it all out." Montgomery's focus was now in the far wall, ringing the cemetery. "There were threats from the Black Oak Pack, of course. I was called apostate for turning my back on the Wolf, traitor for allying myself with the Bat, and worse. But Dad couldn't bring himself to raise a fang against me."

"So, some of those threats were directed at him?" Jordan guessed. It really wasn't much of a guess when she thought about it.

"Yeah. I don't know how seriously he took them. I don't think Marcus was concerned at all. I'd overheard him say that they were the yapping of angry dogs." He must have seen a slight compression of her lips or narrowing of her eyes. "He didn't say it to my face, so don't ever repeat it."

Jordan nodded, and Montgomery continued, "That night, we had been out to a movie. Something about an adventurer preventing a quartz alien skull from falling into the hands of Communists." He shook his head and dropped his free hand to his lap. "Haven't been able to watch it or any of the movies in the series since then."

Jordan placed her hand on his and wrapped her fingers around it.

"This wasn't the theater at The Row. Christine had said that she wanted to get out from under Marcus' eye for a few hours. So, we had picked a late showing at a theater at the other end of town. We were walking back to the car. Some werewolves I didn't recognize stopped us. Another set of strangers cut us off from behind. And..." His voice faded as he stared at the statue.

"And you were attacked," Jordan said, trying to spare him the pain of saying it. "And Christine died."

"She told me to run. I didn't. I shifted as the others did and tried to protect her. For me, it was three on one." He grimaced, his fangs showing in a bitter smile. "I was able to fight one off. I think I snapped his leg, but the two were holding me and made me watch what happened to Christine. Or they did until I bit someone and was hit on the back of my skull. I can still hear the crack."

"I woke up in human form. Christine lay a few feet away, a stake through her heart. It was a miracle we weren't seen by any mortals. Or if we were, Marcus was ruthless cleaning up the breach we made. It's a bit of a blur until Thorn showed up with some of Marcus' family to help. I was cradling Christine and a bit feral. He said I snapped at him, and it took about ten minutes before he could talk me into letting him help."

Jordan leaned against his shoulder. "I'm sorry you had to go through that."

For a second, she thought Montgomery would remain stiffly staring at the statue. Then he leaned against her, his cheek resting against her hair. "Thanks."

They sat there silently until Jordan's phone buzzed. She pulled it from her pocket, looked down at the screen, and scrunched her face. "Angela wants to know when I'm showing up for tonight's lesson."

"How are you doing?"

"I haven't broken my arm again, if that's what you're wondering." She sighed. "She and Alpha Shane keep saying that if they had a month, they could make a decent fighter out of me." She didn't add the follow-up thought. They didn't have a month. "I probably should get going."

"No," Montgomery said. His arm wrapped around her waist. "I'm supposed to meet with Blevins in a while, but let's stay here for just a few more minutes."

She didn't have to ask if he was ordering her as a Patron. That teasing comment was the wrong thing for this moment. "We'll stay as long as you want."

28

Montgomery had seen Jordan off in an Uber and promised to pick her up at the Black Oak Pack's ground. There was no further way to delay what was about to happen.

It had been hard to arrange a location for them to meet. Most of the late-night businesses that Montgomery was familiar with were along The Row. Or, in other words, under the watchful eye of Elder Marcus if not outright owned by him. The envoy refused to set foot anywhere near them. But one location was open late at night, and while vampire owned, it was considered a neutral-enough location for them to meet.

He wondered if Enya would still feel that way if she traced through the shell companies and discovered he was the owner of the Bowling Bonanza.

Montgomery walked into the lobby and passed the store that catered to bowlers with professional aspirations, or at least who didn't want to rent shoes. He saw the manager on duty speaking with one of the customers. Steve did pause and nod to acknowledge Montgomery, then turned back to the customer. Artificial light glinted off a gold ring with an imbedded wedge of ivory and a ruby. The design was the same as the pendant Jordan wore on a necklace. All Family had it somehow. And while Steve was technically Marcus' famulus, he assisted Montgomery in keeping the business he had been gifted as the Elder's bloodchild running smoothly. And reported anything of interest back to Marcus.

On second thought, he should have pushed for the meeting to happen at that coffee shop Jordan always seemed to be slipping off to.

Further through the foyer, the building opened out to the main area. On his left was a counter for paying and renting shoes. On the right was the bar with the usual fried snacks and bagged chips for sale. Further to the right was a nook with a pool table tucked in it. In front of him, a barrier wall with stairs cut through led down to the lower floor with twenty bowling lanes. About half of them were in use, adding a semi-regular crash of balls against pins to the music piped in overhead. A counter lined the barrier wall. Bar stools tucked under the edge of it, forming areas where people could eat and watch the bowling without interfering with the playing area.

Enya had arrived before him. She had claimed one of the stools and leaned against the table, a basket of onion rings and a beer in front of her. Montgomery settled on a stool to her right. "Envoy Enya Blevins," he said with a polite nod.

"Chaos Wolf Montgomery Cooper," Enya returned without looking at him. He winced slightly at the use of the title. He hadn't considered himself a chaos wolf for a long time. And from the curl of Enya's lips, she knew she hit a soft spot. "I'm surprised you said yes to this."

Montgomery shrugged and placed his hands on the table. "Call me morbidly curious. And I'm surprised you asked, given I haven't heard from you since you ended our relationship."

"I'm surprised you call it a relationship, given that we talked maybe for a half hour total our entire lives."

Montgomery quirked an eyebrow. If he read her tone right,

she sounded hurt. "Would you have really gone through with the arranged marriage?"

Enya turned to him and looked him up and down. "No."

Montgomery folded his arms over his chest. "Then don't pretend that I insulted you by breaking the proposal."

Enya scowled. "Very well. Now, what did you want to talk about?"

Montgomery schooled his features to stay neutral. Getting mad at her wouldn't help the situation. Besides, that mess had squarely been his fault. Like the current situation. He knew the answer before he spoke, but he still had to try. "I assume there's no way we can come to some sort of alternate arrangement as far as weregild goes."

"No," Enya said, her expression a mask. "We're long past that."

And there it was. Montgomery sighed. "I was afraid of that."

"Were you?" Enya said. Her mask cracked as anger seeped into her voice. "You seem to have been maneuvering for this exact situation from day one. You knew what pack my brother was from."

"We didn't learn that until after he had bitten Jordan and killed a famulus," Montgomery protested. "He didn't present himself to the Pack for a proper introduction. As far as I know, he was already dead when Alpha Shane first saw him."

"That may be true," Enya said. "But you didn't make much of an effort after you learned about him."

"It's hard to do when you're bound and gagged in a footlocker. Or did Shane not mention that Rhys kidnapped me in a bid to lure Jordan to him?"

"And how do I know it wasn't collusion between you two to lure Rhys to his death?"

"Your brother had problems," Montgomery said. "Jordan told him no. She tried to leave with me without violence. He was the one who attacked her. She was only defending herself."

"I know my brother had problems! But he was my brother!

Doesn't that mean I can't demand justice for him? Did you ever think for a moment that he was obsessed with her because he had problems? And nobody tried to help him?"

"He never presented himself to Black Oak, so we had no way to reach out to him." Montgomery paused. "We heard rumors that Jordan wasn't the first." They hadn't, but it was something Montgomery suspected. And the way Enya's gaze cut to the bowlers with sudden interest confirmed it. "How many?"

Enya didn't look back at him. "Three women we knew of," she mumbled. "None of whom survived."

"Three others." The sound of a bowling ball clashing against pins emphasized his words. An unexpected surge of anger rolled through his chest. "You knew he had issues. And yet you kicked him out and made him someone else's problem."

"We told him that he had the option of leaving the pack to seek a mate after several females rejected him. Once he left the Pack and declared himself a chaos wolf, he was no longer our responsibility."

"Except he is suddenly when he turns up dead."

She glared at him. "Don't tell me you've forgotten that an insult against one of us is an insult against us all."

"Vampires feel the same way," Montgomery countered. "I think you're using this to your advantage, and if I weren't involved, this would be handled much differently."

"Oh yes, I definitely blame you. Not for abandoning me and breaking the arranged marriage. That I thank you for. But you started this by interfering with Rhys and not handing her over to the Black Oak Pack." She stepped forward into his space. "But don't think this all falls on you. Alpha Shane is as much at fault for not dealing with the root cause long before my brother bit that pup. Same as Alpha Cooper."

He clenched his fists to keep his fangs from dropping. "Leave my father out of this," Montgomery ground through clenched teeth.

"Your father and mine are the reason we're in this mess," Enya growled. "I'll never understand how your father talked mine into an arranged marriage."

"The story I got was your father suggested it," Montgomery countered.

"It doesn't matter who initiated the betrothal. What matters is that you were the one who broke it off."

"And that makes me somehow responsible for your brother not being able to find a woman who would accept him as a mate?"

"No, what makes you responsible is that you didn't hand the pup over to Shane. If you had, none of this would have happened. I have to admit I'm curious about one thing." Enya leaned back as she studied his expression. "So, why did you do it? Why are you helping her?"

He heard the quotes around the word helping. "She didn't ask for any of this," Montgomery said. He didn't want to say why this was his fault. "Jordan didn't know what she was getting into when she agreed to your challenge."

"And whose fault is that? Who was supposed to be guiding her, warning her ahead of time? She's worse than a pup because we don't know what the gaps in her education are. Was it her idea to take the fangs? Did anyone tell her? Didn't you warn her?"

Montgomery looked away from her. "No"

Enya's jaw dropped. "Why?"

There was no point in hiding his reasons. "Because he was a chaos wolf from a long way outside of our territory, and I didn't think anyone would come looking for him."

"Even though you knew he was from Green River," Enya said. "And don't bother denying it. Alpha Shane said that he informed you in front of the girl."

Ice coated Montgomery's voice. "She has a name."

"And the title of alpha. That doesn't mean I have to acknowledge it."

"But you acknowledge Alpha Shane."

Enya shrugged. "For as long as he is still Alpha." Before Montgomery could follow up on that, she changed the subject. "So, be honest. Whose idea was it to desecrate my brother's body?"

There was no point hiding what happened. "Rosanna, the Patron of the Famulus Rhys killed. Jordan heard me talking about it and decided to try to make things right."

She shook her head. "So that girl will be taking your well-deserved punishment."

Montgomery shook his head. "You don't have to go through with this."

"The hell I don't!" She slammed her fist on the table. "I've threatened her in front of another pack. I can't back down and let that dishonor stain my reputation. That doesn't mean I'm looking forward to killing her."

"She'll be fighting you to yielding, not death. You can change the fight to first blood."

"That will make no difference. I'll make sure my first blow is a killing one." Enya shook her head. "If you insist she's an alpha, then not only am I fighting her, there's also her territory to be considered. If I defeat her, it's mine. And unlike Alpha Shane, I won't tolerate a chaos wolf in my territory." She paused for a moment. "Even a dead one."

A chill ran down Montgomery's spine. "Is that a threat?"

"It's a promise, vampire. And here's another for Alpha Shane for you to pass along. Clearly, he's weak for tolerating vampires so close to his holdings, let alone allowing a chaos wolf barely older than a pup to somehow gain the title of alpha. Therefore, once I defeat her, it's within my rights to challenge his leadership."

"You saw the Wolf Herself give Her blessing to Jordan."

"I saw something," Enya said. "I wouldn't put it past it to be some sort of trick that you pulled to further manipulate Alpha Shane."

Montgomery rolled his eyes. "So, I'm both a vampire who has

betrayed the ways of the Wolf, but I also have enough of Her favor that I can pull off this massive con." He shook his head. "Really, how much of this is about him and how much about a chance to take a shot at me?"

"Inflated ego much?" Enya snorted. "Montgomery, I'm serious when I say thank you. It was a relief when you broke off our engagement. I'm grateful, because it would have never worked out between us."

"No, it wouldn't have." He never understood why his father had agreed to the arranged marriage to begin with. Did it have to do with his mother having died young and feeling a need to secure his son's future in case something happened to him? Or had his father realized that he had made a mistake? Maybe that was why he had pushed him so hard to join the Conclave as an observer. He would have been 'tainted' by his association with vampires and could break the engagement without problems. Little did his father know how far things would go. "I do have one question."

"If this is about the girl—"

"Not the one you're thinking. It's about Angela Shane." He paused, figuring out the best way to voice his suspicion. "Your sister is her mother."

Enya nodded. "How did you figure it out?"

"A gut feeling," Montgomery admitted. "Jordan mentioned that Angela said her mother was living in Green River, but not who she was. It didn't take too much for me to connect the dots."

Enya sighed. To Montgomery's surprise, she looked tired. "Gwen wasn't supposed to have a pup with Shane. Or rather, she was supposed to have a son."

That made Montgomery pause, filing through his memories of what his father had told him about the Green River Pack. "I thought in your pack, gender of the alpha didn't matter."

"It doesn't, but we have a tradition. In the distant past, a male alpha was followed by his daughter, who was followed by her son, who was followed by his daughter. And so on, and so on, and so on. So, when my sister had a daughter, she raised her until she was weaned and sent her to live with her father."

Which explained why no matter how much he tried, he could never figure out who within the Black Oak Pack was her mother. He had thought that Shane was shielding her from Marcus' machinations. "Does she have a son?"

Enya nodded. "Yes. Angela is out of any potential succession in Green River."

Which suddenly made Enya's ambition for taking over the Black Oak Pack much more understandable. And why Angela saw Jordan as such a threat. And even why Angela was willing and eager to help Jordan kick her aunt's ass.

"What was her name?"

Enya's sharp question pulled his focus back to the here and now. "Her who?"

"The vampire slave my brother killed." Enya's lips curled into a triumphant smile. "You don't know her name, do you?"

Montgomery bit back the urge to say famulus but focused on the challenge. At least Rosanna had spat the name often enough at him that he had it memorized. "Bridgette was killed because she was taking a dress that Jordan had worn to the cleaners." He dropped his voice a half-octave, a trick his father had taught him when he needed to be intimidating. "Now, you tell me the names of the women Rhys killed."

Enya's mouth dropped, revealing the points of her fangs. She didn't hide the snarl in her response. "This isn't about his victims, vampire."

Montgomery tensed with the effort to keep his voice quiet. "That's just the thing. This is all about his victims. You're choosing to punish the one who managed to survive." His eyes narrowed. "And we are in public."

Enya closed her eyes as she sat up. She sucked in a deep breath, eyes still closed. Her fingers relaxed from claw-like curls, and her shoulders dropped. Her eyes opened, but there was still a glare in her eyes. "You and I have nothing more to talk about." She slid off her stool. "I will see you next at the challenge when this mess will be settled once and for all."

Montgomery nodded, not trusting himself to speak. He watched as Enya turned and walked off. The automatic doors had hissed shut when one of the servers came over to him and handed him a tray with an order tab on it. "I'm sorry?"

The server, in his late teens if the beard he was trying to grow was any indication, gestured to the half-eaten fries. "She said you'd be covering the bill."

Montgomery rolled his eyes as he reached for his wallet. He could call over to the manager and have the bill taken care of. None of the other employees were aware of who he was, and he'd rather keep things that way. And of course, Enya would be trying to get under his skin any way possible. He slapped down the card on the tray. He looked at the doors as the server scuttled away. "This," he muttered to himself, "was a waste of time."

29

Sentry Rodrigues let him through the gate to the Black Oak Pack's home territory with only a stony look. Normally, when he came to pick up Jordan, he'd wait for her outside the gates, both men studiously ignoring each other if she were still working her way down from the main buildings. This time, the gate rolled open, and Rodrigues gestured him forward. "Shane says to head up and meet him in the gym."

Montgomery nodded once. "Thank you, Sentry." Rodrigues turned away without any further words, something he was more used to. He started the drive up. Although his eyes were on the road, he occasionally caught a flash of fur paralleling him out of the corner of his eye. He wasn't that surprised. Trust only went so far.

He parked by the main house. Instead of checking in there, he went to one of the side paths that led away from it. He walked to the entrance and turned to face the way he came. "I know you're watching me," Montgomery said in a conversational voice. "I'm here as a guest of your Alpha. I grew up here, so I know the way to the building he's in. I don't need the escort, and I promise to stay on the path."

He wasn't surprised to hear a few low whines and rumbles more reminiscent of a conversation than a growl. Then it went quiet, followed by the deliberate crunching of paws on leaves. The sounds faded into the distance.

Huh, Montgomery thought. *I didn't think that would work.* He turned and walked down the trail. It could have been because it was only a ten-yard walk to the building that served as a gym and sparring area. And as he walked towards it, memories flooded back. Him barely more than four years old, riding on his father's shoulders. He and Shane racing for the door, loser having to do the dishes after the evening meal. He paused at the doors, resting his head on the hand, trying to push the sorrow back into the emotional closet that he kept it locked in. Once he was sure he had it under control, he opened the door and walked inside.

He bypassed the side room with the shower cubicle without a glance, focused on the main room. There was a set of free weights in the corner, as well as a treadmill and a rowing machine. But what had his attention at the moment were the two werewolves sparring. The white-furred one's movements appeared serene compared to the heavy panting of the black-furred one. Shane sat on a bench opposite the gym equipment, watching every move the two wolfwomen made.

Montgomery made his way over to the bench. He didn't sit next to the man. "Has Angela broken Jordan's arm again?"

Shane shook his head, for the moment focusing his gaze on the sparring women. "Not this time."

"Well, that's an improvement." As if finding out that Jordan wasn't in immediate danger, the energy drained out of him. He slumped, letting the wall support his back.

Shane looked at him, keeping an eye on the sparring werewolves out of the corner of one eye. "Well, Blevins didn't kill you, so it must have gone okay,"

"Yeah, it was such a pleasant conversation." He dropped the

sarcasm from his voice. "Are you aware that if she does defeat Jordan, she also intends to challenge you?"

"No, but I'm not surprised. Probably after that, you and Marcus will be her next targets." Shane sounded tired. "Jordan is as ready as we can get her. Angela's taught her everything she can in the time we had. It's up to her now."

Montgomery nodded, watching her and Angela spar. Jordan was fighting well, given the fact she had only been training a week. It was obvious to him she was thinking through her blocks and counters instead of letting her body react. The same with her attacks. Maybe if they had another month, she'd rely more on muscle memory and instinct.

He watched as she charged in, slipping under Angela's guard, or at least that's what she thought she had done. There was a grin of triumph on her face as she pressed her nose against Angela's throat. Her wagging tail froze. Angela was balanced on one hind paw, holding onto her shoulders. The other was against her abdomen, claws lightly poking into her fur.

Montgomery sighed. "That's the move she used to kill Rhys."

Shane shook his head. "She's lucky he didn't gut her." He raised his voice so both women could hear. "Break apart and try again. This time, Jordan, try something else."

Montgomery recognized the look she shot at Shane, the one that said, 'Like what?' with a snarl of frustration. "At least she's not answering back," Montgomery said.

"It would be better if she would," Shane said, watching the two werewolves circling each other again. "It's amazing what a little back sass can cause in the middle of a fight."

Montgomery arched an eyebrow. "You always complain about her mouthing off."

"No, I complain about her mouthing off at me." Shane's lips curled into the barest of grins. "There's a difference." He cocked an eye at Montgomery. "You think we're being too hard on her?"

He watched as Jordan lunged. Angela saw the move coming as if she had broadcast it on the news. She sidestepped and kicked Jordan just above the tail as she passed. Arms pinwheeling, Jordan stumbled and fell, chin skidding against the ground. Montgomery sighed. "Sometimes I worry we're not being hard enough."

"What do you think her problem is?"

"She's scared, but not angry. Or not angry enough," Montgomery said. "She beat Rhys because she was pissed about what he did to me. From what she told me, she was done with Angela's bullying, but she hasn't reached that point with Enya." He arched an eyebrow. "Or am I reading the situation wrong?"

"No, I think you've got it right," Shane said. "I was hoping we could poke her into unleashing the beast."

Jordan swiped for Angela's head. She yelped as Angela blocked her blow and twisted her arm, sending Jordan reeling back several steps. Montgomery shook his head. "Doesn't look like any of us were successful."

Shane shook his head. "No, it doesn't look like it worked." He leaned back against the wall again. "How did the meeting with Blevins go?"

Montgomery leaned back against the wall. "About how you expected. Neither of us could come up with a compromise the other would like."

"Compromise?"

"I asked if there was anything I could do to get her to back out of the fight. She told me to go pound sand."

Shane chuckled, slapping his shoulder. "At least you tried."

"Yeah." Now, he had to deliver this information with caution. "There were other things we discussed.

"Such as?"

"Enya told me about Angela," Montgomery said.

Shane froze. "She what?" he said in a low growl.

"She confirmed who her mother is." The current theory that Marcus held publicly was that Angela's mother had died. While that was possible, Montgomery didn't believe it. Turns out that he was right for once. Too bad he wouldn't be able to share the fact he was right.

Shane looked away and swallowed. "So, what are you going to do about it?"

"Nothing." He shook his head. "She's heir apparent to Black Oak, but she's not an alpha now. And from the way Enya talked, she's not in line to Green River. For now, she's just another pack member. Her maternal lineage is none of Marcus' business." Marcus would have a different opinion, but Montgomery would deal with that when he found out.

He saw Shane studying him out of the corner of his eye. Shane was familiar enough with the Elder that he knew what Marcus would do when he found out that Montgomery was withholding information. "Why?"

Montgomery didn't need any clarification on the question. "She doesn't need the burden of dealing with him in addition to everything else."

"I would have expected you to protect Jordan this way," Shane said. "And I thank you for giving my daughter the same consideration."

"Consider this thanks for helping Jordan get through this. I know it would have been easier for you to side with Enya and not declare her an alpha."

"Yeah," Shane said. "But it was worth it to see her expression when the Wolf showed up and anointed Jordan." He elbowed Montgomery's side. "Yours too, Mr. Skeptic."

"Don't call me that," Montgomery said. "But you're right. I didn't truly believe until then."

A loud oof and the sound of a body thumping against the floor pads. They looked up to see Angela and Jordan getting back on their feet. Jordan was a little slower than Angela. Angela said something, gesturing towards them. Jordan shook her head and took a fighting stance, hackles spiking and ears flattened. Angela shook her head and took the same pose. Then both werewolves were sparring again.

"Be honest with me, Shane. What are her odds?"

Shane shifted his jaw from side to side. "Not good." As if to emphasize his pronouncement, Angela tripped up Jordan as she charged. Jordan overbalanced and fell onto her stomach. Shane stood and clapped his hands to get their attention. "Angela, Jordan, take a break," Alpha Shane called as Jordan rolled to her back. "Both of you, please come here."

To Montgomery's surprise, Angela offered Jordan a paw. Jordan took it without hesitating and levered herself up. "Let's have this conversation human," he said, tossing each of the women their robes as soon as they came within throwing distance.

As the women shifted, Montgomery flipped open the cooler he noticed on the floor by Shane. He pulled out two bottles of chilled sports drink, condensation clinging to their sides. He handed the neon yellow one to Jordan, who took it, saluted him, and unscrewed the lid. "Thanks."

While she drank, he held out one bottle to Angela. She eyed it, eyed him, and at her father's nod, accepted the bottle. "Thank you, Mr. Cooper."

"You're welcome, Angela," Montgomery said. The girl did seem to be learning some manners, or Shane had lectured her that she didn't need to make an enemy of a vampire when she had allied herself with that vampire's famulus.

"Now, Jordan." Shane leaned back against the wall. "You've beaten Angela before. Can you tell me why you're not able to now?"

Jordan shook her head. He had seen similar blank expressions on students who were lost in an algebra problem. "From what you and Angela have been hinting at, I'm thinking about how to do it instead of just doing it?"

"Something like that," Shane said. He glanced at Angela. "Do you have any input?"

"The problem is that you fight like a human," she said. "You don't listen to your instincts.

"And you've done your best, daughter," Alpha Shane said. "You wouldn't be able to train her out of those in a year, let alone a week."

"I'm right here," Jordan snarked.

"And you need to hear this," Alpha Shane said. "You're about to fight a werewolf. And while I won't discount the two fights you've had, you're about to go against someone who has spent her whole life as a werewolf. She's going to know tricks that you can only dream of."

"You're supposed to be encouraging me," Jordan grumbled.

Shane continued as if she hadn't interrupted. "And you're not going to know how to counter them as a werewolf would, no matter how much you train with Angela."

Jordan snapped her gaze to Montgomery. "Are you going to let them talk about me like that?"

"Yes," Montgomery said. "You're running out of time, Jordan. You need to listen and figure out why you're blocked. You need to learn what they're trying to teach you."

"You don't think I'm trying to?" Jordan snapped. She glared at each of them in turn. "I've been doing everything you've been telling me, and I can't get it. Okay?"

He didn't like how her voice's pitch was getting higher. "Jordan, I know you're doing your best—"

"That's just it!" Jordan's eyes were wide as she spat out the words. "I'm doing my best, and it's not enough. I'm going to die! Alpha Shane is going to lose the Black Oak Pack! And then, the Conclave will be wiped out." Her voice dropped to a whisper.

"And it'll all be my fault!" She spun on her heel and fled out the door.

Montgomery was up and following her. He heard Angela behind him yell, "Jordan," and then Alpha Shane rumble.

"Let them go, Angela. He'll bring her back."

At least someone has faith in me, Montgomery thought as he headed out the door.

30

Jordan ran. The cotton robe wrapped around her body was too thin to protect her from the night air. She clutched at the fabric, ignoring the hard stones mixed with sharp sticks and loose dirt under her pounding feet. She bolted up the path, even though she didn't know exactly where she was going. She just needed to get away from the training, from their words, and from the impending sense that everything was closing in around her, and that there wasn't a damn thing she could do about it.

Her feet ached, not having the protective layer of fur and thicker skin of paw pads to protect them. Her lungs burned as she tried to suck air in. Jordan stumbled to a stop, leaning against a young oak tree, eyes closed. Her fingers gripped the bark and closed her eyes, concentrating on regaining her breath.

She heard footsteps crunching towards her. She sniffed, but her nose was too stuffed to smell anything. She could guess who it would be. There would only be one in three people looking for her.

"Hey."

Jordan twisted around to look at Montgomery, then turned away.

"I know you're scared," Montgomery said. "And I'm sorry I didn't realize that earlier."

Jordan swiped at her eyes with her forearm. "I don't want to go back," she sniffled.

"You don't have to." He slipped an arm around her shoulders. Jordan stiffened, expected to be turned towards the house. "Let's keep walking. There's something I want to show you."

She relaxed against him as they kept going in the direction she had been heading. They walked down the path without saying anything. This wasn't the one that led to the field with the large oak. In fact, she didn't think she had been this way before. But Montgomery had grown up here, so she had to trust that he remembered where he was going.

She heard the sound of running water. Eventually, they came across a little creek. Montgomery led her along it to where the trail widened to a pebbly beach. There was a stone bench near the tree line. "Oh good, it's still here," he said as he guided her towards it. "Pretty, isn't it?" he said, gesturing towards the creek.

"Beautiful." Legs shaky as the last of the adrenaline left her, Jordan sat. She remained close to Montgomery, wanting comfort even if there wasn't much physical warmth he could offer. She looked out at the water, more hearing than seeing it flow past, and sighed. "I'm no alpha, not like Shane is."

"No, you're not." She jerked away, staring at him in shock. She had expected Montgomery to counter her statement with some argument about how she had been doing her best, and she was too hard on herself and of course, she was an alpha. "You've been granted the title, but you don't have the support system that Alpha Shane does. You don't have years of experience. Nor do you have a pack of werewolves backing you.

"What you do have is the blessing of the Wolf herself, which is more than a lot of werewolves can claim. You also have Alpha

Shane helping the best he can, at least in this situation." He rested his hand on Jordan's shoulder. "And you have me and Thorn backing you."

She swiped her arm across her eye again. "But you're my Patron. You're supposed to have the power over me. Not vice versa."

"I've never wanted power over you, Jordan. I know we have to appear that way in public to keep you safe, but I don't see you as a famulus. I see you as a friend."

"Then what do we do?"

"What we've always done," Montgomery said. "We figure out our next steps and go from there."

"Then we better figure out something fast," Jordan said.

"That's part of why I thought we should come here instead of heading back," Montgomery said. "Shane and I used to come here to think."

"Think about what?"

"About what would happen when I became alpha," Montgomery said. "He was going to be my right hand, and we were going to be the best damn pack there ever was."

"He was your best friend," Jordan said.

"Yeah, until Dad sent me to live with the Conclave." Montgomery shook his head. "I'm still not completely sure what he hoped to accomplish with that. I'll probably never know."

She didn't know what to say to that. Instead, they sat, watching the creek bubble past. "Montgomery, be honest," she said. "Do you think I have a chance of surviving?"

"I don't think you'll survive," Montgomery said. "I think you'll conquer. I don't know why you're having problems now. But I've seen you fight. Rhys wasn't going easy on you, and still, you managed to beat him. Same with Angela." He squeezed his arm around her. "I know you can do this, Jordan."

"Then why can't I seem to beat Angela again?"

"From what you told me, you were pissed at her the last time.

You didn't think, didn't plan, didn't strategize. You just fought. And that might be the problem. You're overthinking everything. You need to find that anger, that instinct, and use that to fuel your attack."

"Instinct." Jordan shook her head. "I still don't get it. Angela keeps telling me to use my instincts. And when I do, she kicks my ass."

"You have wolf instincts," Montgomery said. He gestured from her head to her toes to her head. "They're just buried under all that."

"So how do I unbury them?"

Montgomery shook his head. "Hell if I know." He sighed. "While Angela and Shane may not, I trust you. When you're in a clutch situation, you've managed to come through. Your instincts kicked in when you rescued me. They kicked in when you fought Angela. And I know they'll kick in when you face Enya."

"Glad one of us has faith in me."

"Two of us," Montgomery said. "You forget that both Thorn and I will stand by your side."

She caught the inside of her lip between her teeth. "And if I fail? If Enya kills me?"

"Then we will damn well avenge you."

That was the last thing she expected to hear from him. Jordan gave him a wet laugh. "You sound like that superhero from the movie we watched the other night."

Montgomery shrugged, but there was a hint of a smile in the corners of his mouth. "It had a lot of catchy one-liners." Then his mouth widened to a full smile. "Feeling better?"

"Some. But I'm still panicked, still have no idea what I'm going to do. " Jordan pulled away to look at Montgomery. "We probably should head back."

"Yeah, we should," Montgomery said. "You ready?"

Jordan sighed and stood. "Yeah, let's go."

They walked up the path silently, his arm still around her. Or more accurately, Montgomery walked while Jordan limped. Barefoot and without the adrenaline of her panicked flight, she felt each of the stones and sticks that littered the forest floor.

She wasn't surprised when they stepped out of the trees next to the gym, Alpha Shane and Angela stood there waiting. "We've done enough," Alpha Shane said. "I'm calling it for tonight. Go on home and get some rest."

Jordan stiffened, mouth opening to protest. But she stopped when Montgomery squeezed her shoulder. "He's right," Montgomery said. "Exhausting yourself before the fight won't help."

Jordan sighed, seeming to fill and empty her lungs with the entire breath. She pushed out from beneath Montgomery's arm and headed with Angela to the room where they had changed clothes earlier. As she stepped into the building, she heard Shane say, "If drama were something we could weaponize for this fight, she'd win, hands down."

Jordan snorted but said nothing as the door shut behind them. She went to the side room where her clothing had been stashed. She had rinsed the mud off her bare feet and pulled on everything but her shirt when Angela reappeared, human and also dressed. "I've been thinking," the blonde said. "You might as well take tomorrow off too."

Jordan's brows furrowed. Angela had insisted they spar every night since she had been declared an alpha. The one exception had been the night of the Conclave's gathering, and Angela still attempted to guilt her into showing up that night. "You think I'm going to lose."

"No," Angela said, annoyance creeping into her voice. "I'm thinking that there's no point in tiring you out the night before the fight." She closed her eyes and put her hands up, visibly relaxing herself before she continued, "Dad may think that, but Dad hasn't fought you. I know you can beat her, Jordan. I don't know why you're holding back, but I hope you figure it out in time."

One corner of her mouth curled even as she fought the sarcastic smile. "So, you're giving me twenty-four hours to unpack whatever trauma is setting me up to fail?"

Angela shrugged. "I would have gone for forty-eight, but Dad insisted that you needed to practice tonight."

Jordan snorted a laugh. "Okay. I'll spend the next night in deep meditation, trying to figure out everything that's wrong with me."

Angela considered her words, then shook her head. "Nah, you don't have to figure out everything. Just what's blocking you from kicking my ass. And if that's going to translate to you being able to kick Enya's."

"And if I can't?"

"If she does kill you, I'm going to summon your ghost so I can personally beat you up for shaming my teaching skills."

Jordan's eyes widened. "You can do that?"

"Yeah, we talk to the dead all the time." Angela's voice was deadpan. "Last time was to tell your Patron that you took the path to the creek."

Jordan shook her head, face pressed into her palm. "Walked right into that one, didn't I?"

"Yeah, you did." Angela gestured with her head. "Go home, Jordan. Get some rest. Figure out what's going on."

She nodded and turned towards the door. "I'll do my best."

Angela grabbed her arm, halting her. "That's part of your problem. Don't do your best. Just do it."

Jordan nodded. Angela let go of her arm. Without any further words, she turned away and walked out to where Montgomery was waiting with Alpha Shane. She steeled herself, preparing for him to yell at her as well. Instead, his words were gentle and cautious. "We'll see you for the ceremony in two nights, Jordan. Be here as soon as you can after sunset."

Jordan nodded. The way the time was phrased, Montgomery

and Thorn could attend with her. "I'll be here, Alpha Shane. And I thank you and your daughter for the support you've shown."

If he was surprised at her response, Alpha Shane hid it. The respect in his voice didn't sound mocking, at least to her. "Until then, Alpha Abbey. Mr. Cooper."

Montgomery nodded goodbye as she gave a small wave. She wasn't surprised when her Patron opened the passenger door and gestured for her to get in. Either he was treating her like an alpha and not a servant in front of Shane, or she looked that tired and out of it. She thought it was more the latter than the former, but she couldn't be sure. She sat back in the seat and closed her eyes.

She heard Montgomery ask a question. "Do you want to grab something to eat on the way home?"

And she thought that sounded great. She hadn't eaten anything since she left the apartment before her visit to the cemetery. But she couldn't wake up enough to say so.

31

———

Jordan woke up in a tangle of limbs later than she had for the last week. She had a fuzzy memory of Montgomery driving them home, helping her out of the car, and putting her to bed. Normally, she would be up a few hours before sunset, warming up blood and having her own breakfast or rushing out the door to run errands so she could be back when Montgomery and Thorn woke up. For the last week, she had also been running off to meet with Angela for her fighting lessons.

But tonight, she wouldn't be doing that. Tonight was a night to relax, or at least as much as she could relax knowing that tomorrow night, she could die.

She felt someone nudge her shoulder with a feather-weight tap. "You awake?"

Jordan lifted her head and nodded at Montgomery's whispered words. "Yeah."

Montgomery smiled, stroking her cheek. "You feeling better?"

She leaned into the touch, grateful for the comfort. "Yeah, I guess I was having a panic attack last night. Or it was hitting that I won't be getting out of this without fighting." Jordan shrugged. "I was hoping that some sort of miracle would happen, and it would all go away."

"I know, Jordan." Montgomery rubbed her arm before taking her hand and squeezing. "To be honest, I was hoping for the same thing. I just haven't had a chance to panic about it yet."

"Maybe that's what we should do tonight. Panic. Or see if there's some place we can run away to." She glanced over at a sleeping Thorn.

Montgomery followed her gaze. "We already talked about it. There's no safe place that we can all go. Or at least not now."

She softened her snort, not wanting to disturb Thorn. "Figures."

She felt Thorn's arm twitch against her, as if he could feel their eyes on him. It was some sort of vampire instinct, or they had woken him up with their whispers. "Evening," he said, then yawned.

"Evening, Thorn," Montgomery said.

Thorn tilted his head at Jordan. "Shouldn't you be meeting up with Angela?"

Jordan shook her head. "She said she's taught me all she can, and that it's not worth risking injuring me right before the fight."

"So, you've got the night before the big fight off? Cool."

Jordan shrugged. "I think I'd rather be sparring. At least that would make the night go faster, and I'd exhaust myself so I can sleep until tomorrow night."

"You think you're going to be up all day?"

Jordan nodded. "You haven't noticed that days before big events, I'm not able to sleep? Or at least not for more than an hour or two?"

"Can't say that I have," Montgomery said.

Thorn elbowed Montgomery in the side, a playful grin on his face. "Insert 'sleeps like the dead' joke here."

Jordan ignored the swat that Montgomery aimed at Thorn. "I

did the same the night before a big test at school. Or a trip. It's how I process stress I think."

"Okay," Montgomery said. "In that case, let's give you something to focus on. Did you ever return your parents' calls?"

Jordan shook her head. "No. Every time I thought 'I'll do it tonight,' some other emergency came up, and it was too late in the evening. She and Dad would have already gone to bed."

"That's a really good excuse, Jordan. One that I'd buy if I didn't know you were up in the early afternoons and could make a call then without disturbing me or Mac," Thorn said. "What's the real reason?"

She drew in a deep breath as she tried to figure out the best words to explain. "I don't know what to tell them." Jordan raised her hands and then let them fall to her sides. "They're going to ask why I quit school. Why I haven't moved back home. And they'll be horrified that I'm rebelling against what they taught me by living here."

"Having two boyfriends?" Montgomery asked.

"Living with one man while unmarried is enough to make them wail about where they went wrong," Jordan said. "Finding out that I'm living with two would probably give them a heart attack."

Thorn squinted at her. "I don't get the vibe from you that you were raised in a strict religious household."

"Yeah, well.," Jordan rocked back and forth as she looked away. "I kinda started the rebellion thing in high school and have been figuring things out ever since. It's part of why I was at a community college but living on my own. I couldn't afford to go to state without their help, so I was trying to save up money and get some classes out of the way. It wasn't going well, even before I got bit."

"We've never really talked deeply about this," Montgomery said. "So, what have you told your parents? Exactly?"

There was a probing urgency in his tone. And Jordan, for the first time, wondered if Marcus had his spies watching her parents. "As much of the truth as I can without directly lying. I guess you'd call it lying by omission." Jordan shrugged. "They know I broke up with my ex-boyfriend. By the way, they think I was an idiot for doing so, even though he was cheating on me. They know a roommate of mine was killed in the dog attack that was on the news. They know I dropped out of college and quit my job after that. And they know I moved out of the apartment when Molly went to live with her parents."

Thorn leaned closer to her. "Do they know what happened with Molly after that?"

Jordan shook her head. "I have no idea how to handle that part. It seemed better not to talk about it."

"Smart idea." Montgomery gently stroked her shoulder. "Do you know how they got my phone number?"

Jordan shrugged. "I left your information with my old apartment manager so he could forward mail and stuff. He's the only person I can think of who could have given it to my parents. Or maybe they got it from my old job since they mailed the last paycheck here."

"He shouldn't have, given he's also a famulus," Montgomery said.

"I'll make some discreet inquiries," Thorn said. "I don't want to get him into trouble, but he should know better."

Jordan winced, a twist of nausea in her stomach. She hadn't wanted to get someone in trouble, especially since she had no idea who his Patron was. "Guess it could have come from the police report, also."

"Either way, how much does she know about us?" Thorn asked.

"They know I'm working for someone as a personal assistant. They know I have a new boyfriend, and I'm living with him singular." Jordan shrugged. "I didn't give a name, so I'm assuming they think it's Montgomery."

"I haven't talked to them yet," Thorn said. "But seriously. You should call them, if only to back her off."

"There's a chance that this will be the last time you may be able to do so," Montgomery said.

"I know!" Jordan snapped. "I know! But they're already disappointed in me for dropping out of school! I don't need to add to their disappointment when they find out I'm living with two men!"

"Jordan?" Montgomery's voice was quiet. "Are you ashamed of your relationship with us?"

"No, it's not that." She sighed and looked up at the ceiling. "It's just hard to fight some of the 'values' that I was raised with."

"I know, Jordan, I know." Montgomery put an arm around her shoulders, scooting closer. "If you're not comfortable with our relationship, we can change it. You don't have to share a bed with us if you don't want to."

Thorn nodded. "You don't have to decide right now. Or if you change your mind in the future, we can work it out."

Jordan arched one eyebrow. "You were just telling me that I might not have a future beyond tomorrow night."

Thorn shrugged. "You know me. Plan for all possible outcomes."

Jordan sighed. She was losing the battle and played the last card she had. "If I talk to them, they'll want to meet my boyfriend."

"We can worry about that when we're making dinner reservations," Montgomery said.

"Says you." Thorn rubbed his stomach. "I had to fake eating a meal the other day. I forgot how nasty purging everything was."

She recognized the playfulness in Montgomery's voice. "Were you on a date and forgot to tell us?"

Thorn's response was flat. "Business meeting."

Montgomery arched an eyebrow.

"I have to wine and dine suppliers on occasion," Thorn protested.

Montgomery threw up his hands in surrender. "If you don't want to tell us what you're doing, Thorn, you don't have to."

Jordan looked back and forth between the two men. "Will this be an ongoing trust issue? Cause we're all going to have things we can't discuss. But we can't be constantly picking at each other that we're untrustworthy."

"You're right, Jordan," Thorn said. "I had a meeting with someone from Black Oak." He held up his hand. "We were old friends, but we kept it secret. They didn't know I was in the area until long after you found Jordan, Mac. I met with them to get a different opinion on the whole alpha wolf situation, as well as get a read on what was going on within Black Oak."

Jordan shifted her jaw, not sure how to feel about this revelation. "Are they how Marcus found out about me being caught by Animal Control?" she asked.

Thorn shook his head, an emphatic, sharp shake. "No. I'd stake my life on that. They're not a spy for Marcus."

"And you're not going to tell us who it is?" Montgomery said.

"Can't," Thorn said. "Too much of a risk to them if they're found out. But trust me, they have no love for Elder Marcus and can't be bribed by him or Shane. They're not the leak." He looked at Montgomery, a hint of worry in the downturned corner of his mouth. "This is something you're going to have to trust me on."

Montgomery swallowed, but he did nod.

"Thank you." Thorn elbowed Jordan in the side. "And we're supposed to be talking about your parents calls, not my friendships."

Jordan rolled her eyes. "Damn it, I almost got out of that."

Montgomery nudged her side. "No such luck."

Jordan let out a heavy sigh. "Okay. Give me an hour to wake up and get something to eat. Then I'll give my parents a call."

Now Montgomery rubbed her shoulder. "Good. And afterwards, we'll figure out something to do for the evening." He glanced over at Thorn. "Can you take tonight off?"

Thorn nodded. "I'll make a few calls. After Jordan does."

Jordan shook her head. "Neither of you will let this go, will you?"

Both men shook their heads, both wearing the same sly smile.

Jordan held up her hands, looking at the ceiling in defeat. "Okay. Let me get dressed, then I'll make the call. Do you want to listen in, or can I have some privacy?"

"If you want it." Montgomery slipped off the bed. "Want to use the shower first?"

"Yeah," Jordan said. She slid out of bed. "I'll heat breakfast and then make the call."

"Or I could heat up something while you're in the shower," Montgomery offered.

Both Jordan and Thorn looked at him. "You remember how to cook?" Thorn asked.

"I was thinking of heating something in the microwave, How hard can it be?"

Jordan and Thorn shared a look with each other that spoke volumes without saying a word.

"Oh, come on!"

32

———

Hair still damp from the shower, Jordan sat at the table next to the kitchenette. She stared at the black, glassy surface of her phone as if she were facing down Angela in one of their sparring matches. She wished she were facing Angela. At least then, the pain would only be physical and would eventually recede.

She took a deep breath and tapped the screen to wake the phone. It scanned her face and opened the app screen. Jordan took another breath and scrolled through her lists of contacts to find her parents' phone number. She tapped the number and confirmed that she wanted to make the call. She closed her eyes as it rang three times, then a familiar voice spoke. "Hello?"

Jordan's eyes opened. "Hi, Mom."

The voice at the other end of the phone caught. "Jordan?" She could almost see her mother's hand raising to her mouth to keep a gasp inside. "It's been too long."

"Yeah." *Because you yell at me every time I try to talk to you,* she thought. Her family didn't know the reason. "I know you've been calling, and I wanted to make sure everything is okay."

"Of course everything's okay, Jordan," she said. "Dad and I are worried about you. You weren't the same after you and Scott broke up, but you wouldn't come home. And then you quit your job and school and went to live with a stranger all within the same week."

Scott. Her parents had thought he was perfect for her. What they didn't know was so did Tammi's mom and Michaela's dad for their daughters. Tammi, Michaela, and Jordan all had different opinions on Scott's suitability when they met each other. "Mom, I told you. I have a new job as a personal assistant. The room in his apartment is part of my compensation." Of course, she left out the part about the truth being a little more complicated than that.

"And exactly what do you do?"

It was a little too easy to rattle off the statement that she had prepared. It wasn't a lie, but a careful editing of the truth. "He has a health condition that doesn't allow him to be out in sunlight, so I run errands for him. Drive him around if it's after dark."

She wasn't sure if she didn't sound as practiced as she thought she was, or if her mother's instinct for knowing when their child was lying kicked in. "Wouldn't he need someone with medical training for that?"

"I know it sounds weird, Mom, but you have to trust me."

"You know every time you said that to me, you'd go and do something you knew I wouldn't approve of."

"Mom, I'm an adult now—"

"Then you should act like one!"

Jordan's finger moved towards the disconnect button.

"Wait, Jordan!" It was like her mom could see what she was about to do. "I'm sorry I yelled."

She froze, finger hovering over the disconnect button.

"Jordan?" Another pause. "Jordan?"

She sighed and pulled her hand away. "I'm still here, Mom."

"Good." Her voice was much softer. "I know you think you can get yourself out of whatever trouble you've gotten yourself into,

Jordan. But remember that Dad and I are here to help you. You can always come home."

As if that would be any better. She drew in a deep breath through her mouth and blew it out her nose. "Okay, Mom. I'll call you if I need help."

"And if you don't need help too, Jordan. I miss you."

While something didn't break inside her, she felt a lump shift and soften. "I miss you too, Mom."

"Maybe you could come home for dinner in a week or two." She recognized the bouncy, faux bright tone in her mom's voice. "Maybe you could bring your new boyfriend along. Your dad and I would like to meet him."

Jordan closed her eyes. That would happen over her dead body. She wasn't exposing Montgomery or Thorn to her parents. "We'll see, Mom."

"Or we could meet somewhere for dinner. Pick a restaurant you're comfortable with and a date. Dad and I will be there."

Jordan closed her eyes. That might work, but there were problems with it too. Mostly if they noticed her boyfriend wasn't eating or drinking anything. But at the same time, it would be in public, which had the benefits of everyone being on their best behavior. But at least her mother was making an offer. "I'll have to talk to him, Mom, and get back to you with a date." She tensed, waiting for the arguments and the questions about when they would be able to do it.

"Thank you, Jordan."

She was a bit shocked that her mother wasn't pushing against her. "Give me a couple of days," she said. "I have to figure out some scheduling with my boss."

"I understand, Jordan." Her mom's voice was a sweet neutral that she used when she thought Jordan was making a mistake and would have to find out herself. "Call me in a few days. Our schedule is wide open."

"I will, Mom." And oddly enough, she meant it. "Love you,

Mom. I'll call next week." Her stomach clenched as she thought the words, *if I survive the fight.*

If her mom caught her lie by omission, she didn't give any hint of it. "Love you, Jordan."

This time, she allowed herself to hit the red button. Her phone chirped as the picture of her parents faded to black. Jordan blew a breath out between her lips as her shoulders dropped. She sat back and looked up at the ceiling.

"How did it go?" came Thorn's voice.

Jordan jumped, laughing at herself. She should have expected Montgomery and Thorn to step out of the bedroom once things went quiet.

"As well as can be expected," Jordan said. "She said she's disappointed in me without actually saying she's disappointed in me. And we need to decide which one of you is my boyfriend, because Mom and Dad want us to meet for dinner."

Montgomery and Thorn looked at each other. Thorn gestured to his blue hair and then tapped one of the tattoos on his wrist. "You'd probably make a better impression on them than I would."

"You're the one who owns a successful business," Montgomery said. "And Jordan's supposed to be working for me. I doubt they'd like that her boss is her boyfriend."

Jordan bit the inside of her lower lip. "I told her I'd call back next week, so we can debate it after the fight with Envoy Blevins is done.

Thorn grinned. "Now, who's making plans for surviving the near future?"

Jordan grabbed the closest pillow and threw it at Thorn, unable to hide the half-smirk, half-smile on her face.

33

Jordan woke up on the outside edge of the bed, back pressed against Montgomery's stomach. She reached for her phone and squinted at the screen. It was two in the afternoon. She put the phone down and then thumped her head against the pillow. Her alarm wasn't set to go off until five PM. The sun wouldn't be down until six. And they wouldn't be expected at the Great Oak Pack's cabin until eight. She had plenty of time to sleep.

Except she knew she wouldn't. Like she had pointed out earlier, if there was ever a high stress event coming up, she wouldn't get a full sleep cycle beforehand. Deciding that if she couldn't sleep, she should go watch a movie or get something to eat, she scooted towards the edge of the bed.

A hand slid up and down her arm, halting her movement and offering comfort. "Hey," Montgomery whispered. "Are you okay?"

"No," Jordan whispered. The tremor in her voice matched the tremor in her body. "I don't know I can do this."

She felt lips press against the nape of her neck. "Roll over." She squirmed onto her right side to face Montgomery. He wrapped his arms around her, drawing her close and tucking her head under his chin. "We'll get through this, Jordan," he whispered. "I believe you can do it."

She stopped shivering, soaking in the comfort of being held. Lips pressed to her forehead. "Listen to me. You've fought her brother and won. You've beaten Angela and won. She will just be another notch on your belt."

Something about that phrase struck her funny. "I don't wear belts," she said with a wet giggle.

"Maybe you should start," Montgomery said. His hand slid down her side, over the dip of her waist to rest on her hip. "It would be fun taking them off you if nothing else."

Thorn piped up. "Who's taking off a belt, and can I help?"

Both Jordan and Montgomery laughed. "I'm about to fight for my life, and you want to take off my belt?" Jordan giggled.

Thorn made a humming noise. "To be fair, I'm interested in taking off more than just your belt."

"And what about my belt?" Montgomery pouted.

"You're not wearing one," Thorn pointed out. "Guess I'll have to make do with your shorts."

She felt Montgomery squirm as he yelped. Part of her wanted to protest that they shouldn't be indulging now. Not when she would be facing a fight for her life. Again. But if not now, when? Why not have one last pleasant memory for them just in case? Grinning as she felt the fabric brushing against her thighs, and Thorn tugged it down Montgomery's legs, she pressed her lips to Montgomery's.

He kissed her back. And it didn't take long before she felt one set of hands working her shirt over her head while the other traced the waistband of her panties. She pulled back from Montgomery's mouth and lifted her arms up so he could pull the shirt off. Then Montgomery's tongue slid into her mouth as his hands cupped her breasts. She moaned as she felt Thorn's hand slip between her and Montgomery's bodies. Montgomery grunted as

Thorn's knuckles brushed against her pussy as his fingers wrapped around Montgomery's cock.

Her eyes closed, and her head tilted back as she felt Montgomery's kisses move down to her neck. Her werewolf friends would say that it was stupid to bare her throat to a vampire, no matter how much she trusted him, or how soft his lips were. There was a hint of fang in his more aggressive kisses, but nothing that ever broke the skin. It was stupid, but it added a certain dark spice. She hadn't been brave enough to give him permission to bite her, but the potential did send a thrill through her.

Then Thorn turned his hand so his fingers were rubbing her through the thin cotton of her panties. She gasped and jumped, earning a chuckle from both men. Montgomery's fingers began a slow swirl around her nipples. Thorn worked his hand under the hem of her panties to cup her pussy. Then his fingers slowly worked between her lower lips. She squeaked when his fingers brushed over her clit.

Thorn chuckled and slowly pulled his hand out, letting his fingers tease as they withdrew. Montgomery nipped at her throat as her hands roamed up and down his and Thorn's shoulders and backs. Someone, she wasn't sure who, pulled her underwear down her legs. Jordan squealed as a hand traced up the ticklish muscle of her calf. "No fair!"

"Very fair," Thorn countered. His hand moved up her thigh as Montgomery's kisses moved down her collarbone. Then she heard the slap of flesh against flesh.

Montgomery yelped. "Easy there."

She could just see Thorn's smug grin over the edge of Montgomery's shoulder. "Want me to kiss it and make it better?"

"Don't answer that," Jordan warned. "Cause he'll do it."

"You say that like it's a bad thing," Montgomery countered.

Thorn snorted. "Oh, trust me." He reached over Montgomery's shoulder to roll her nipple between his fingers. "There's many things I want to do to both of you." Montgomery resumed his kisses downward, coming to focus on her other breast, his hand nudging Thorn's out of the way.

Jordan arched into their touches. It was time to do some touching of her own. One hand slid down Montgomery's stomach, over taut skin and through his dark curls, only to discover that Thorn was already stroking him. Thorn lifted his head to look over Montgomery's shoulder and smiled. His hand slid away, and Montgomery moaned. Jordan was pleased that the moan turned to a gasp as she stroked Montgomery.

She heard the rustle of sheets and felt the mattress shift as Thorn turned away. Montgomery surged up to kiss her. In the middle of their tongues tangling, Montgomery let out a sharp gasp, and Thorn a rumbling growl. "Roll over, Jordan."

She kissed his nose. It took some cautious squirming to keep from falling off the side of the bed. Montgomery's arm went around her stomach and drew her back against his chest. She arched one leg up. Thorn placed a hand on her thigh, bracing her leg. She shivered as she felt Montgomery's fingers trace over her pussy, circling and then rubbing against her clit. Then there was a pressure against her pussy, and he was pushing inside.

She grabbed the edge of the mattress and locked her elbows to keep herself from skidding forward. All three were panting, catching their rhythms so they moved with each other. Thorn's hand pulled away from her thigh, to be replaced with Montgomery's. Now, Thorn's fingers stroked her clit. Pleasant pressure grew, feeling both men exploring the sensitive area of her body.

Montgomery's thrusts turned erratic, and he grunted into her shoulder. Thorn's fingers moved faster, applying more pressure. The pleasure throbbing between her legs crested and flooded through her body.

Jordan closed her eyes as Montgomery helped lower her leg. A wave of relaxation followed her orgasm. Jordan twisted her head around to look at the two men the best she could. "You know, I almost fell off the edge of the bed twice."

Montgomery nuzzled her neck and shoulder. "Don't blame me. Someone wanted the middle of the mattress."

"Guilty," came Thorn's sleepy response.

Jordan smiled and resettled, snuggled back to belly with Montgomery as Thorn wrapped his arm around both their bodies. She felt the light sheet being pulled up over her shoulders, Then it was pressed down by a heavier blanket. "Get some sleep, Jordan," Montgomery murmured in her ear. "We have a long night ahead of us."

She wanted to counter with 'what do you mean 'we,'" but sleep overtook her before she could.

34

Jordan and Montgomery were let through the gates. The Sentry didn't tell them they were expected or give them any instructions. There was no reason for him to. Angela had called with instructions earlier in the evening about where she was to meet up with everyone and what the procedure would be. And it wasn't like she and Montgomery, who had offered to drive, hadn't been to the main house multiple times.

They pulled up to the main house. Outside by several of the parked cars waited Alpha Shane, Angela, and Talespeaker Diana. Jordan counted the number of vehicles. "Great," she said. "All of Black Oak is here to observe."

"This affects them as much as it will you," Montgomery said. "Are you really surprised?"

Jordan shook her head. "No," she said. "I just hoped that they wouldn't all be here."

They got out of the car and walked towards the three were-wolves. "Alpha Shane, Ms. Shane, Talespeaker Diana," Montgomery greeted then.

Shane nodded in acknowledgement. "Alpha Abbey. Mr.

Cooper," he said before turning to Jordan. "Are you ready for tonight?"

"As I'll ever be," Jordan said. She heard the crunching of gravel under tires coming up the driveway towards them.

"You've fought challengers and won before, Alpha Abbey," Talespeaker Diana said. "And now, you have the blessing of the Wolf in addition."

"Doesn't the envoy have that blessing as well?" she asked.

"That remains to be seen," Diana said. "And tonight will determine that for certain."

"You're going to let the lands of your pack be desecrated by a vampire?" The group turned towards the newcomer's voice. Enya walked towards them, already shifted into her werewolf form. Jordan swallowed, recognizing the brown on gray pattern, so similar to Rhys'. Talespeaker Lucas stood next to her, fully human.

That was a weird statement, Jordan thought. Montgomery was here the first night they met. Why was Blevins objecting to his presence now?

Shane drew himself up to full height, arms crossed over his chest. "As a chaos wolf, Montgomery Cooper is allowed here. He doesn't have a lighter or an axe, Envoy Blevins. And I doubt his bite could harm any of the oaks, even if he wanted to."

"Yes, but what about him?" Blevins jerked her head towards the way they came.

Jordan looked back to see another vampire and human making their way. The dark-haired woman she didn't recognize, but she walked the three respectful steps behind as a proper famulus would. Her stomach dropped as she recognized Nicholas.

"Per the treaty he and I have, it's Elder Marcus' right to be here to observe this challenge," Alpha Shane growled. "He has sent his oldest bloodchild in his place." His voice lowered. "I much would have preferred it was only that blue-haired vampire that's always hanging around you two."

Her eyes narrowed at Alpha Shane. "His name is Thorn."

Alpha Shane dipped his head to her. "I stand corrected, Alpha Abbey."

Jordan turned away, not wanting to show how uneasy that title made her. Part of her was suspicious that he only used it because it irritated Enya. She watched as Nicholas walked up to the group. Of course, Marcus would send him to observe, since he couldn't trust Montgomery or Thorn to be unbiased, and Rosanna would start a fight. She tried not to make a face when she realized he would see her naked when she shifted. That sent a cold chill up her spine.

Focus, she growled to herself. Montgomery, Thorn, and even Reginald's warnings had settled somewhere in her gut, given her reaction. Right now, he wasn't the threat. The woman standing at Alpha Shane's side was.

When the vampire reached them, he bowed, the picture of respect. "Alpha Shane," he said as he straightened. "On behalf of Elder Marcus, I thank you for allowing me onto the land of the Black Oak Pack." Jordan noted that he didn't mention his famulus. "I swear that I'm only here to observe and report back to my sire and won't interfere with the outcome of this challenge."

Alpha Shane nodded. "You're welcome to observe as long as you obey the strictures I've discussed with your sire." He glanced at Montgomery. "Of course this goes for all vampires present."

Montgomery also bowed his head but said nothing. His hand brushed against Jordan's, grabbed on, and squeezed. Jordan squeezed back. She wasn't sure if that meant he would try to protect her if things went wrong or reassuring her that everything would be all right. Either way, it was a physical reminder of his presence that she needed at that moment.

"Now that we're all here," Shane said. He gestured towards the cabin. "Alpha Abbey, if you would care to go and shift."

Jordan nodded and started towards the cabin. She was a little surprised when Angela fell in step beside her. Enya wore a smug smile as she passed. And she could hear Nicholas' question clearly. "She's not comfortable shifting in public? Pity. I had hoped to observe it."

Alpha Shane's response floated through the closing door. "Angela needs to make sure that she's briefed on a change of the setup we had to make."

She looked at Angela. "There's been a change in the setup?" Now, what would she have to adapt to on the fly?

Angela shook her head as they passed into the living room. "I noticed it's hard for you to shift in front of strangers. Dad and I thought we'd make things a little easier."

"Thanks." She continued into the bathroom. Once inside and undressed, she paused in front of the mirror. Her hands shook, making it hard to unclasp the Family necklace, but after the fifth attempt, she managed it. She drew in a deep breath. "I can do this," she whispered and reached inside for the shift.

And for once, despite the worry and the stress, it came easy. She kept her eyes closed, afraid that watching her transition in the mirror would somehow stop it. When she opened them, a black-furred, brown-eyed wolf stared back at her. For a moment, she thought The Wolf had appeared for a last-minute pep talk. Except that the motions of the furry head in the mirror matched hers. She knew she had black fur, but she had never looked at herself while shifted before.

Knowing that she was stalling, Jordan stepped out of the bathroom. Angela stood leaning against the wall. "All set?" she asked.

"Ready as I'll ever be," Jordan said.

"There's something I wanted to talk to you about privately," Angela said. She pushed off the wall. "Remember everything Dad and I have been teaching you about fighting?"

Jordan nodded, wondering what last-minute nugget of

wisdom she would drop now, and why she had waited so long. "Yeah?"

"Forget it. Do whatever it takes to win however you can do it."

One ear flipped back. "Are you telling me to cheat?"

Amanda shook her head. "No, I'm telling you to use whatever you have in you. We keep forgetting you beat her brother. And you beat me." She stepped up to her and poked her in the center of her sternum. "Whatever that was, use that to beat her."

"Your dad said not to. And every time I tried that on you, you almost gutted me."

"Yeah, but I knew that trick. Blevins doesn't."

Jordan rolled her eyes. "You could have pointed that out before you broke my arm."

She heard the suppressed snort/laugh from Angela. "Come on. Let's get out there so we can get this over with."

They walked outside. To Jordan's surprise, Alpha Shane had shifted to a werewolf form. *At least Nicholas got his chance to see a shapeshift,* she thought as she stepped into her place in the procession. Alpha Shane took the lead, followed by Envoy Blevins and Talespeaker Lucas. Jordan had the next position with Angela and Talespeaker Diana flanking her on either side. Montgomery walked behind her, positioned ahead of Nicholas and his famulus. She bet, from what little she had seen of him, that annoyed him that his younger bloodbrother was before him.

Jordan focused on her breathing as they walked down the path that led to the clearing. She wasn't sure if the silence as they walked was part of the tradition, or if nobody had anything more to say. In the next hour, it would be over with.

That changed when they stepped out of the trees to the meadow. She heard Montgomery's footsteps pause behind her before resuming. *This has to be the first time he's been here since he was turned,* she thought.

The oak was one of the four corners of the roped-off square the size of one of the wrestling mats she had seen in the high school gym.

She remembered the briefing that Talespeaker Diana had given her earlier. The tree would be one corner, the Black Oak Pack's symbol, and a stand in for the Wolf. The vampire guests would take the opposite corner. The other two diagonal corners would be for those who stood with her—Montgomery, Angela, and Talespeaker Diana. *Not a Pack,* she thought. Unlike the other werewolves fanned out behind at the opposite corner, holding a blank space clearly meant for Alpha Shane. She met Billy's eyes. He smiled for a fleeting second before his face returned to a studious neutral, like most of the others.

But to her surprise, most of Montgomery's attention was focused on the tree. "Been a while since I've been out here," Montgomery said, studying each limb.

To Jordan's surprise, Angela asked the question she also wondered. "Has it changed much?"

Montgomery looked around. "Field's a little bigger, but so is the oak." He placed his palm on the trunk like he was reaching to comfort a skittish horse. "So, it all evens out." He took a step towards the tree and then looked at Shane, as if asking permission. When Shane nodded, he walked over to the tree. His fingers brushed against a set of claw marks that the bark had almost covered. Eyes closed, he looked like he was communicating with the tree.

"If you're done walking down memory lane," came Enya's cutting voice, "let's get this over with."

Montgomery glared at her but withdrew his hand. He hugged Jordan, his cheek pressed to her furry one. "Kick her ass," he whispered in one ear.

"Will do. I promise," she whispered back.

He reached up to dig his fingers into the fur just under her ears, pressing his forehead to hers. He kissed her forehead and then stepped back. Without any further words, he stalked back to the corner where Nicholas stood.

Shane positioned himself in the center of the field and

gestured Jordan and Enya forward. But before she moved to take her indicated place, Angela put a hand on Jordan's shoulder. "Good luck, Jordan. May the Wolf watch over you."

"And you, Angela," Jordan said. She felt Angela's hand withdraw as she kept an eye on where Enya and Lucas spoke in low tones. Then he turned and retreated to the corner opposite Diana.

This was it then, Jordan took a deep breath as Alpha Shane stepped towards. "We gather here under the light of Luna," he intoned, "to settle by combat the accusations between Envoy Enya Blevins and Alpha Jordan Abbey. If Alpha Abbey wins, she'll be deemed blameless regarding what happened to Rhys Blevins." She could hear Montgomery repeating the words in English for Nicholas. "If Envoy Blevins wins, Alpha Abbey will pay restitution, namely her pack lands of Mount Ponderosa and her life. Are these terms acceptable?"

Jordan nodded. "Yes."

"Agreed," Enya said, also nodding.

"The combat is until the other yields, be it in word, deed, or death. If you step outside the marked boundary, it's an instant forfeit," Alpha Shane continued. "The fight will begin when my howl fades. May the Wolf witness and judge your actions."

And that was it. Shane retreated to his corner with his Pack. She and Enya stared at each other. She tried to hide the shivers that Enya's sneer sent down her spine. "Any last words, pup?"

"A few." She smiled, trying to match her attitude. "But now isn't the time to say them."

Enya shook her head. "You do have potential. Sad to see that you're wasting it."

"Then stop this," Jordan said. "You could call it off, and we can figure something out."

Enya shook her head. "No. It's gone too far. I couldn't stop this even if I wanted to."

Jordan's toes curled into the grassy ground. "Then let's get this over with."

That was when Alpha Shane howled a sharp, brief call, "Begin!"

The howled word still echoed in Jordan's ear when Enya leapt for her throat, claws and fangs bared. Jordan yelped and spun to the side. She felt claws scrape along her arm and saw bits of black fur float in the night air. Jordan dropped to all fours without shifting to full wolf. Her arm stung, but it held her weight.

"Well done," Enya said. "I hoped you would last for more than a bite or two." Enya dropped to all fours and circled. Jordan pivoted so she was always facing her, both watching for a weakness or unguarded step. "Come on, little Alpha. Attack me," Enya taunted. "I'll even give you a free bite."

Jordan tensed in preparation to leap but growled, "Like I'm stupid enough to fall for that trick."

Enya sniffed. "Don't ask me to estimate your intelligence, given the choices I've seen you make."

Jordan bolted forward a step before she checked herself. *She's trying to goad me into attacking.* And she almost fell for it. And she still had the urge to attack. As if to confirm her realization, Enya taunted, "Too afraid to attack?"

"No, just waiting for my opportunity." Wanting a better angle, she circled as well, making sure she stayed far from the rope border.

"Well then, let me give you that chance." Enya charged, but this wasn't a bluff. Jordan twisted out of the way at the last moment. She bit her hip as Enya passed. Her fangs barely penetrated the fur to scratch against the skin. But from Enya's insulted yelp, Jordan thought she had torn a chunk of flesh from her. Enya spun and glared at her. "Okay, pup," she snarled. "You want to fight? We'll fight."

Jordan thought she had been prepared by Angela's sparring. She blocked and countered her movements as fast as she could.

But half the slashes still landed. She backed up to gain some space and reset. Enya charged forward but tripped on the uneven ground. Jordan saw her opportunity and rushed her.

She realized, too late, that she had made the same exact error she had with Angela. She had slipped in too close and too slow; the Envoy had been waiting for her. Enya lifted her leg between them, claws flexing for a disemboweling kick. Jordan backpedaled, tripped, and fell on her ass. She flipped and pulled her feet under her, pushing upwards. Enya stomped down, claws digging into her back above her tail.

Pain shot up her spine to curl around the base of her skull. Jordan stumbled and fell. Her teeth clenched as her chin scraped along the ground.

Behind her, Enya tsked. "You know what your problem is, pup? You don't fight like a wolf. You only have human instincts."

Something inside her growled at that comment. "Well, if all I have are human instincts," Jordan said as her fingers closed around a handful of grass. Claws flexed, breaking the clod free from the earth. "Then I'll fight like one!" Ignoring the pain, she pushed up to her feet, flinging her handful at Enya's eyes.

The werewolf reared back and snarled as she swiped the dirt and grass out of her eyes. Jordan leapt onto her feet. She charged, leading her right shoulder to slam into Enya's stomach in a tackle. They went down in a tumble of legs, arms, and claws. Jordan rolled to the top and slammed a fist into Enya's muzzle. Fangs cut her knuckles, but she didn't stop, landing blow after blow. Her shoulder ached with each impact, but she didn't stop. She could taste blood between her clenched teeth. She wasn't sure if she had bitten her tongue, or it was from the spray from Enya's nose.

"Stop! Please!" The voice was wet with the bubble of blood that escaped with the words.

Jordan froze, one arm cocked for another blow. Her teeth were bared in a rictus of a snarl. She could almost hear Montgomery whispering in her ear, *Asking you to stop wasn't good enough.* "Are you yielding to me?" When she didn't answer, Jordan pulled her arm back for another punch.

Enya's eyes slid to the side, staring at the tree. "I yield to Alpha Abbey of the Mount Ponderosa Pack," she growled through gritted fangs.

Jordan drew in a deep breath and rose to her feet, but she didn't look at her friends. From their lack of reaction, they hadn't heard Enya's statement.

She took a step back, studying Enya's face. There were puffy spots around the eyes and cuts. She didn't think she had broken Enya's nose. The curve in the muzzle had to be because of the blood-matted fur. Not sure how it would be accepted, she offered her bloodied paw to Enya to help her up.

Enya looked from her paw to her face and back to her paw. She took Jordan's hand and levered herself up. She then pulled in close. "This isn't over, pup."

Jordan pushed her back, hooking her leg and sending her tumbling to the ground outside of the rope boundary. She smiled around a mouth full of fangs. "That's Alpha Pup to you. Now, are you going to address me properly, or do I need to beat you down again?"

She was sure that Enya wished the daggers shooting out of her eyes were silver plated. Slowly, Enya rose to one knee, lowering her head. "My challenge has failed. I acknowledge you, Jordan Abbey, as the alpha of Mount Ponderosa."

"And don't you forget it," Jordan growled.

She heard the padding of paws nearing her. She turned enough that she could keep an eye on Enya while watching the approaching Alpha Shane. He flicked a look at Enya, still on one knee, and then nodded approval. Alpha Shane offered her his hand. She thought he would shake it. Instead, he lifted it above her head in a victory salute. "Let me present to you the undisputed Alpha of Mount Ponderosa!"

35

It was an hour after dawn when Jordan dragged herself up the stairs to the apartment. *Some famulus I am.*

Most of the night after the fight was a blur between exhaustion and the adrenaline crash. But there were snapshot images in her mind like clips of a video spliced together without transitions. Howls and cheers breaking out. Being mobbed by the young wolves of the Black Oak Pack. Sitting on Angela and Billy's shoulders. Ryan staring at her with grudging respect. Nicholas clapping as if he were observing a golf tournament. Shane and Diana nodding. Montgomery beaming with pride. And out of the corner of her eye as she was being hustled off to the main house, Talespeaker Lucas tending to Envoy Blevins. And the look of pure hatred in Enya's eyes. The one weird thing was that the half-second glimpse she remembered of Pamela, the werewolf hadn't been looking at her, but above her. Something in the tree? At that point, she had been dropped to her feet and hustled towards the main cabin and didn't have a chance to follow Pamela's eye line.

Jordan had been so focused on trying to win the fight, she hadn't given much thought to what would happen after. And right after winning, it was party time. And werewolves knew how to party.

She hadn't even noticed when Montgomery had disappeared. Nicholas had demurred coming to the celebration and left before they returned to the cabin, famulus in tow. The last she had seen of Montgomery, he had been keeping to the corners, politely chatting with Shane and Diana. When she looked down at her vibrating phone and saw the text, she realized he wasn't around. His message had been short and simple. *Have fun and see you at home.* Then she was pulled back into the story that Shane was telling about his and Montgomery's First Hunt and what a disaster it was.

As the sun rose, Jordan ordered herself a rideshare and said goodbye to everyone. Most of the ride, she spent in the backseat of the car, head leaning against the seat, split between wondering if that had really just happened, and falling asleep.

The short nap did refresh her. She opened her eyes just as the car pulled to a stop at the apartment building. While her steps weren't peppy, she wasn't dragging as she made her way to the apartment.

She placed her keys into the bowl, fingers wrapped around the metal to muffle any clinks. For all she knew, Montgomery and Thorn were already asleep since the sun was well up. She glanced at the refrigerator, decided against a snack, and padded to the bedroom. The two bodies curled together seemed to confirm her guess. Keeping quiet to not disturb them, she stepped out of her shoes and pulled off her clothes except for her underwear. She slipped on the oversized tee shirt that she preferred sleeping in. She slipped into the bed, taking the innermost spoon spot against Montgomery.

Montgomery shifted, slipping an arm around her waist, followed by Thorn doing the same. "How was the rest of the party?"

"You missed the good stuff," Jordan said.

"Like?"

"Like Alpha Shane wearing a lampshade."

Montgomery squeezed her waist. She heard the grin in his voice. "Liar."

"Okay, maybe not that. But we could have left together. You didn't have to dip out and leave me a text."

"Yeah, I did. The celebration was about your accomplishment. If I tried to be more present, it would have been a distraction. Besides, you seemed to be getting along with everyone, and I didn't want to mess that up."

"I'm not sure if it was that, or if they were happy that I kicked her ass. Apparently, she was a jerk to the entire pack." She waited for the two men's chuckles to die down. "As much as I want to hope, it's not over, is it? She's always going to hate me and want revenge."

"And me," Montgomery added. "But there's one thing that can be said about Enya Blevins. She is a creature of honor. She won't attack you again, unless you give her a new reason to."

"Oh wonderful," Jordan said. "Knowing me, I'll accidentally bump her in line and give her a new excuse to challenge me."

Both Thorn and Montgomery chuckled. "Probably something a little more dramatic than that," Montgomery said.

"Mac," Thorn chided. "If you haven't noticed, drama is what we do."

This time, Jordan joined in the laughter. There was a warm, peaceful moment she wanted to revel in. After the week they had, they all deserved it.

And Montgomery shattered the moment. "You realize we have a new set of problems?"

Jordan nodded. "I've confirmed my position as an alpha." Not once, but twice. While it could have been seen as a technicality of Angela, and the blessing of the Wolf could be passed off as a mass hallucination, there was no way the argument would be accepted having defeated Enya. "Elder Marcus will see me as a threat."

"More of a threat," Montgomery corrected. "And while Shane is an ally right now, there's a chance that might change his mind too."

Jordan sighed. "So, what do we do?"

Thorn rested a hand on her shoulder, his thumb tracing over the curve. "We take things one night at a time."

"What comes next?"

Montgomery shrugged. "For the werewolves, there will be a ceremony where Blevins takes leave of Shane. You'll be invited under your new title most likely, and you should make an appearance."

"Maybe I should designate someone to go in my place." Jordan leaned her head against Montgomery's shoulder as she took another sip. "Are you sure I can't send Rex?"

That got a chuckle from both vampires. "No," Thorn said. "And before you ask, you can't send me or Mac either."

"Why would I?" Jordan looked back and forth between Montgomery and Thorn. Neither of them looked directly at her. The line of sight was a deliberate choice they made. In fact, it reminded her of how she used to look at Alpha Shane. "Wait, are you telling me that the two of you are part of my Pack?"

Montgomery and Thorn shared a look. "It's been suggested," Thorn said.

"By more than one person," Montgomery confirmed. "It's one of the main concerns Marcus has now," Montgomery said. "They think that I'm favoring the werewolf I once was instead of the vampire I now am."

"Because of me," Jordan said. She studied Montgomery and Thorn closely. "So... are we a pack?"

"Jordan, that's a dangerous question," Montgomery said.

Jordan held up a hand to cut him off. "You're my Patron, and I swore an oath of lifelong service to you. But you're also my friend and lover. Just as Thorn is. That makes us family." She hoped they heard the small 'f' in her sentence. Jordan placed her hand down in the center of the table. "Doesn't that also make us a pack?"

Thorn and Montgomery shared another look. "She's not wrong," Montgomery said as he placed his hand over hers. "I've been in denial about it for a long time. But she has a point. Packs have been founded on looser relationships than ours."

Thorn looked at the two of them. He placed his hand on top of Montgomery's, fingers curling around to touch Jordan's palm. "Yeah, you're both in denial. Just like me." He squeezed their joined hands. "This will be very difficult."

Jordan laughed. "Since when have we done easy?"

"Yeah, but there's a lot more than the usual," Montgomery said. "Rosanna suspects, and she has Marcus' ear. He's already asked me flat out if that was how I felt."

"And what did you tell him?"

"That I was his loyal bloodchild and member of the Conclave," Montgomery said.

"He's asked me similar questions about you, Mac," Thorn said. "But so far, he seems to trust me as his spy. Or at least as much as he trusts anyone."

"In other words, he has his spies spied on," Jordan said.

"That's what I mean about this being difficult," Thorn said. "We can't act that way in public. Jordan, you're going to have to still defer to Montgomery."

"I don't want this to be the kind of pack that Alpha Shane is running," Jordan said. "It can't be."

"Then what do you want it to be?"

"I want things to keep going like they've been. Or a little more open, a little more honest. We're all hiding stuff, and we've seen how that leads to more trouble. Or at least let's be upfront when it's something we can't share."

"So, we're making it official," Montgomery said. "Which do you want to do, matching rings or matching tattoos?"

Thorn yanked the pillow out from under Jordan's head and thwapped Montgomery with it. Jordan yelped a 'hey' of protest as he said, "For that cliché, you're not getting the couples discount."

36

This discussion with Marcus was different from his usual. When he stepped into the office, Montgomery discovered Nicholas was there, sitting next to the empty chair by the desk. Of course, he should have expected it since Nicholas had been at the fight. He bowed to his sire and nodded to his bloodbrother. "Sirs."

Elder Marcus didn't bother with social niceties. "So, Nicholas has informed me your famulus has fought and won against Envoy Blevins," he said. "This is the third werewolf she's beaten."

"Yes, sir," Montgomery said.

"While she started slow," Nicholas said, "once she found her footing, she was quite formidable."

"At least she'll make a good bodyguard," Marcus said. "Assuming she's still loyal to you, Montgomery."

"I don't think there should be any question as to if she's loyal," Montgomery said. He would have to choose his next words with caution. "She informed me that Green River's Talespeaker attempted to sway her over to their side. And she refused to entertain the thought."

"So, she has some wisdom." Marcus sat back in his chair. "And are they still considering her an alpha wolf?"

"There's no question about it as far as the werewolves are concerned," Montgomery said. "She's been challenged twice and won both times. She's an alpha wolf."

"And she now believes it," Marcus said.

"Belief is a strong word." Montgomery made an equivocal motion with his hand. "She knows that it's in name only, that she doesn't have a pack that will back her. But she now has a reputation that she can fall back on, so others won't challenge her without thinking twice."

"What about the possibility of her allying with Alpha Shane?" There was a sly look on Nicholas' face "Say, a political marriage."

That caught him flat footed. "She wouldn't do that," Montgomery spluttered. *But would she?* he thought.

"It doesn't have to be to him specifically, although I do see if his daughter doesn't make a suitable Alpha, him wanting another heir. And it would make sense to join the two Packs."

"Except other than land and a potential child, she has nothing to offer," Montgomery countered. "He could take over Jordan's territory easily if he wanted to, despite her defeats of Angela and Blevins. As for children, there are other packs which would be better political picks. Besides, Shane already has an heir."

"Who was beaten by Jordan," Nicholas pointed out. "Won't that be seen as a weakness in Ms. Shane since Jordan is so... unconventional for an alpha?"

"Jordan has shown no interest in taking over Great Oak," Montgomery said. "She wouldn't be considered a threat unless she made a move against Alpha Shane. And despite her growing reputation, she's in no position to do so without a huge risk."

"For a huge reward," Nicholas said. "A couple of those young male pups are about her age. I'm surprised they haven't attempted to get to know her better."

"One of them is her friend, yes, but I believe his interests lay elsewhere."

"You're sure of that," Marcus asked. "I remember one of them running up to her to speak the night she proved to Shane she was able to shapeshift."

"Under Alpha Shane's orders," Montgomery said. "While he has remained in contact with her, the boy has made no attempt to woo her over to the Pack since."

"That you're aware of," Nicholas said. "For all we know, being friends would be the next step in trying to seduce her into the Pack."

"I've observed him and Jordan interacting several times," Montgomery said. "Aside from one ham-fisted attempt, I haven't seen him make any further overtures to Jordan. If anything, if I'm guessing correctly, he may leave the Black Oak for other reasons."

'If she seduces him," Nicholas said.

Montgomery shook his head. "There are other reasons to leave a pack aside from love. And right now, Jordan can't offer any of them. More than likely, he'd end up leaving the area entirely."

"What's to keep her from swaying other werewolves to her side."

Montgomery held out his hands to his sides, as though the explanation were self-evident. "I know the Conclave is concerned about me being under her sway and having transferred my devotion to her. However, they keep forgetting that I'm anathema to other werewolves. Alpha Shane tolerates my presence because of the truce he has built with you, sir. He knows killing me would start a war with you, a war he's not sure he could win. But Envoy Blevins made it clear that after Jordan was dead, I would be next, followed by the entire Conclave. Many more werewolves will share her beliefs than his." He dropped his hands. "As long as I'm associated with Jordan, Alpha or no, she can't amass the power that would make her a threat to him, or to you, sir. She will be seen either as a joke being played by Alpha Shane, or a technical error he hasn't taken the time to correct."

Marcus sat back, thinking over Montgomery's words. Nicholas' gaze stayed on him but did flick towards Montgomery for a second before returning to Marcus. After a minute, the Elder nodded. "You still need to keep her on a tight leash, Montgomery. She cannot be seen publicly disobeying you, now more than ever."

"Of course, sir."

"How long will Envoy Blevins remain in Rancho Robles?"

"She's scheduled to take leave of the Black Oak Pack tomorrow night."

"I'm certain she would have liked to leave tonight," Nicholas added. "But she doesn't need to be perceived as fleeing with her tail tucked between her legs, given what Jordan did to her."

Montgomery nodded confirmation. "She won't want to return to her Pack too quickly, just for that reason. Jordan and I will be expected to be at her sendoff since we were there for her official introduction."

"Keep a close eye on both her and Shane," Marcus said. "I want to know if they even blink at each other hostilely." He glanced at his watch "Now, unless you have anything you wish to discuss, you're both dismissed."

Both vampires rose and bowed to their sire. "Have a pleasant evening, sir," Montgomery said. Without any further words, he turned to leave.

He reached to push the door open. "Montgomery," came Marcus' voice. "I still expect you to publicly punish Jordan for her earlier disobedience, alpha or not."

Montgomery turned back, making sure his face was a mask. "She has been," he said. "Why do you think I allowed Angela to repeatedly beat her up under the guise of training when I could have done the same for her myself?"

This second silence of Marcus' felt heavier. His spine tightened, waiting for the berating and scolding that was about to come. Instead, Marcus nodded. "Be sure that the Conclave is made aware of it."

"Yes, sir." He turned to the door and opened it. *Bullet dodged.*

He allowed Nicholas to go first, as was the proper etiquette. Nothing was said as they walked through the hallway or the outer office. It wasn't until they stepped into the lobby and his shoulders relaxed that Nicholas spoke in a voice pitched only for him to hear. "Well played, little brother," he said. "I was thinking that I would have to keep an eye on your famulus. You just proved that it would be a mistake to overlook you as well."

37

———————

It didn't take a letter this time to prod Montgomery to call Alpha Shane. There were some questions he needed answered, and not just because Elder Marcus had asked him to. He waited until Thorn had left for his tattoo studio and Jordan a meeting with Angela to place his call.

The phone rang twice, and he was mentally preparing a message to leave on Shane's voicemail when the werewolf picked up. "Montgomery? Is something wrong with Jordan?"

"Uh, no. I, ah, wanted to talk to you."

"Okay." Shane sounded puzzled. "You should have stayed for the party. "We had a freshly dressed deer and could have served you some blood from it."

"Thanks, but if I had stayed, it would have been awkward. It was Jordan's time to shine."

"Yeah, but if Jordan's going to be around, you're going to be around. So, at least the kids need to actually learn how to play nice and not just pay lip service to it."

Montgomery chuckled. "Did we ever learn to do that?"

"You ended up with a vampire girlfriend. So, you tell me." The light, almost friendly tone shifted to a serious business tone. "You talked with Elder Marcus?"

"Yes. After Nicholas informed him of what he witnessed, Elder Marcus has... concerns about Jordan and her new status as alpha. Mostly how seriously are you taking it."

"You mean if I'm going to propose that we join forces and run all the vampires out of Rancho Robles?"

"Something like that," Montgomery admitted. "Or that you might propose, period."

There was dead silence for a moment. "Wow. I mean, I know age differences don't mean much to you vampires, but Angela is her age. As pleasant as she is to look at, I'm not going to add to my daughter's issues by making Jordan her stepmom."

"I didn't think so but—"

"You still had to ask to report back to your sire," Alpha Shane finished. "You can reassure him that I have no intention to take a mate right now, and if I did, it wouldn't be Jordan."

Something in his chest eased at Shane's words. "Don't take this wrong, but that's good to hear."

"I get it," Shane said. "One less entanglement to deal with." He paused. "Besides, she's being discreet, but I think she's already taken. And if I'm not wrong, so are you."

"It's a complicated situation," Montgomery sighed. "I didn't mean for things to happen this way."

To his surprise, Shane also sighed. "We never do." There was another pause. When Shane spoke, there was a tentative tone, not of an alpha addressing a potential enemy, but an old friend attempting to reconnect to someone they hadn't spoken with in years. "It was good interacting with you when we weren't trying to bite each other's heads off. You can call me whenever you want, if you need to discuss things."

"It's hard to talk to you," he admitted. The next words slipped out before he could stop them. "Not after what you did to Dad."

"What I did to... Montgomery?" There was a heavy silence

before Shane spoke again, "Did you think I had something to do with Alpha Cooper's death?"

"You ascended after him." There. He'd finally said it. He steeled himself for the denials, the justifications, that Alpha Shane was about to spout.

He didn't expect the softness and hurt in Shane's voice. "Montgomery, listen to me and get this through your thick skull. I had nothing to do with your father's death."

Was he wrong? No, he couldn't be. There was too much that he had been involved with. "Just like you had nothing to do with Christine's."

"I said get it through your thick—grrrr. Listen to me, Montgomery. I swear on the Wolf, Luna, Sol, and Gaia that I had nothing to do with your father's death. I'll even swear on the Bat if that's what you want."

The phone slipped through numb fingers and rattled on the floor as the oaths echoed through his head. Montgomery didn't know what to say. For so many years, he had blamed Alpha Shane for his father's death. It had gone from white-hot fury to the cool anger that still burned. Having to work with him to help Jordan was something he could do but didn't mean he wouldn't poke the werewolf when he had a chance. To let that go seemed impossible. Except that Shane was willing to swear by the Bat, a god considered anathema to werewolves.

It took a second before he could make out the words coming from the phone on the floor. "Montgomery? You still there?"

He picked up the phone and tightened his grip, not wanting to drop it again. "Let's say I believe you," he said. "Who did it?"

"That question has bedeviled me for the last twenty years," Shane said. "Believe me, if I knew who it was, I'd be after them myself. This isn't how I wanted to become alpha."

"Do you think it's connected to... what happened to me and Christine?"

"I don't see how it couldn't be, but I've never been able to find out who it was." Shane sighed. "Are you ready to talk about what happened?"

Montgomery closed his eyes. He wanted to say yes, wanted to know if what he suspected had any foundation. But he couldn't bring himself to say yes.

And to his relief, Shane read his silence and came to the correct conclusion. "When you're ready, let me know. I'll tell you the story about that night."

He nodded, then remembered that he was on the phone. "Give me a few days," he said. Enough time for him to come to terms with Shane's information and see how it slotted into what Thorn found out.

"Of course, Montgomery. Like I said, let me know when." Shane paused. "I need to take care of some things before Envoy Enya and Talespeaker Lucas leave. I'll see you at the official send-off. Have a good evening, Montgomery."

He swallowed. "You too, Alex." This time, the use of his name wasn't a slip but a choice.

38

There wasn't much time before the coffee shop closed, but Jordan hoped this meeting wouldn't take too long. She had scooted out of the apartment just as Montgomery and Thorn were awake enough to hear that she was going to meet with Angela. "Have fun getting your butt kicked," Thorn called as she closed the door.

At least that wasn't happening tonight if Jordan's plans went right. The future was wide open though.

She made it to the coffee shop, hoping she could snag the corner table that she liked the best. Unfortunately, Angela had beaten her there and selected the table next to the central window in the middle of things. The blond woman already had a tea, if Jordan was scenting it right, She waved hello and ordered her latte and two cookies. She reached into her pocket and fingered an envelope, hoping she was making the right decision.

Once her name was announced, and her coffee was in hand, she headed to the table where Angela was waiting. The other woman was pulling her tea bag out and setting it to one side. "Jordan," she said with a nod.

Jordan sat opposite her. "Angela." She held up her coffee, half in greeting and half in salute. Angela matched her motion, and both women sipped. Jordan pulled one cookie out of its paper pouch and nudged the bag towards Angela. "Cookie?"

Angela arched an eyebrow. "You know alphas are supposed to eat first."

"I'm not here as an alpha," Jordan said. "And I'm waiting for you to take a bite so I can at the same time."

"We're equals then?"

"For tonight, at least."

Angela pursed her lips and nodded. She picked up the cookie studded with dark and light spots and studied it. "Chocolate chip macadamia?"

"Yeah. I know we can handle chocolate, but triple chocolate seemed a bit too much like a threat. And they were out of snicker-doodles, so..." She gestured to the cookies. "Chocolate chip macadamia."

Angela shook her head. "You are one weird wolf, Jordan Abbey."

Jordan grinned. "That has nothing to do with me being a wolf. Overthinking things can be blamed complexly on my human side."

"Huh," Angela said. "Then my statement still stands." She held up her cookie, and Jordan did the same. Both women took a bite at the same time. She saw Angela's shoulders relax, and felt the tension leave her neck as they both munched and sipped their drinks. "So, tell me, Jordan," she said once the cookie was only crumbs. "Why did you ask me here?"

"I figured we needed some sort of postmortem on the fight," Jordan said. "That, and I have a question. And while we were cele-brating didn't seem the proper time to ask."

"Fair enough. Ask away."

Jordan paused, making sure she had picked the right words. "You told me to fight like a human," she said. Her smile and a laugh pulled the sting from her question. "So, tell me. Were you trying to get me killed?"

Angela shrugged. "I didn't think you'd use that exact same move, given how many times you ended up on your ass," she said. "But werewolves claw and bite. We don't punch. So, with the element of surprise, you won following my advice."

Jordan rubbed her right hand's knuckles, feeling the ghosts of the impacts through her arm. "Yeah. About that." She reached into her back pocket and pulled out a small green envelope. She held it out to Angela.

Angela sniffed hard enough that Jordan felt the air displace from her hand. "What is it?"

"Gift card to The Pizza Palace where we first met," Jordan said. "I wanted to say thank you, but I wasn't sure how." She held out the envelope steady, waiting for her to accept or reject it. "If you'd rather have a gift card for somewhere else, just name the place."

Angela narrowed her eyes. "Is this a tribute from one Pack to another? Or some kind of bribe?"

"I'm hoping it's a gift from one friend to another. A 'thank you' for helping when you didn't have to."

Angela looked at the hand holding out the small envelope. Just as Jordan was about to withdraw her hand, Angela took it. "Thank you," she said. "Despite what I said, you were a good student. Too bad we didn't have more time for more lessons."

"About that." Jordan scratched the back of her head, looking at her from an angle. "Would you be willing to teach me more?" She held up her hand to cut off any protests. "Not just the fighting. The alpha stuff too. There's a lot more I need to learn. And I need someone to teach me. And let's face it. Montgomery can't, and I'm not sure that Diana's way of stuffing my head full of stories will work for me."

Angela looked her up and down. "And what's in it for me?"

Jordan arched an eyebrow. "The chance for you to continue regularly kicking my butt with my consent isn't enough?"

Angela mirrored Jordan's expression. She crossed her arms over her chest. "Maybe I'm worried that you'll beat me up."

"Fair." She had managed it once before. Jordan frowned, considering her options. "How about this? Loser buys coffee afterwards?"

Angela pursed her lips and then countered, "And pastries?"

"And pastries." Jordan held out her hand to shake. "Deal?"

Despite Jordan agreeing to her counter, Angela hesitated. Jordan wondered if she had blown it again, broken some sort of obscure werewolf tradition about sealing a deal. Maybe they were supposed to bear throats instead? Just when she was going to withdraw her hand, Angela spoke. "I'll toss in language lessons too. Your accent needs a bit of work." She took Jordan's hand and shook it with a firm squeeze. "Deal, Chaos Alpha."

Jordan's eyebrows lifted. "Chaos Alpha?"

"That describes you best," Angela said. "You're an alpha, but you've got a weird pack, and you're not exactly bringing peace and harmony with you."

"Chaos Alpha." Jordan chewed over the words, tasting how they felt in her mouth. Angela didn't seem to be insulting her. And the title did fit. She wasn't a traditional alpha by any means. She'd ask Billy to make sure this wasn't some obscure trap she was falling into. "I think," she said, her grin widening. "I like it."

39

Thorn sat at his desk, sketchbook propped up with the help of a clipboard at a comfortable angle. Dark pencil in hand, he scratched away at a rough design. Jordan had told him and Montgomery how Angela had referred to her as a chaos alpha. The words sent a flash of an image in his mind, one he wanted to make at least a rough sketch of. Refinement would come later. At this moment, he wanted to grab the concept before it disappeared.

He was deep in his concentration, so he didn't register the yelling heading in his direction. "Ma'am," a female voice yelled. "You are not allowed back here unless the boss says so."

Thorn stood as the door to his office opened. Pamela shouldered her way past it, a red-haired woman following hot on her heels. "It's okay, Charla," Thorn said. "I'll see her. Keep an eye on the front, please."

Charla met his eyes, hesitated for a second, and then nodded, light sparkling off her nose ring. She turned and pulled the door closed behind her. He sat. "To what do I owe the pleasure of this visit?"

"Don't bother with pleasantries, Kelly," Pamela snapped. "Where were you last night?"

"Keep your voice down." Thorn glanced at the closed door. "Charla already thinks we're having an affair, and you talking like that won't help me convince her otherwise."

Pamela's lips pressed together "You're not answering the question." Each word was spat with perfect enunciation. "Were you there last night?"

"No! I won't step foot on Pack ground unless invited." He bristled at her raised eyebrow. "Want me to show you the log books for last night?"

"You were inking someone while Jordan was fighting for her life?"

"No, because Marcus sent Nicholas, I couldn't show my face, I had to stay here. Ordered the same damn ink three times because I couldn't focus."

"So, you weren't hanging out in the field?"

Thorn rolled his eyes. "There are bats native to the area. If you saw one hanging from your sacred oak, that wasn't me."

Pamela stared at him. He met her gaze, not saying anything more. Both of them looked away at the same moment. "So, you weren't trespassing on Pack land last night. Are you going to show up in her dreams every night from now on?"

Thorn crossed his arms over his chest. "Only when I think you'll be there. We agreed you wouldn't try to influence her and yet here you are, doing the same thing."

"I'm trying to give her advice she's not getting from either Montgomery or Diana."

"And you can't speak to the Talespeaker about it?"

Pamela looked away. "She won't listen to me."

"I thought the two of you were close."

"Once. But she and I haven't spoken in those terms for a long time."

Thorn raised his eyebrows but said nothing. It wasn't his

place to pry into Pamela's relationships that didn't directly affect him, even if his curiosity was burning. He expected her to snap that her relationships were none of his business. The werewolf's next words caught him off guard. "Look, if you care for Jordan like you say you do, leave her alone."

The thing that stung the most about Pamela's words was that they were gentle, almost caring. "I'm sorry? So, you can wrap her around your little finger?"

"No. You saw what happened with werewolves that you get close to. Things don't end up well for any of them. My firstborn and Montgomery to start."

Thorn's eyes narrowed. "I'll take the blame for what happened to your firstborn, but what have I done to Montgomery?"

"Who put it into Marcus' mind that it would be a good idea to turn him after the loss of his blooddaughter?"

Thorn reeled back. "That wasn't me." *Or was it?* "I made an offhand comment once that Montgomery had potential as a vampire, and it was a pity he had been born a werewolf, but that was before Christine was killed. I never went as far as suggesting he be turned."

"And what offhand comments have you made about Jordan?" Pamela asked. "You're not thinking like who you are. You're lost in the role you're playing."

"And you're the one trying to take on a motherly role," Thorn said.

"Yes, and like all mothers, I know that I have to let my children make their own choices. I can advise Jordan, but I cannot force her to do anything she doesn't wish to."

"And I'm not forcing her into this relationship," Thorn said.

"No, but you aren't exactly discouraging it either. Don't get me wrong, I like her. She has the potential to be a good alpha."

"If she quits her relationship with me."

"And Montgomery. If it's any comfort, it's not just you I'm concerned about."

"Then answer me this. Do you really think she can break her Vow of Family and not suffer repercussions? Do you think that you can convince Alpha Shane to protect her from the wrath of Elder Marcus and the Conclave? Or she'd be able to protect herself alone?"

Instead of answering him, Pamela locked eyes with him a second time. This time, she looked away first.

"Exactly. We need to deal with her where she's at, not where we want her to be." Thorn sat back, his arms crossed over his chest. "Unless you have a plan for us to break up where she comes out of it alive, don't bring it up again."

Pamela nodded. "She's putting things together. She doesn't know who we really are yet, but she knows that we're out there, and we're interested in her."

"I know." Thorn studied the pencil markings on the sketch-pad. "Is that such a bad thing?"

"She trusts you. She hasn't tried to figure out how to block you from her dreams. And she trusts me—"

"Gaia knows why."

Thorn ignored the muttered outburst. "—So, why don't we reward that trust?"

Pamela's jaw dropped. "Have you finally gone mad in your old age? Are you saying we reveal ourselves to her? Do you remember what happened last time we did that?"

Thorn wiped away her concern with a wave of his hand. "Nothing so bold, nothing so drastic. A test to see if she's worthy of more information. We confirm that yes, we're out there and see what she does with the information."

"And what do you think she'll do with it?"

"Talk to me, Montgomery, and Diana about it, but she won't actively try to figure it out. We'll have to be careful, of course, but I don't think it's that big of a risk."

"You're putting a lot of trust on a girl who has only known about the supernatural world for a little under a year."

"Has it only been that long?" Thorn shook his head.

"Yeah." Pamela sat in the chair on the other side of his desk. "Are you sure she's up to this?"

"She's faced everything that's been thrown at her and come out the other side."

"Point."

"So, what happens next?"

"That's a good question." Thorn's frown turned into a grin. "Guess that depends on what mess she gets herself into next."

Pamela laughed. "I think you're right."

40

Jordan was sitting in the center of the squared-off area, dirt still churned up from the fight. In front of her sat the Wolf, head hanging over hers. "This is another dream?"

"I decided you didn't need a nightmare about losing the fight, so I'd interrupt what your subconscious had planned," the Wolf said. "You fought with honor. Well done."

"Thank you," Jordan said. She sighed and looked down at the ground, plucking at a few leaves of grass. "I'm not sure that I won the proper way. I mean, I didn't grab her throat with my fangs. I broke her nose with a right hook."

She jumped as a cold, wet nose nudged under her chin, lifting it so she was looking the Wolf in the eyes. "You won," the Wolf said with no hesitation. "You used your deadliest weapon. Your mind." The Wolf's tail thumped once against the ground. "Claws and fangs are sharp and deadly, but without a mind to guide them, ultimately useless."

"Okay then. That was a worry in the back of my mind. Because of how I beat her up, Blevins would say I hadn't won properly, and the fight was invalid."

"Oh, Blevins will probably whine about it privately to her

sister. But she won't want to complain too loudly or for too long. When word gets out that the werewolf she lost to had been changed for about a year while she's been a werewolf since birth, it won't be a good boost for her reputation.

"For once, my inexperience is an asset." She shifted to look the Wolf in the eyes, or at least the best she could given her angle and closeness. "Why did you help me?"

"It's time you claim your rightful place. And you can't do that if you can't communicate. You were already learning. I just sped up the process."

"That..." Jordan paused, not sure what the repercussions would be if she voiced her thought. *What the hell.* This was her dream. The Wolf had swallowed her before, and all that happened was she woke up. "That sounds like cheating to me."

The Wolf tilted her head. "Do you want me to remove my blessing."

Jordan shook her head, hands to her chest and palms out. "No, no. No need to go that far."

The Wolf laughed, tail wagging. "Do you have any other questions?"

"Of course I do, but I'm going to stick to the ones I think you'll actually answer." Jordan licked her lips. "The giant bat-like creature who attacked me during our last meeting in my dream. That was the Bat."

It wasn't a question, but the Wolf answered as if it were. "Yes." There was a weariness of the ages on Her slumping shoulders. "Given who you are dealing with, it's not surprising that you drew His attention."

Jordan nodded. That made sense, but she didn't like the implications of having the attention of two gods on her. "Am I in danger?"

The Wolf barked Her almost human laughter. "Alpha Jordan Abbey, you live among vampires, walk with werewolves, and dream with gods. When would you not be in danger?"

Jordan nodded. "You have a point." She considered for a second. "Do I know you?"

The Wolf's head tilted to one side. "What do you mean?"

"The way you're talking, you're either omnipresent, or you have eyes on me somehow. I don't get the feeling you're omnipresent. So, that means you're physically watching me?"

"Why can't I be doing that from the spirit world?"

"You could. Except Thorn and I have had talks about the Bat. He believes that He is walking the world and is out there somewhere. I haven't talked to too many werewolves about religion, so I haven't gotten a feel for their beliefs." She met the Wolf's eyes. "So, do I know you?"

The Wolf met her eyes. Jordan held her stare, despite the growing urge to drop her gaze. She was about to blink to relieve the growing sandpaper itch in her eyes when the Wolf spoke. "Yes. You do."

Jordan inhaled, a sharp breath as her lips parted.

"No, I'm not going to tell you who I am." The Wolf rose to her feet. "That you have to figure out on your own." She turned and padded towards the wood line. Then she turned. "You should also be aware that your friend Thorn is right. The Bat is out there as well. And He has His eye on you in the real world as well."

"Great." So, not one god stalked her, but two. "So, what happens next?"

"That's up to you. But I don't suggest you try to figure out who we are. That will lead to problems for all of us. And I like it here. I'd rather not have to move on again."

Jordan tilted her head, still trying to keep eye contact. She settled on looking into her right eye. "And if I do accidentally figure out who you are?"

"Then I'd keep my guesses secret. There are those who believe in us, enough to want to put an end to us." Jordan felt the cold, wet, pebbly skin of the Wolf's nose between her eyes as a warm exhale surrounded her. "We may be immortal, but we don't know if Gaia's curse made us invulnerable." With those parting words, the Wolf rose and turned away.

Jordan watched The Wolf as she padded off into the tree line, her black fur blending in with the shadows. She stared for a few more seconds, expecting to see the reflection of eyeshine staring back at her. She noticed a bat-shaped shadow detach itself from a tree and slip into the sky, momentarily blotting out the moon.

Even knowing she was in a dream and safe, Jordan shivered, remembering Talespeaker Lucas' words "It appears you've managed to pique both their interests. But beware. Their interest can be both a blessing and a curse."

41

Jordan drove up to the entrance of Black Oak Pack's territory. Technically, she didn't need to be here since Envoy Blevins and Talespeaker Lucas were under the auspices of the Alpha Shane. But then Shane had personally invited her, and she agreed. She wasn't about to let them think she was weak and afraid, despite beating her. She may not have her footing on Mount Ponderosa, but she wouldn't be seen like that publicly. She had earned the right to be an alpha, and she would act like one. And if Montgomery and Thorn would be rumored to be her pack, then she would lean into it. It was a pity that she couldn't convince Mrs. Clarke to let her bring Rex. But then, given how the Rottweiler had reacted to Talespeaker Lucas, that might have been a good thing.

Sentry Rodriguez did a double take when she lowered the car windows to show that there were two vampires in the car. Montgomery shook his head as Thorn wiggled his fingers in hello. But he recovered and addressed Jordan. "You're expected at the main house, Alpha Abbey." He paused. "And might I add that it was an impressive display you put on the other night."

"Thank you, Sentry Rodriguez," she said. She rolled up her

window and started the drive up to the main house. "Anyone want to bet on him calling ahead about the two of you coming?"

Montgomery shook his head while rolling his eyes. "You know I don't take sucker bets, Jordan."

Billy was waiting for them on the porch when they pulled up. He didn't show any surprise at her bringing not one, but two vampires with her. "You're expected. All of you," he added.

"Thanks," Jordan said. "Is the envoy here?"

Billy shook his head as he opened the door for them. "They're on their way up now. Alpha Shane wanted to make sure you were here first."

The trio stepped through the door. Jordan had cleared the threshold when Angela hustled over to her. "Dad wants you to stand by him," she whispered.

Jordan glanced at Montgomery and Thorn. Montgomery had an eye on Shane as he spoke with Diana. Thorn and Pamela were in some sort of conversation. Deciding that it would be better if she went with the request, she followed Angela over. "Surprised that you didn't drag me over to him by the arm."

Angela shrugged. "I would have, if I didn't think Dad would chastise me publicly, Alpha Abbey."

Jordan shook her head. "I don't think I'll ever get used to that title."

"You better," Angela said. "Cause you're going to be hearing it a lot from now on."

Angela led her to where Alpha Shane was talking to Talespeaker Diana. "Ah, good, you're here, Alpha Abbey," he said. "Montgomery went over the ceremony with you?"

Jordan nodded. "She announces her intention to leave and asks for safe passage out of your territory. You'll grant it, and she drives off. Sounds simple."

"You'd think, but now that your territory is in the mix, I wouldn't put it past her to try something," Diana said.

"I want you to stand on my left side," Alpha Shane said.

"A united front," Jordan said.

Shane nodded, smiling and revealing pointed teeth. "Exactly."

Three knocks sounded on the door. Or was it three stomps on the wooden porch? Either way, it was a signal because all the werewolves looked towards the door. Diana stepped to the right, and Jordan took her place on his left. Angela slipped into the spot between and behind her father and Jordan.

No sooner than they were all in position than the front door opened. Envoy Blevins and Talespeaker Lucas strode up the hall. Despite the stern expression, there was something different in her bearing. Jordan could make out the faint outlines of bruises and lines of scrapes down her cheeks.

She walked up to stand square with Alpha Shane, Lucas on her right and just behind her shoulder. She would have thought that Lucas would be positioned opposite his counterpart rather than her. "I wish to return to my homelands," Enya said. Her words had the weight of formality and politeness, but her glare through a still puffy eye said what she really wanted to.

She lifted her chin, while Alpha Shane stood immobile as he spoke, "You're free to go of course, and both I and Alpha Abbey wish you safe and quick travels to Green River."

Enya winced at the use of Jordan's title. Both waited for Shane to continue. Traditionally, there was some sort of comment regarding peace between their packs. When it became clear that Alpha Shane wouldn't say anything more, Enya dipped her head. "Then I and my Talespeaker take leave of the Black Oak Pack. My treatment here will always be remembered."

That was a polite threat if Jordan had ever heard one.

Talespeaker Lucas fixed his eyes on Jordan's. "Alpha Abbey, remember what I told you about the Wolf and the Bat."

Jordan nodded, looking at him through narrowed eyes. "I'll keep it under advisement."

Lucas looked away from her with a slight snort. Angela leaned over to whisper in her ear, "What did he say to you?"

She inclined her head to the other werewolf and whispered, "We had a discussion about religion." Jordan straightened her head. Angela hovered over her shoulder as if waiting for more of an answer. After a second, Angela leaned back.

"Do you wish an escort to the main gate?" Shane asked with overly polite concern.

"No," Enya said. She cast a sour look in Montgomery's direction before addressing Shane's question, "I wish nothing further from you." With that, she spun on her heel and marched outside.

Alpha Shane looked at Jordan. "Well, that answered that," he said and followed.

Jordan followed, more sensing than seeing Montgomery and Thorn take up flanking positions. They walked outside. Alpha Shane and members of the Black Oak Pack were gathered to the left side of the porch, leaving an open spot for her and the vampires with a modicum of privacy. Enya and Lucas were already opening the doors to the car.

"I wish to speak."

Jordan blinked as Ryan stepped forward. He was carrying a duffel bag that was packed to the point of bursting. He stood in front of Alpha Shane, straight as a board. "I wish to withdraw from the Black Oak Pack."

If Shane was surprised, he didn't show any sign of it. "You wish to become a chaos wolf?"

"No," he said and looked to where Enya and Lucas waited. "Not a chaos wolf."

Shane also looked at the members of the Green River Pack. "May I ask why?" he rumbled.

Ryan's gaze shifted to Jordan's direction. "There are too many painful memories of my brother here. I need a fresh start."

Jordan's eyes narrowed, but she didn't say anything. Her hands balled into fists. Would he challenge her for Mount Ponderosa?

"Very well," Shane said. "You're released from any obligations you hold to the Black Oak Pack."

Ryan bowed his head in acknowledgement. He turned on his heels and walked down to where Enya and Lucas waited. Ryan said something in a voice too low for Jordan to catch. But Enya's response was loud and clear. "Of course. Green River will welcome you without hesitation." Enya ushered Ryan into the backseat. While the Talespeaker slipped inside, disappearing without so much as a final glance at anyone. Enya however took a moment to smirk at Shane, Montgomery, and Jordan each in turn. Then she was inside the car. The driver's door slammed shut.

"Amazing," Thorn said. "I've never seen a car pull away in a sulk before."

Good riddance, Jordan thought. She turned to Alpha Shane. "Is there anything I need to be concerned about with Ryan leaving?"

"No," Shane said. His shoulders slumped. Angela and Diana also had similar expressions of disappointment. "It's his choice to leave and find another pack."

She glanced at Montgomery, who nodded in confirmation. Jordan sighed. "Anything else we need to do?"

Alpha Shane shook his head. "No, we're done here."

She noted that he didn't say they were free to go, but he wasn't saying they needed to stay either. "In that case, we'll head on."

She didn't know whether she should be annoyed or amused at Shane's inquisitive glance at Montgomery. "This is her show," the vampire said with a shrug.

Shane snorted. "This isn't helping your image, Montgomery." He looked back to Jordan. "I'll inform you when they've arrived home. There shouldn't be anything more, but I'll let you know if I hear anything, Alpha Abbey."

"Thank you, Alpha Shane," Jordan said. "I look forward to hearing from you."

Again, Alpha Shane snort-laughed. "Why couldn't you have

had those manners when we first met?" He waved a hand. "Have a pleasant evening."

"You too, Alpha Shane." Jordan stepped off the porch, waiting to hear the door close behind them before indulging in an eye roll. "Didn't expect Ryan to leave."

Montgomery nodded. "I don't think any of us did." He paused for a moment. "You know that wasn't your fault. It was purely his choice."

"I know," Jordan said. "And I know he's hurting over the loss of his brother. And I'm a constant reminder of his loss." She shrugged. "I know it's not my fault. I just wish he hadn't run into the arms of Green River." Montgomery nudged her shoulder and shook his head, but he had the same bemused expression. "What?"

"You're growing up," Montgomery said.

"Me? I'm not the only one." She bumped Montgomery's shoulder back. "You were in Alpha Shane's presence for a half hour without poking the werewolf once."

"Huh," Montgomery said. "I guess we all are acting more mature."

"I'm not," Thorn chirped. "I refuse to grow up."

She was about to respond when a female voice behind her called out, "Hey Jordan! Wait up!" She turned to see Angela walking towards her at a rapid clip. When she was within reaching distance, Angela held out a digital key fob, the kind used to open electronically locked doors. "For the back gate, so you can get in easier. See you tomorrow at two pm."

Jordan nodded as she took it. "Thanks. See you then," she said as she slipped the fob into her front pocket.

Angela nodded and walked away as the three of them continued to Montgomery's SUV.

Montgomery arched an eyebrow. "You don't have to check in any more? You're moving up in the world."

Jordan shrugged. "So it seems. Or Sentry Rodriguez is sick of letting me in. He's always at the gate. Does he ever get time off?"

After Montgomery's chuckles died down, Thorn gestured back at the cabin. "You're seeing Angela tomorrow?"

"Yeah," Jordan said. "Enya's not going to be the only person who challenges me, and I can't depend on the few tricks I know. I need someone to continue teaching me to fight. And she's the best option I have."

She expected Montgomery to have an opinion. To her surprise, Thorn protested. "I'm not sure I like this."

Jordan turned her head to look at him. "I'm not sure we have a choice."

Montgomery exhaled, seeming to empty his lungs entirely. "I'm afraid you're right."

Jordan studied him for a moment. He looked thoughtful and a bit wistful. Worry twisting her stomach, she asked the question that had been on her mind since Montgomery read them the letter. "Regret not marrying her?"

Montgomery spoke before Jordan had stopped. "Hell no! Not for one minute!"

Montgomery had replied with no hesitation and so much vehemence, both Jordan and Thorn laughed. And after a second, he laughed as well. Arm in arm, the three of them walked to the car to head home.

The End

Curious about how Rex went missing? What happened with Animal Control? Why was Jordan wearing a rhinestone collar? Subscribe to my email list at www.sherylrhayes.com and get an exclusive story *Chaos Unleashed* to find out the answers to these questions and more.

ACKNOWLEDGMENTS

I would like to thank the following people:

- Colleen for help figuring out where to put a pack in New Mexico.
- Truly Bellamy, for being honest when an idea had legs and when it was a dead end.
- Alex, for poking and prodding me to make word count.
- Tabitha, for yelling, "Keep going!" when I informed her I made word count.
- Fiona Jayde for her usual kick ass work on cover.
- Shenandoah Frederick for asking questions that got me looking at things from a different angle.
- Michelle Dunbar for her editing chops.
- Sue Soares for making my words make more sense.
- Tammy Payne for finding all those little typos after I eyeballed the document four times.
- And last but not least, Mur Lafferty's I Should Be Writing Fabulists Discord for supplying suggestions, distractions, support, and general shenanigans.

ABOUT THE AUTHOR

Sheryl R. Hayes can be found untangling plot threads or the yarn her three cats have been playing with. She is equally likely to be shooing one of them off the keyboard as she is working on her novels and short stories. In addition to writing, she is a cosplayer focusing on knit and crochet costumes. Follow her at her blog at http://www.sherylrhayes.com.

ALSO BY SHERYL R. HAYES

Jordan Abbey Series

Chaos Wolf (Book 1)

Chaos Hunt (Book 2)

Chaos Unleashed (Book 2.5) Exclusive to my mailing list!

Chaos Kin (Book 3)

Short Stories

Pangram in *Ink: Queer Sci Fi's Eighth Annual Flash Fiction Contest*

Reading the Leaves in *AlternaTeas*

A Smoking Hot Proposal in *Clarity: Queer Sci Fi's 9th Annual Flash Fiction Contest*

The Tenth Life in *CatsCast Episode 15*

The Twisted Princess *Exclusive to my mailing list!*